EVO⎽⎽R

A Novel

By

KINGSTONE JUDGES

COPYRIGHT

Copyright © 2020 Kingstone Judges

First published 2020

for my mother, Rossah.

TABLE OF CONTENTS

CHAPTER 1

"That's all Your Honour." Jack adjusted his tie and turned to the chair.

Silence covered the courtroom ceiling. Few coughs were faintly audible, so were the restless people who couldn't keep their feet still.

Neythan felt his heartbeat rise. The outcome was out of his control and the metal around his wrist wasn't as tight as the thick chain around his waist. Possible scenarios had raced in his mind. No hope. Not that it mattered that much. A slight right movement of his eyeball summed up the situation. The look that masked his Lawyer's face was like walking into the rain and hoping that not a single drop will fall on your flesh.

The Lawyer had done his part. But was it enough to influence the jury?

"May the defendant rise?" The Judge said.

Neythan stood. He fought the urge to look back and see if Alisha had come for the final hearing. He had not told her his side of the story. It was more than a fact that all she knew was what every person in the country knew. Which was only what the News had been saying for the past seven months. He was an enemy of the people. The time had come to see if he was also an enemy of the Jury.

The Judge looked at the man who stood on his right side. The man held an A4 bond paper with both his hands. "Mr. Foreman?" The Judge said. "Has the Jury reached a verdict?"

"Yes. Your Honour." The man cleared his throat. "Case number VC99543269. Neythan Evock against The County Durham People and The Police Department." He wiped his nose and gave the Judge a glance. "On two counts of first-degree murder. We find the defendant--." He paused then proceeded. "Not guilty."

An eruption of swear words, boos, insults, and shouts proved that the people didn't agree with the outcome. Warmblood flowed at the tip of Neythan's fingers. The noise behind him began to sound more like his own salvation's anthem.

The Judge dropped the hammer a few times before he got back the attention of the people. His voice echoed. People had now stood. "You may now proceed Mr. Foreman." The Judge wiped his forehead with the back of his hand.

"On one count of armed robbery, in which the defendant allegedly fled the scene with 7 million pounds." He continued after a deep exhale. "We find the defendant, not guilty your honour."

"That's just bollocks." The Prosecutor threw his folders on the floor.

While papers floated in the air, The Foreman duked as a shoe flew above his head.

A hard, metallic object burst its contents after it landed on Neythan's head, just above his ear. The foamy liquid sprayed past his right side.

"You need to calm down my friend," Jack said.

"Fuck this man," Neythan said while he slammed the table with his fists again.

He applied force on his Lawyer's chest with his palms. Watched his Lawyer wobble backward the same time his vision caught another can of ginger beer flew past where must have been his Lawyer's face's position. The can might have found its way to the Judge but Neythan failed to confirm that.

His hands had now been locked. He felt the force of the two police officers pull him. Both their heads were beneath his shoulders, but they managed to maneuver Neythan from the chairs towards the exit door next to the Judge's chair.

They locked his arms with the inside of their elbows. The chains on his ankles failed him to make strides that would compensate the pace of the police officers. Neythan tripped. It didn't bother them. They just dragged him while the tip of his shoes scratched the old wooden floor. He cracked a smile when one of the police officers kissed the sore of a flying boot.

They had now passed the door to the corridor. Dim, but he could still hear his salvation anthem.

"Hey?"

The police officers stopped after they heard the shout. Neythan knew who it was. They all turned.

"What?" The police officer on the left said. He breathed heavy.

"I think that's far enough," Jack said. "My client is a free man now. Remember?"

"We are very much aware of that." The one on the right said and caressed the gun on his hip. "But we need to process the prisoner out of the system."

Neythan had already accessed possible scenarios if Jack was to fail to deal with the situation. Both scenarios would leave the police officers unconscious or worse. They were too close to him, within range of maximum damage. They still had their arms around his hands. And one thing above all, they had the keys.

"I don't think that's necessary Sir. Given the nature of this case and not to mention the verdict." Jack walked forward. "I think for the safety of my client, you should let him find his way out."

"He's safe with us." The one on the right said and rubbed his foot against the floor. Something he had done a few times before.

"Take these chains off me man." He loosened their grip.

The police officer withdrew his gun. "What are you trying to do? Huh?" He raised his voice and aimed at Neythan's face.

Neythan stared in the policeman's eyes then on the hand that held the gun. He breathed out with a slight head shake. "Keep that gun on my face and your friend here will pull your head out from that wall behind you."

"What? What did you just say?" He cocked the gun. "Did you just threaten me?" He rubbed his foot against the floor again. "Turn around and move forward."

"Ok. Enough of this." The Lawyer said and stood beside the other police officer who still had not caught his breath. "Sir. You seem to be the rational one here. Could you give me the keys? Please?"

"No. You are not." The one with the gun said. "You need to back up."

"Don't point that gun at me, my friend," Jack said. "You have already broken more than four laws right now."

"I am the law."

"If I don't get the keys right now." Jack adjusted his tie. "I will take you before the Judge and we will see if the keys are worth the years, I will pin on both of your heads."

The quiet police officer threw the keys to Jack.

"What..."

"You know how smart this shite is. I am not going to prison for no bugger." He then walked forward towards the end of the corridor.

Jack unlocked the cuffs before he unlocked the chains around Neythan.

The sound from the courtroom had decreased. The police officer beside them put his gun back in the holster. Looked at Neythan then at Jack. No word, just the sound of his footsteps along the corridor.

Neythan smiled and rubbed his wrists. "No words can describe how grateful I am man." He put Jack around his arms. "Thanks. You the man."

Jack breathed. "No problem my friend." He gave a nod. "You need to bring Alisha to an understanding of what really happened. We might have jumped this hurdle my friend, but you know your wife." He laughed.

"About Alisha still," Neythan said and scratched his eye. "Is she here?"

"Yes," Jack said. "I made sure of that. Take this corridor, it will take you right outside. She's waiting for you." He shook Neythan's hand. "I have done my part. I am going underground now. Remember, eyes open and your gun close. We still don't know what we are up against."

"You know me, man." He took the left corridor.

It was dim. Dust tingled his nostrils but that didn't interfere with the joy which boiled in his heart. A free man with only one desire. To reunite with his family. Only seconds away.

Spider webs covered the door handle. Visible layers of dust covered the door frame. He felt the resistance when he tried to pull the handle down. He applied more force which welcomed the sound of locks as they released. He pulled the door towards him. Light escaped in. So was a scream.

He opened it wide and stepped outside.

Raised his hand to shield himself from the rays. Tanya ran towards him. Her braided hair floated in the air. Neythan set his right knee on the ground and welcomed his daughter into a warm hug. He fought the urge of tears as he felt her heartbeat on his chest and her sharp melody scream of joy.

"I missed you, daddy." She said with her arms wrapped around his neck. "Mama said you are coming home today."

"Yeah, I am." He said. "And this time, I ain't going anywhere."

"You promise?"

He recognized the voice and turned his head. Stood up. Looked straight into her small eyes. Took a moment to breathe in her beauty. Then held her around the waist. Pulled her closer. He then felt the wetness and softness of her lips on his, he pressed his hands against her bottom while he felt her tongue inside his mouth. A vibrated feeling ran through his body and he smiled. "Yes, 1 promise. I am not going anywhere."

Her thick lips formed a smile. The sun worshiped her brown skin and made her dark hair sparkle while the breeze maintained its curls.

"Where's Travis?"

"In the car," Alisha said and turned.

#

"I think we should go on holiday Daddy." Tanya leaned forward.

"Sit back Tee," Alisha said.

Neythan turned to the back seat. "Yes. I think that's a great idea sweetie." He looked at his son. "What you think Travis?"

Travis raised his head from his phone. "Yeah," He shrugged. "I guess so."

"I think that's a great way to celebrate your case win," Alisha said while she checked for oncoming cars before she emerged on the roundabout.

"It sure is," Neythan said and smiled while he relaxed on the seat. It was a great day. Great outcome. Great weather. He admitted that most of the thanks had to be given to Jack. The Lawyer had pulled down a huge tree.

"How did you even find Jack?" Alisha glanced at Neythan. "He one hell of a smart man. He was confident from the beginning." She indicated. "To be honest, I had a few doubts. Didn't even think you would find a lawyer who would want to represent you."

He sighed a laughter. "He kinda popped out of nowhere." Scratched the back of his head. "He said he knew Layan."

"Layan?" Her tone changed. "Neythan. Did you go back?"

Neythan checked the rear-view mirror again. The black Jeep was still behind them. "Take that next left turn." He said with calm. He had noticed the Jeep five turns before.

"What? Why?" She said with a frowned face.

"Just do it," Neythan said. "Don't indicate."

Alisha kissed the cab with the tires.

"We should go to the Caribbean islands," Tanya said.

Neythan looked. The Jeep still followed. That was the confirmation he needed.

"Where exactly were you thinking of going Tee?" Alisha said.

In that instance, something broke through the back windscreen before it hit the radio, which then turned off.

"Put your head down," Neythan shouted as the rear-view mirror reflected two automatic rifles outside the back windows of the Jeep.

"What's going on?" Alisha chocked on her words.

"Just put your head down and drive as fast as you can." He slid his right hand underneath his seat. "Keep your eyes on the road."

"Daddy!" Tanya screamed.

"It's gonna be fine Tee," Neythan said. "Just lay down on the seat."

He pulled out a pistol from under his seat. Checked the mirror. Smoke rose from bullet holes. Checked the magazine. Full.

"Is that a gun?" Alisha shouted while she swerved to avoid an oncoming van.

"Eyes on the road." Neythan cocked the gun. "Keep your hands steady."

"Why is there a gun in your car?" Her voice carried anger. "Why Neythan? You promised to …" An involuntary scream of shock interrupted her when the side window beside her exploded into fragments of broken pieces.

It wasn't time for domestic conversations. Not when bullets sprayed towards them. He checked his mirror. It wasn't there anymore. He turned to the back. Clear view. Tanya and Travis screamed. He shielded with the seat and took aim. The back windscreen had webs of cracks. Bullet holes. As the car swerved the wind carried it away providing Neythan with a clear view to the Jeep behind. The bouncing lid of the boot was only a minor distraction.

Two shots into the Jeep's tinted windscreen seemed to have caused a mechanical error to the car. He watched it as it lost control before it kissed an oncoming bus.

Neythan breathed. "It's ok now Evocks." He sat back and looked forward.

Alisha kept her foot on the accelerator.

"Daddy?" Travis said. "The door is open."

"Shit," Neythan said. "Slow down Alisha."

Alisha sniffed. Tight grip on the steering but didn't seem like she heard anything Neythan said.

"I am moving away from the door."

"No," Neythan shouted. "Keep your seatbelt on." He then turned to Alisha. "Stop the car."

She didn't react. She didn't turn. She didn't slow down. She didn't blink. And she fast approached a sharp bend.

Before Neythan reacted to Travis standing from the seat, he felt a violent force that shook the car. Alisha's head hammered his shoulder. He threw his right hand on the steering to regain control of the car. It might have been too late as the car swerved away from its rightful lane. The oncoming red Benz blasted a horn. Three sixty steering turn made Neythan's car only graze the side of the Benz, but it also took him over the cliff.

He felt the car go on its side in a violent motion. For a moment he could see the sky and then not, and then again. He felt the sting of pieces of glass as they pierced through his flesh. Fast. Only reflex actions. He didn't feel in control of anything. Only felt the pain every time his body made contact against the car.

Neythan couldn't hear his wife or his children, only the sound between life and death. Panic suffocated him. He closed his eyes.

Everything then stopped. His heart pounded. Relief ran cold in his veins. He felt the pain. He knew he was still alive.

Stillness. He opened his eyes, blood stung them. His hands felt the roof of the car which was now on the ground. He felt the resistance in his neck muscles when he turned to Alisha. She didn't seem conscious, but she breathed. There weren't visible injuries on her face. Her hair swept the broken glasses on the bottom as her head dangled.

Neythan released the seatbelt. He groaned when he fell. At the back, Tanya laid on her back, but the oxygen made her stomach expand. She had a cut on the side of her eye. He turned to his left.

"Travis. Trav-Travis. Travis?" Neythan shouted while his eyes moved everywhere.

Panic poisoned him. He knew calmness was exactly what he needed. He faced forward, backward, and sideways. Still, no sign of his son. He tried to block the worst thoughts and kept his breathing steady.

"Travis?" He shouted louder than before.

Tanya raised her head.

He kicked his door to open. It must have been jammed. He applied more force with a roar. He heard the hinges loosen. Another effort did it.

Crawled through the broken glasses. Looked forward. Hollow forest filled with considerably spaced thin long trees. Dead brown and dirty leaves. Sticks and dried up broken branches and ancient fallen trees on the ground. No sign of grass or maybe it was buried underneath the leaves.

He pushed against the ground. Rested his chest on his knee. Applied effort which stood him upright. Couldn't ignore the pain in every part of his body. His joints complained with every movement he made.

The sting of blood in his eyes blurred his vision. But he still felt the heat from the rays that penetrated the long tress from above. The right arm felt heavy as he raised it to wipe blood off his eyes. While his shirt sleeves moved slowly against his eye lids. Impact. Pain exploded on the side of his right knee, just a fraction off his knee cap. It sent him to the ground. He could not hold his scream as he rolled.

Something hard had struck him. He glanced up and a tall man advanced toward him with a silver pole raised. Ready to strike again.

Neythan seized his glance and ran his eyes around him.

To his right side, he saw Tanya who looked like she was coughing and in front of him, he saw Alisha who hung on the seat belt with her head down.

The image pumped him with adrenaline as he dogged another strike but felt the brush of air past his face. Neythan pushed himself closer to the wrecked car.

He saw it at the corner of his eye. Extended his right hand to reach it but he wasn't faster than the pole which barely missed his ribs but sunk perfectly into the side of his stomach, forcing a cough out of him.

Another inch of movement, he felt it in his hand.

The man breathed a sound with his hand raised, mounting the momentum for a third strike.

In a reflex. Neythan turned, faced the man, and squeezed.

The man froze in motion. The metal pole escaped his grasp. His chest bled. It coloured the white shirt he wore. Then he fell on his knees like his legs got chopped.

Neythan sprung to his feet with his eyes fixed on the man.

He roared his words. "Who the fuck are you? Who send you?" He wanted to break the man's neck, but he needed answers.

The man didn't say a word. His eyes slowly shut. He weakly gasped for breath. Then fell forward, with the dirty leaves welcoming his face first.

"Shit." Neythan stood up.

"Travis!" No one responded. Just the sound of the spinning tires and the exhaust still smoked.

Blood and sweat flowed down his body. His right leg felt numb. His eyes scanned everywhere, and his son's name breathed loudly out of his mouth. Still, no response.

He walked up to the road. With every step, he called Travis.

No cars passed by. Heat radiated from the sweaty tar. The heat waves seemed like invisible flames.

He took in a heavy breath with his mouth. To his left, the road seemed endless and nothing other than the stretching white lines in the middle. He turned to his right and saw a blue hat just before the dip.

Relief.

The pistol in his hand, cuts on his face bled steady.

He brushed his eyes with his sleeves. Ran forward and fell. The pain in his knee had suddenly intensified. Neythan limbed toward the dip and never stopped shouting his son's name.

He picked up the hat and a few feet away, next to a granite stone, Travis was there.

Neythan moved closer and noticed not only the blood that covered his son's face but a visible cut on the side of his head. The stone had opened Travis's skull, brown tissue exposed itself out of the skull.

He felt like air was being pumped inside his lungs that he couldn't exhale. He didn't know what to do but to throw himself next to his son.

"Travis talk to me, talk to me man. No, no, no." Neythan shouted but his son remained unresponsive. Tears blurred his vision. He put his fingers below Travis's ear. He didn't feel anything.

He cried aloud. "Somebody help me?" Not that anybody could hear him.

He held Travis's hand. Sniffed and calmed. "You are an Evock," Neythan said. "We are strong, we are strong," He sniffed. "We are survivors. You don't do this man." He swallowed saliva. "Don't do this Travis, don't do this." He looked at Travis's closed eyes. "Talk to me, I am listening." Slightly shook his head. "Say something. Say something please." He said with a soft voice. "I am here ok, I am here, I am listening." Tears still washed the blood off his face. "Say something man. Say. Something." He raised his voice like he was in a choir band.

Neythan bowed his head. Closed his eyes and sobbed.

Few minutes went by.

He could not gather any thought in his mind. He couldn't even feel the heat from the sun. Just pain within him.

A car pulled over next to him. He raised his head and the police officer was already stepping out of the car. "Call an ambulance please." He shouted with a voice filled with hope.

"Already done it." The police officer said. "Less than two minutes away."

#

Alisha tried to remove the seatbelt to no avail. It trapped her on the seat. She looked to her side, Neythan wasn't there. She heard a cough from the back.

"Mama are you ok?" Tanya asked and moved toward her mother.

"No Tee, can you pass me a piece of a broken glass please," Alisha said while she tried to pull the belt.

"Mama?"

"Yes, Tee."

"Why is the ground …" Tanya breathed a sharp scream that would have driven away any birds nearby.

A chill ran through Alisha's body. Before she could ask her daughter.

"There's dead man's body outside," Tanya said with a shiver.

"Dead?" Alisha wrestled the seatbelt with panic. "Who's it?"

"I don't know." Tanya turned to face her mother. "He's full of blood and has army trousers."

"Can you see Dad or Travis?"

"No mama," Tanya said. "The man looks scary."

Alisha kept wrestling with the seatbelt. "The glass, Tanya?"

"Oh." She handed the broken piece to her mother.

"Good. What else do you see?"

"The ground is wet."

Her daughter's statement seemed to have penetrated the fear and panic she felt and renewed her sense of smell. She could now detect the smell of gasoline. Steam also escaped from the naked bonnet. She slowly inhaled trying to achieve the impossible. To calm her nerves. "Tee, I want you to listen to me ok." The pace she attempted to cut the belt with defeated the purpose she intended with her words. "Go as far away from this car as possible ok?"

"No mama." She affirmed. "l am not leaving you here. We will only leave together."

"No Tanya. You need to go now. Run." Alisha's tone exploded.

With a sad face, "No Mama," She said. "Let me help you cut the belt."

Alisha continued at the belt. Not much progress shown.

"We will wait then," Tanya said. "I know Dad will be here."

#

"What happened here?"

Neythan embraced the silence of his thoughts. Kept his eyes on his son. Everything around him sounded like rushing waters in his ears.

"Was this an accident? Are there any other casualties?" The police officer asked again.

With a faint voice, "My wife and daughter." Neythan spoke.

"What?" The police officer stepped closer to Neythan.

Neythan raised his head. Another man approached.

"My name is James." The paramedic introduced himself. "How long has the boy been unresponsive?" He asked and checked Travis's pulse and his pupils.

Two ladies in navy blue outfits were already fastening Travis to the bed. They pushed him to the ambulance.

"The boy needs urgent medical attention, Sir," James said while he wrote something in his book. "This is a critical injury. Are you with him?" He looked at Neythan. "Would you come with us to the hospital?" The paramedic asked.

Neythan was still. He looked like he was daydreaming. He never responded or never heard anything?

"Sir!" The paramedic said, "Are you ok?"

"Is my son alive?" The only words that escaped Neythan's lips.

"Yes, but he needs medical help, urgently. Could you come with him?"

"We need to go." A lady shouted from the front of the ambulance.

A thunderous explosion stole everybody's attention. A cold chill traveled in Neythan's body and snapped him back to reality, "Alisha?" He shouted and took off towards the thick dark smoke that rose higher than the trees.

He dragged his right leg. The pain was present, but he paid no attention to it. He ran.

The police officer ran beside him.

He slipped on the gravel as he descended towards the car. A few more strides, the horror was within view.

The last flames danced with the steady wind. The smell of burnt tires filled his lungs. His knees felt weak that he threw himself to the ground. There was no sign of life in the ashes and flames before him.

It had turned out to be the most disastrous, painful, and tragic day of his entire existence. He was supposed to be celebrating the victory of his trial, but life has a way of taking everything away just when you thought you had everything.

CHAPTER 2

"Are you sure about this?" He studied the profile.

"Sending a legend is the best approach General." Lieutenant Dough said. "Engaging directly with Evock might cause noise. Noise equals attention. And that's something we can't afford." He looked down at the folder on the desk.

"Might cause noise?" The General widened his eyes. "He just neutralised an operative."

The Lieutenant maintained silence.

"I need an effective mission plan Lieutenant. Effective." He closed the folder. "The longer the Xenner stays in a civilian's possession the higher the risk of everything falling apart." He stood from his chair. "I can't have that."

Lieutenant Dough cleared his throat. "Shall I activate the Legend Sir?"

"Should have been done yesterday."

\#

Ten minutes had passed. Not a movement was made. He had turned the engine off. Parked the car by the side of the road, just before the gate. A clear view to the entrance of the Catholic Cathedral, downtown of Newcastle.

The heart was willing to proceed inside and enter the confession room but his will was weak. He was a man of faith and values, but the situation he's in contradicted his core beliefs. Could be that he didn't have a choice or maybe, sometimes a man must do whatever is necessary to protect his own family.

He surely had crossed a line, but was it the last time to do so? If not, no point to see the Priest. Though, it is important in the eyes of the Lord to repent. It is also of greater importance for a man to protect his family in the eyes of the Lord. Damn.

He closed his eyes and contemplated for another two minutes. Still no will. Maybe a hit of nicotine will do. He thought.

Reached into the inner pocket of his jacket. Pulled a pack of cigarettes with his right hand. Opened his door. Stepped out of the car. Weak wind danced together with the late morning sun. Clear sky. A troubled mind.

After this cigarette, I will go in. I must. He said to himself before the spark on his lighter produced a flame.

Something about the moment when the flame touches the tip of a cigarette. The way it slowly consumes and keeps on until the cigarette burns out. It's the same way guilt eats a man's heart. Difference with a cigarette is, guilt only stops when the heart stops beating. He wondered if there're men out there who carry guilt in their hearts. If there were, he believed they would also want redemption just like he did. The hope of redemption is the only comfort for a heart consumed with guilt.

He blew the smoke out with calm. Few more puffs.

He turned toward the gate. Moved away from the side of the car. Walked past the bonnet. Foot on the pavement. Extended his left arm to push the gate while his right hand flicked away the butt of the cigarette. He disabled hesitation and quarreling thoughts in his mind. Just a quick shuffle of his feet towards the entrance.

Nothing much on the outside. Just a pavement tiled with ancient stones. The Cathedral itself looked just about the same as the most Cathedrals in England. Difference was, it wasn't situated in the Town Centre. Quite place on the border of Town. Surrounded by what seemed like abandoned business buildings and houses.

Stepped on the first step of the entrance. His phone vibrated in his side pocket.

"Yes?" He answered.

A pause. Like the person on the other line had gone mute. "Granick?" He knew the voice. The cold chill that traveled down his spine confirmed who it was. "It's time." The voice said again.

"Alright. I'm on it." Granick turned to his car.

\#

Stared at the family picture, hoped it could wash away the pain with memories. Gulped the ice-cold whisky. It felt warm down his throat. Guilt and blame ran through his veins. Loyalty surely does come at a price. He only wanted to help an old friend. He damned himself for not thinking things through and for choosing to fight the prosecution. Maybe they could still be alive, but he would be in some prison with no hope of seeing his family ever again. He had to get out even though the reality didn't feel like he was free. The one thing he fought to be close to is what was taken from him.

Many voices spoke in his mind. The same as the previous day. Was it his fault? It seemed like it to him. It seemed like good motives can also have devastating consequences.

Neythan stood up. Drained the remains of the whisky in his glass. Approached the door.

A police officer stepped in after the door was opened. "Jesus?" The police officer walked forward. "You look like…" He didn't finish the sentence. "Have you had any sleep?"

"What do you want?"

"Well," He cleared his throat. "I came to see how you are coping. Given the recent circumstances." He sat down.

"Circumstances?" Neythan turned. "Say that again and that's the last thing you will ever say." He poured another full glass of whisky and sat down opposite the police officer.

"Ok," He rested his elbows on his knees. "I have one question for you. Just one."

Neythan didn't respond.

"What would you do if you knew who was behind the accident?" He rubbed his palms together. "Not that you think it was an accident. Do you?"

"Who was it?" He felt a heartbeat in his stomach.

"Oh no." He waved with his index finger. "That's not how it works."

"So, what do you want then?"

The police officer stood up. Straightened his trousers, reached his suit jacket. "Here." He handed Neythan a card. "You need to sober up and clean up, then give me a call first thing tomorrow morning."

"You better have something." Neythan took the card. Looked at it. "DC Granick, huh?"

"You got that right." He turned to the door. "Tomorrow. First thing." He shouted before he closed the door.

Neythan placed the card on top of the picture frame which was on the table. Lifted the Jack Daniels bottle. "Shit." It was empty. Sat back and rested his head on the sofa.

He had felt something off about Granick, he just couldn't pin-point it. Neythan liked the idea of working with him. The Detective could get access to useful information, something Neythan needed. He needed to know who killed his wife and daughter. When he does know who killed them and who was involved, they would have to die. The one thing Neythan doubted Granick would agree with. Not that it was a problem, he just didn't want to kill the Detective, but if the Detective stood in the way, Neythan would have no choice.

#

It was just after eight. They were the only customers in Costa. Neythan could see the waters of the sea through the window. One lady swept the floor and the other one was behind the counter.

"I am good. Thanks." Neythan leaned to the table. "Let's just get to the point of why you made me leave my bed this early."

"Ok," Granick said while he emptied the sugar sachets into his coffee. He stirred then looked at Neythan. "Why would anyone want to kill you?"

"Alright," Neythan cracked his middle finger with his thumb. "There's one thing you need to get straight, you are not fucking police to me. You are either with me and give me the information you have or against me, well," He sat back. "In that case, I will have to get it out of you." He looked Granick in the eye and ripped a sugar sachet, emptied it in the Detective's coffee. "The sooner you stop asking questions and start telling me what you know, the better we get along."

Granick cleared his throat then made an exaggerated loud exhale.

"What do you have?" Neythan said.

"The car that hit you, you know, the one..."

"Yeah yeah, I know." He interrupted him. "Go on."

"It's registered to an address in Newcastle," Granick said. "The weird thing is, he's the brother of the guard you allegedly murdered."

"What?"

"But," Granick paused with his mouth open. "There's no evidence that puts him at the scene though since the driver was never found." Granick looked at Neythan like he expected him to comment about the missing driver, then continued. "He had also reported the car stolen."

"Bullshit," Neythan said. "What a coincidence? We pay him a visit." He stood up.

"For what?" Nearly choked on his coffee.

"To pay my condolences."

#

It was no surprise that the traffic in A19 was slower because of the road works. They weren't far from their exit though.

At low volume, the speakers played a gospel song. Neythan figured the Detective might be a religious man but he didn't bother to ask. He was busy trying to figure out who would want him dead. The guy they were going to see had a reasonable motive but Nyethan had thought that was just a floating threat in a vicious tornado. It just didn't seem plausible that the guy would hire a hitman and a gang unless they were different people. That posed the unanswered question, was the shooting, and the lone hitman connected, or they were different people?

Granick slowed the car to let a young boy cross the road on his skateboard. Some skids ran about and shouted along the sidewalks. At the corner were the road end, Neythan noticed two boys who wrestled on the lawn before a young girl appeared from behind the corner with a brick in both of her hands. Neythan burst out a loud laugh after one of the boys on the lawn received the brick to the face.

"What?" Granick said after he made a right turn.

"Don't tell me you didn't see that." He tried to suppress his laugh.

"See what?"

"You must be blind." Neythan coughed.

"We are here." Granick climbed the curb and turned the key. "You stay in the car; I will go in."

"I see, you ain't just blind," Neythan opened the door. "You are crazy too."

"No, Evock," Granick said. "I get that you wanna get some answers and all but think for a sec." He paused for the lady walking her dog to pass. "If this guy is involved in what happened, do you think he's just gonna let you in?" He looked at Neythan. "My priority here is to prevent things from escalating. The last thing I want is dead bodies or violence." He said with an even, low tone. "Let me do this."

"Five minutes." Neythan closed the door. "Five minutes is all you get."

Granick nodded and got out.

Neythan agreed. Avoiding attention from the police was a good idea to an extent.

He checked his wrist. 09:30am. Third day since he left the courtroom. He had to visit Travis later in the afternoon. The image of his bloodied son kept flashing in his mind. Family was all that mattered in his life. For a man who had never experienced much affection from family, he had sworn to love and protect his own.

He had to find who was responsible for the death of his wife and daughter. There was no limit to what he was willing to do to his transgressor.

The streets were quiet. The sky was spotless. Granick had not been back. Ten minutes had passed. Neythan searched the car.

He couldn't find a gun. It didn't matter much than understanding what happened that day. He knew the guy would either shed some revelation or shed some blood.

Neythan stepped out of the car. Didn't process anything in his mind. He just headed straight to the door. He knocked.

A moment passed before the door slowly opened. The first thing he saw was a gun pointed at him.

"You came to kill me too hmm?" The man chewed something.

Neythan raised his hands. "Look, man, I only want to talk."

"About whaa hmm?" He instructed with his gun to make Neythan come inside. "How do you even know where I live hmm?"

Neythan didn't respond, he stepped inside.

"Drop the gun." Granick now had his gun attached to the back of the man's neck.

"What the hell Detective?" The man turned. "Do ya know who this fucker is?" He chewed while he maintained a disgusted look towards Neythan

"Put the gun down." The Detective cocked his gun.

The man surrendered his gun to the carpet.

"I thought you understood me," Granick said.

"Well, five minutes is long past." Neythan walked forward. "It's my turn."

"You need to leave," Granick said. "Let me do my job."

"Don't point that gun at me," Neythan said then impatience over-powered him. He motioned his right fist and connected his knuckles with the man's chin.

"Jesus Christ Evock," Granick shouted.

Neythan pressed his right foot on the man's throat.

"What do you think you're doing?" The Detective shouted again.

"Getting answers." He pressed harder. "Something you should have done already." He watched the man struggle for air and the man's eyes seemed like they were about to explode out of the socket.

Neythan lifted his foot after he felt a tap on his leg. "You ready to talk?"

The man coughed, spat whatever he chewed, it was red and drooled saliva on the dark carpet. He caressed his neck while taking in heavy breaths. "Ya sins are catching up with ya hey?" He laughed. His beard was now covered in thick brownish saliva.

Neythan stomped hard on the man's fingers.

"Evock, you need to stop," Granick said while the man rolled on the carpet with his mouth open producing a sharp scream like a dying goat.

"Stay back," Neythan said while he crouched. Yanked the man off the carpet and slammed him against the side wall. Neythan then connected his forehead with the man's nose.

The man let out a cry. "Do something Detective." He tried to turn towards Granick but Neythan's grip prevented that.

"Are you ready to talk?" Neythan loosened his grip.

"Aye?" He said and sniffed blood in his nose. "Let go of me neck."

The man slid down against the wall till he was sat. He tilted his head up. Wiped blood off his lips and noes. "Nobody was supposed to die." He coughed. "They wanted you alive." He spat out blood.

"Who?" Neythan fixed his eyes on the man.

"The Russians." He took in heavy breaths.

"Names?" Neythan raised his voice.

"I don't know any names." He frowned his face. "But the man who's looking for you." He spat and looked at Neythan. "They call him The B ..."

A bullet drilled the man's skull, just above his right eyebrow and stopped him from finishing his sentence.

Neythan turned and released a quick kick to Granick's extended arm. The gun floated across the room. A reversed motion found Neythan's back heel sunk in the Detective's neck. The wall might have supported Granick's fall but not Neythan's chock. "Why did you do that?" Neythan whispered through his teeth.

He released his grip and moved towards the gun on the floor.

Neythan cocked the gun. "This is what we came for." He said. "To know who's behind what happened."

"I had to kill him," Granick said. "To protect us, to protect me."

"Protect?"

"Yes." Granick looked at the dead man. "He had seen us. He was going to the police after we left."

"That wasn't your decision to make."

"This is your fault," Granick said. "You should have let me do my job."

"You clearly don't know shit about your job."

"So, you do?" Granick widened his eyes. "I work within the law. This is not how things are done. I ask people for information not beat the crap out of them."

"I see," Neythan said. "You kill them instead?"

"You wanted him to go to the police?" Granick said. "You should have just stayed in the car."

"You should have let him finish talking." Neythan lowered the gun. "Next time you do something like this, you better kill me too because I will." He headed out.

CHAPTER 3

Granick pulled out his phone and dialed.

"Hello." The voice said. "Who's this?"

"DC Granick." He cleared his throat. "Daniels said to call this number if an accident was to happen."

"Is this your first time?"

"Why?" Granick stretched his neck.

"You should never say your name." He sounded like he had food in his mouth. "Anyways, just send me the postcode and leave right now."

Before Granick responded, the phone was down.

He typed in the postcode and send the text. He then searched the dead man's pockets. Found a card and a mobile phone.

He straightened his back. Unlocked the mobile phone, numerous unnamed contacts. Most things on the phone didn't make sense to him but he knew Brian would be able to understand it. The card was a restaurant business card with a Russian name on it.

Granick ran his eyes around him, picked up his gun and left the house.

He breathed heavy and the sweat itched his left eye. First time is always the hardest, as they say. That felt a different meaning to what that common saying says. A Catholic who's also a representative of the law had just blown a civilian's brains out. To what cause? To what limit? Had the line of being humane disappeared?

It was a very conflicting experience. The line between law and necessity was gradually blurring. Granick's heart was burdened. He felt like he had no choice but had that eye that says, "I will do whatever it takes."

Started the engine and headed to Peterlee. At least that was the idea until he found himself pulling over at the car park next to the pub.

The hot air breathed heat over his face. He scratched his back and felt his shirt stuck against his skin. He thought about lighting a cigarette, but he believed his thirst was greater than his craves for nicotine.

#

"How is he doing now Doc?"

"He's stable." Made a lazy sigh. "He got here on time, which was a very good thing." Another sigh and continued. "But, uh, there are things you should know Mr. Evock."

"What you mean Doc?" He scratched his chin. More like a distressed subconscious reaction. "Is everything alright?"

"Can you follow me." The Doctor stopped in his tracks when he realized Neythan wasn't moving. "He may still hear us. I think it's best if we leave this room."

It began to feel like the day couldn't get any better as he followed the footsteps of the Doctor.

"Have a seat." The Doctor said while he pulled out a folder from the top drawer of his desk. He then slapped it on the desk before he sat down. Took a deep breath, looked at Neythan's unblinking face and opened the first page. "Mr. Evock, your son suffered a very severe critical injury to the back of his head. This damage affected his skull and his brain." He moved in his chair. "However."

"What?"

"The operation was successful. Your son is a fighter." The Doctor said in a calm voice. His facial expression seemed like there was something more sinister to where the conversation was headed.

Travis was alive. It was better than the dead end he had had earlier. That was something he had to reflect on and form an effective plan to find out who the Russians were. There wasn't a starting point and Neythan knew it. But then again, what did the Detective and the man spoke about before he came in? Neythan questioned. All that was for another time, the present time was to hear what the Doctor had to say.

"What exactly are you trying to say Doc." He said like he had had a flash back.

The Doctor cleared his throat. "Your son's stable. He hasn't regained consciousness yet, but I assure you, we are going to give him the best care possible."

"How much time are you talking about here Doc?" He could feel his palms getting warmer.

"I am sorry Mr. Evock, I cannot answer that." The Doctor said. "It is up to him now. We can only hope he regains consciousness sooner rather than later."

"What you mean by that Doc?"

"We did everything we possibly could Mr Evock." He closed his folder. "We ran some tests after the operation, and I have been monitoring his brain activity these past two days and today." He paused with his mouth open and then went on.

Neythan couldn't understand the words the Doctor went on to say. "What are you saying Doc?" He choked on his words.

"Ok." The Doctor said. "What I mean is, there's a high chance that your son could recover with a severe disability." He looked at Neythan. "Best case could be he might not be able to see or walk."

"How is that even the best-case Doc?" He slammed the table and his eyes became watery. "You did say there's a high chance, right?" Neythan looked at the Doctor like he begged.

"Yes." He nodded.

"Then you ain't certain right?" He tried to fight his tears. "Which means there's also a chance he could recover well?"

"I wouldn't want to raise your hopes Mr. Evock." The Doctor said. "In my experience and my informed opinion, these tests are rarely wrong, and if they are, which is very unlikely, it's by a very slight margin."

The Doctor's words felt like fire blazed within Neythan. He felt like he drowned. The feeling of panic and inability to breath under water felt as real to him as the chair he sat on in the Doctor's office.

Self-questioning in his mind. The questions didn't matter to him. It was the same questions he had been asking himself since the accident. And, he had come to believe he was the one who had caused all the pain to his family. What Neythan couldn't figure out was why it had all happened.

Many thoughts went through his mind. What was more real than the thoughts, was the pain he felt by each breath he inhaled. It haunted him like a ghost.

His reality had become a nightmare he couldn't wake from but to only face it through. Soul torturing questions he couldn't avoid began to pour into his mind. How would he tell Travis about the tragic death of his mother and his sister? Neythan couldn't bear the thought of having that conversation with his son. The more he thought about it was when he wished if it was him who had died that day. Only him.

"Did you hear what l said?" The Doctor asked him. "l can get you, someone, to talk with about this. I understand how hard this can be on people."

"I appreciate that Doc but no. I think I will be alright." He stood up and extended his hand. "Thank you for your time Doc."

"You're welcome." The Doctor shook Neythan's hand. "I will let you know as soon as he wakes up."

Neythan left the office and headed toward Travis's ward.

He stood on the right side of the bed, beside Travis's head. Kneeled and held his son's hand.

The continued beeping sound of the breathing machine irritated him, even though it was the official proof that Travis was still alive. He looked at his son. Helpless. He knew that there was nothing he could do to help Travis. He despised himself. What the Doctor had said soon became a burden too heavy and painful to lift.

Neythan barely saw Travis's face. It was bandaged from the back of his head, round to his forehead and across his cheeks to under his chin. The eyes were spared but they were closed like someone in deep sleep, they didn't twitch, not even slightly. A thick white-grey tube went into his mouth, looked like it choked him. Travis was still, no movement of his body to suggest he was alive but Neythan knew he was. The Doctor had said, and the machine still beeped. They were a few needles going into him. All connected to different tubes that carried different colours of liquids.

His heart ached from the sight of his son laid on the hospital bed. It was a situation he never thought or wanted to see his son in. Not any father would. He could only assume his son was rested, that's how it seemed. He tried to shut down the thoughts of his son still being in pain.

With both his knees on the floor, Neythan moved his thumb on top of Travis's right hand. He uttered words to his unconscious son with desperate hope that his son could hear him.

Just stillness and quietness from his son. Neythan continued to utter more words. "I love you son." He sniffed. "l am sorry this happened to you, l will be with you every step of the way." He didn't move his gaze from Travis's eyes. He hoped for them to open. "I want you to fight son. This is your war." He squeezed his hand. "I will make sure the people who did this are laid next to you with no breath in their lungs. That's my war. We are fighting together son. Evocks are always stronger together." Tears dropped onto the blue gown which covered Travis. "There's nothing that matters more to me than you and your mother and your sister. I love you; I love them." He rested his forehead on top of Travis's hand while he sobbed. "l am going to turn every stone in hell and wash my hands with the blood of the people who made me shed tears." He cleared his throat "When you make a choice son, you should honor it. No love or loyalty must cause you to dishonor it."

Neythan stood up. Reached the back pocket of his black jeans and pulled a blue hat. He placed it on Travis's chest and then kissed his forehead, but only kissed the bandage, he didn't mind. "I love you, Travis," Neythan said and scanned the room. He breathed in and took a moment to let the reality sink in. He then walked slowly to the door and turned, looked at his son like he said goodbye and he left the ward.

He walked down the corridor. Long corridors with light blue walls. He didn't see anyone else.

He threw himself on the chair and sighed, looked up at the ceiling. His hands were spread out on top of other chairs beside him. He closed his eyes and started thinking.

What the Guy had said before the bullet drilled his skull kept on playing in Neythan's mind. Neythan knew that it was the Russians who wanted him alive, he didn't know why. If the Detective had not shot the Guy, Neythan could have known why, but now he knew that that was the answer he had to figure out next. And soon.

What the dead man had said, meant to Neythan that everything had happened because of him. They were attacked because they wanted him. What he didn't understand is why would the Russians want him. He had never crossed paths with Russians before, let alone the ones who come with guns spitting bullets. Did he have something they wanted? That was another question that came across Neythan's mind. He realized he was the focal point; he just didn't understand how and why he became a target.

The person who could help Neythan figure who the Russians were and why they were after him was the Detective. He didn't trust Granick.

A distant female voice snapped him out of his thoughts, and he opened his eyes.

Young lady, mid-twenties, stood right in front of him, dressed in some light blue top and black trousers. Her hair was tied back. She wore an animated smile on her face, with a white plastic cup in her hand reaching to Neythan, "Here, have a drink." She said.

Neythan assumed she was a nurse by how she was dressed, and, why would a random person offer him a drink in a hospital, he thought. Neythan took the drink and seeped, "Thank you." He bowed his head.

"Are you ok?" She asked. "You have been sat here for quite a while now." Her voice was loud, but she wasn't shouting. She spoke to Neythan like she knew him.

"Yeah, who are you?" Neythan gulped another seep of water.

"I am Tracy. I work here. I am a nurse. I was only concerned. You really don't seem well. Are you waiting for someone?" Fast talker.

"No, 1 was here to see my son, he was in an accident" Neythan replied and stood up headed to the nearby bin and threw the plastic cup in it.

A sad face clowned Tracy's animated smile. "I am sorry to hear that. How's he?"

"Alright." Neythan didn't want to continue with the conversation. He thought the nurse read that by the way she stared at him.

"Okay." She slapped her thighs. "I have just finished my shift. Are you driving?"

He shook his head. "Not today."

"1 could drop you home if you don't mind. I don't think it's safe for you to be walking around or staying in a hospital in this state you're in." She said.

Neythan looked at her with surprise on his face but he saw her seriousness. "Why?"

"Don't be silly." She laughed. "It's my job. 1 help people and if 1 leave you like this, 1 would have failed my job." She seemed sarcastic, but she wasn't.

Neythan couldn't understand her but he saw nothing dangerous about her. The way she spoke and moved her hands, her body language was about the honest person he had ever seen apart from his wife and he agreed.

#

Uncomfortable silence in the car rose like mist. Neythan on the passenger seat processing what the Doctor had told him and what that guy had told him. The questions about the nurse ran through his mind too.

"So," She glanced at him. "Are you married?"

Neythan faced her. "How about you tell me more about yourself?"

"Well, you already know my name." She checked the mirror before she changed her lane. "I have been a surgical nurse for nearly six years now and I have always worked at Granite Hospital, where you saw me." She smiled. "Right or left?" Tracy then asked.

"Turn right and stop."

Tracy stopped the car after she turned right. "Are we there yet?" She asked but she looked surprised.

It was barely near his house. Neythan didn't understand why the nurse wanted to help him. He failed to tell between if she only wanted to help or she was after something. He chose not to take a risk to believe in the good heart of the nurse. Not when he knew that there were people after him.

"I am near now, I can walk." He said. "I need the walk anyways. I have spent the whole day sat in that hospital." He opened the door. "Thank you for your generosity," Neythan said and got out of the car before Tracy said anything.

Another thought wanted to believe that Tracy meant no harm, but he still wasn't willing to take that risk. He kept on walking without turning back, till he heard the car took off.

Neythan walked as slow as he could walk. He kept on thinking about what the Guy had said but what really ate his mind was what was he going to say before Granick put a bullet in his head. As hard as he thought, he couldn't come up with a solid answer or plan. That frustrated him.

Maybe it was time to reach out to the Detective and ask what he had.

The distance seemed short. He was already in the driveway of his house. He sat his eyes on the little pink bicycle by the wall of his garage. He almost burst into tears but fought it. What he couldn't fight was the pain.

Seeing Tanya's bicycle made him realize how much he had missed his little girl but that also brought the regret and the blame. He then went inside and went straight to the whisky. He didn't bother about getting a glass and gulped two seeps from the bottle.

The house had a distinctive smell like wet garbage. It looked like it had been a while since it was cleaned. It didn't confirm that someone still lived in it.

Neythan walked across, seemed not bothered by the strong smell. He sat on the sofa. Flicked an empty box of pizza to the floor and he laid down on his back, rested his head on the arm of the sofa, his legs still on floor. He closed his eyes ready to sleep.

With no time the dreams began to welcome him. This had been the only time Neythan had some sleep for the past few days.

Seemed to have rested in a land of peace, far from the chaotic world he lived in. His phone rang. Neythan didn't wake up till the phone went off but it started again.

The second time Neythan woke up but frustrated. He reached his pocket and took the phone ready to turn it off. But the name he saw on the caller id made him awake even more. It was Jack, his lawyer.

CHAPTER 4

"Hello?" Neythan answered with a dry voice. "Why you calling me at this time man?" He yawned. "Some of us need some sleep." He struggled with each word that came out of his mouth.

"Is that a way to great your savior?" Jack laughed. "Considering how hell of a job l did to pull you out of the mud you were in?"

Jack's voice came out sharp, it caused discomfort in Neythan's ear that he reduced the volume on his phone. "Yeah, that was appreciated," Neythan said. "Why you calling me?"

"Sorry to hear about your family," Jack said. "It hurts to know that you didn't tell me what happened, I had to hear it from the echoes of the streets." Jack sounded serious. "Anything you need, I am here my friend. You know that, right?"

"Are you really gonna get all emotional with me right now Jack?"

Neythan understood why Jack felt like that. They had spent more than three months working together, building his case. They had grown closer to each other, became friends. But Neythan's world had not been smooth. Everything had either, drained him or hurt him. The need of catching up with friends or anybody had been sucked out of him. Neythan knew that he might have been wrong for not telling Jack about his wife and daughter but that didn't really move him. He had much denser things to worry about and give attention to.

"I'm just concerned about you. And I hope you haven't done anything stupid." He coughed. "I know everything has been hard for you lately, but you have a tendency of making things much worse than they are."

Neythan heard a laugh after Jack said that and wondered what was funny.

"How is it going, you know, with your son?" Jack continued.

"Stable. He's in a coma ... wait a minute." Neythan raised his voice. "How do you know about my son? Nobody knows about him; nobody knows he's alive. How do you know that?"

"That's exactly how I know because nobody knows what happened to him. His name never came up on the scene." He said. "Only Alisha and Tanya were said to have died that day, Travis is never mentioned anywhere but he was at the court. That means he was there in the car. Which means, he left the scene with you."

What Jack said made Neythan think that Jack knew something, or he was working with someone in the police department. To have that information meant Jack was working with either the police or the people who attacked Neythan. Neythan concluded. "How do you know about this?" Neythan asked.

"About what? I was at the court with you remember?" Jack said. "I know who was there. Unless you are asking me about how I know what happened at the scene?"

"Yeah." Neythan had now fully awakened. His heartbeat was steady, a lot of questions raced in his mind. He had sat upright, and his voice now sounded like he talked with a stranger.

"That doesn't really matter. I have bigger things to talk about. The very reason of why I called you." Jack replied. He sounded like he was doing something, causing his voice to come out distorted.

"Go on." Neythan pressed the phone closer to his ear.

"What l tell you is what you need to know. You don't ask questions about me, ok?"

Neythan made a sound of agreement.

"Right," Jack began. "There was another person involved at the scene."

Neythan agreed with that. It was the man who had tried to kill him with a metallic pole. "You know who he is?"

"No," Jack said. "I got a name though. It raises more questions than it answers."

"Why?"

"Well, according to the name. The man is six months old."

"Ok, that's a problem." Neythan scratched his chin. "What's the name?"

"Gordon Denver."

"Anything else you found out about the guy?"

"I tried all my contacts, but they all said the same thing."

"What?"

"The man doesn't exist, he's a ghost," Jack said. "His name has no history. No bank accounts. No schools, colleges or universities and no addresses. This Gordon Denver name can only be a cover up?"

"For what?"

"That's the question."

Neythan just contemplated but didn't say anything.

"You know what this mean my friend? This is bigger than it looks." Jack continued. "Usually, people who exists like ghosts to the system are government agents, secret agents or some type of high-profile organizations."

All this was unexpected to Neythan but what really shocked him, was how his lawyer had the information. What sources was Jack working with? He asked himself.

Neythan broke his silence. "Why would people like that be after me?" He said. "Any chance he could be Russian?"

"What?"

"Doesn't matter." Neythan interrupted Jack. "So, no idea who he worked for?" This was the information Neythan would kill to get. He wanted to know who exactly was behind the accident and the attack. After what the guy the Detective killed said, Neythan knew he had to know who wanted him and why.

"I don't know but there's something going on." Jack said. "I am sure he wasn't just some common criminal or hit man. There's more to this my friend. You must know what's going on before this get a lot messier."

What more of a mess would it be? When half of his family was dead, Neythan thought.

What Jack said and what the guy Granick killed said got Neythan thinking. There was no denial that something was going on, and if it was to be revealed, Neythan would be the person to do it. He was the common piece. Nothing is a coincidence.

Neythan sighed. "I think I need to go back to the beginning of all this, to see a broader, clearer picture man."

"Yes, you need to know who Layan was exactly working with and why he had to do that job."

"True that. The whole operation was questionable."

"Ok. Enough of that, you know exactly what you need to do." Jack let out a laugh. "There's something serious you need to hear."

"I never said stop talking," Neythan said. He knew more information would make his job easier.

"There's one problem. It may be good news and it may change everything or make everything worse."

"What is it?"

"I have the forensic information from the accident scene." Jack started. "Leaking gasoline and the overheated, damaged engine due to the impact caused the explosion."

"Even I would have guessed that," Neythan said.

"What really got my attention is that there was only one person's D.N.A found on the scene. The evidence shows that there was only one fatality of the explosion. The mystery man." Jack cleared his throat and continued. "Neythan. The evidence suggests that Alisha and Tanya where not present at the time of the explosion."

"What?" Neythan said and stood up from his sofa. "How is that possible?"

"I don't know how but I trust my contacts, it's always concrete information. No mistakes and no lies. Reliable and believable," Jack said. "That's the game, you play it wrong, you get killed."

"I was there man, I witnessed everything," Neythan said. "I didn't see nothing moving around the area."

"They were not there. The evidence doesn't lie my friend."

"Where did you get this information?" Neythan had to ask. It was a strong piece of information and could entirely change everything if it was true.

"You don't need to know that. I have told you what you need to know." Jack said. "This has only one reasonable explanation. Alisha and Tanya might still be alive. They didn't die at the accident. What you need to do now is find them or find out what happened and what's going on."

Neythan didn't say anything. He just paced in his house.

"I trust my sources with my life. Questioning what I am telling you is a dangerous thing you can do right now. Your wife and daughter might still be out there. You must do something. What that is, it's up to you. But you know how this whole thing looks, there's no denial that anything can be possible." Jack said. "You need to start looking at this differently my friend. This is bigger and more complicated by the looks of it, and too many unanswered questions. Some of this doesn't even make sense."

It surely didn't make sense to Neythan, if anything, it raised a lot of questions. He knew he needed time to gather his thoughts and analyze everything. What Jack was saying, what the guy Granick killed said, and any possible cause that could've brought all this. "I hear you man, I will look into it."

"Ok. Be careful my friend. You need to know who the mystery man worked for. It's a dark world you are getting into now. Keep your eyes open. Don't trust anyone. You don't know who is against you, who is after you and who you are fighting with." Jack said. "And most importantly, you don't contact me. Ever."

"Let me know if you find anything else," Neythan said.

The line went off.

Neythan froze for a moment. His chin rested on his chest. His breathing, slow. His eyes closed. His right knee shivered. The phone slowly slipped from his grip.

It fell on the floor. The sound brought Neythan back to reality. He started processing what Jack had said. He had to think till it made sense to him, he thought. He couldn't find a reason of why Jack would lie to him. His instinct told him to believe Jack, but his reasoning couldn't.

Neythan thought. If Alisha and Tanya managed to move away from the wrecked car, they must have moved up to the road. But he didn't see them in the road. They did not even respond when he shouted. So, how could they have not been inside when the car exploded?

He could never really know. There was a considerable time gape between, when he left the car and when he came back. Considering the events that happened that day, Neythan couldn't rule out any possibility. He was shot at. Someone rammed his car and attempted to kill him. If something else was to happen, it could have.

He went into the kitchen. He couldn't shut his mind.

The day had now completely displaced the night. Light escaped through the windows as the curtains were widely opened.

Empty bottles and beer cans covered most of the kitchen surface. Containers of fast foods filled the table and the sink. The lid of the bin was uprightly open, even a grain of salt couldn't find space. Disturbing smells poisoned the kitchen. Neythan extended his hand to the handle and opened the window. He figured the morning air would deal with the smell. Not the over filled bin on his left though. There weren't much dirty dishes, just a few glasses he used to drink his whisky with. He was never fond of cooking. Another thing which made his heart crack. Alisha did most of the cooking. She enjoyed cooking; must have been why she was a successful chef.

Fourteen years he had known her. A humbled woman who wanted nothing but an honest life. Neythan tried. He didn't just try, he embraced it. She had said to him they couldn't raise a family together if he wasn't willing to become a family-oriented person. Neythan looked through the window and wondered, wherever Alisha was, heaven or somewhere if she still wanted him to be an honest family-oriented person or a stone-cold animal on a rampage path of vengeance and judgement.

Thoughts about his wife couldn't calm him. He reached for a Jack Daniels bottle and picked a dirty class beside the sink. He needed some ice.

With no time he was back on the sofa. This time with the Samsung TV on.

He dropped three ice cubes into the glass before he filled it. Then emptied it. He poured another full glass and set back.

Grabbed the remote. Browsed through the channels. He did that again. He threw the remote to the wall behind the TV. It smashed into pieces, with the batteries rolling on the laminate floor.

Emptied the glass.

He rubbed his hands on his head vigorously.

Poured another full glass again, and he stood up. Went back in the kitchen and picked up his phone from the floor. Scrolled through his contacts and stopped on Granick's name.

He put the phone down. Squeezed his head with both hands and let out a thick scream like a heavy engine. His wife and daughter might still be alive. How sure was Jack? Who was the mystery man working with? Why did the man attack him? If Alisha and Tanya are still alive, where are they? What exactly is causing all this? Who's pulling the strings? All these questions shot Neythan at once. The fact that he couldn't answer one of them, made him feel like his tongue was on fire. He picked up an opened bottle of whisky and drained three gulps before he put it down.

He looked up above the fridge. Where the ticking sound came from. 08:12 a.m.

He knew it was going to be a long day.

He picked up the bottle again. Just before the bottle touched his lips, the knock on the door stopped him.

CHAPTER 5

Neythan ran his eyes around the kitchen. He couldn't find the right weapon.

He heard the knock again.

He passed the laundry room door and stopped in front of the washing machine. Dropped his upper body while his right hand reached for the door handle. He opened it and dipped his hand in.

He withdrew his pistol and placed it on top of the white freezer on his right side. He then crouched beside the washer, pulled it slowly away from the wall before he reached the washing powder box which was behind. He stood up avoiding his head to bump against the shelve that covered the top of the washer.

Poured the powder into the small sink under a single window. A black case fell. Reached for his gun and then picked up the magazine from the sink. He checked the magazine. It was full. Then proceeded to insert it.

He heard the knock again.

A firm grip on the gun. He advanced to the main door. Peeked through the window. No visual. The elephant ear flower beside the entrance blocked his view. He cocked the gun, then slowly pulled the door handle. It clicked, he let go.

He watched the door as the person on the other side pushed it. "Hello?"

Granick's voice temporarily calmed Neythan's nerves for a moment.

A thunderous sound filled the air when the door slammed shut. The Detective reacted to the sound by turning back. Neythan connected Granick's jaw with his right fist. He watched the Detective wobble as he tried to grab the thin air for balance.

Neythan followed Granick and released a vicious kick that landed bellow Granick's chest, with a force that jerked him further backwards. The Detective's legs lifted from the floor before his head connected with the radiator on his way down.

Neythan advanced quickly. Only rage in his eyes.

He threw his right hand with wicked force. His palm violently landed on to Granick's throat with an instant grip like a hungry lion does on its prey. "You're gonna start talking." He groaned his words out as he squeezed Granick's throat against the radiator.

The Detective's skin turned pale. A big pumped vein divided his forehead. His legs kicked, but only air. His hands weakly gripped Neythan's hand but to no avail.

Neythan delayed his release until he felt that Granick was on the borderline of blackout, then he threw him to his right.

Granick let out disturbing coughs like something stuck on his throat. And took in a loud heavy breath. Rolled to his side, put his right elbow beneath his body and raised his head. Spat some blood. He tried to lift himself to a sitting position but Neythan's foot laid him back down.

"Tell me what I don't know." Neythan kept his foot pressed against Granick's cheek. "Don't lie. If you do, your brains are gonna be all over this floor."

"What do you mean?"

"You are not in a position to ask questions."

"I don't understand, I thought we were a team." Granick breathed between the words.

"You thought, didn't you?" Neythan said. "We ain't no team. You know something you ain't telling me."

"I think you need to make this clear. I don't know what you are talking about."

Neythan bent his knee and released his heel onto Granick's belly. "I ain't playing games."

Granick echoed a scream while he folded his arms around his stomach. He sprung up, only for his chin to connect with the bottom of Neythan's shoe.

Neythan sat his leg down and looked at Granick. "Now you have broken my table." He said. "Stay down and start talking."

Granick laid in glass. His teeth looked like they were painted in red. Red saliva came out of his mouth. His legs hooked on the frame of the table.

"Ok. Now that you are all comfy. I am gonna start from the beginning." Neythan said. "Why did you come to the accident? How did you know?"

Granick groaned and spat.

Neythan just looked at him. Cold eyes.

Granick tried to move. The glass must have cut him. He stopped trying. "Evock," The Detective looked at Neythan. "What's wrong with you?"

Neythan pressed Granick's back against the glass. "I ask, you answer."

"Ok." He nodded. "I was responding to a burglary call, then l saw you and your son beside the road." He said. "I did what anyone would have done. I stopped. Wanted to know if everything was ok, if you needed help or summet, you know. And it turns out you did."

"Why would you say you didn't see the car my wife and daughter were in?" Neythan said. "It was an accident scene, any person with eyes would have seen that car."

"I told you, I only saw the car that was on the road. Your car? I couldn't have seen it. It was yards away from the road. You know that hill is covered with gravel." He spat some blood. "How could I have seen any traces?"

"Did you see anyone on the road?"

"What? No." Granick frowned. "Just the empty car. I told you, I checked everywhere." He coughed. "I didn't see anything."

"What else do you know?"

"That's everything."

Neythan fixed his eyes on Granick for a sizable amount of time like he read him. Then raised his head and faced to the window. Made a few steps backward. "So," Neythan said. "Tell me about the victims of the accident."

"I know as much as you do."

Neythan stepped forward, pulled his gun, and pressed it against Granick's throat, right below the voice box. "I don't want to ask you again."

Granick's eyes widened and raised his hands. "Please, please, don't do this. I have told you what l know."

"You haven't." Neythan cocked his gun. "I have information that says only one person died that day." He said. "And you can't tell me you don't know about that."

Granick swallowed saliva. "I swear to God, I don't."

Neythan didn't say anything. His knuckles sunk into the Detective's stomach.

Granick produced a deep cough. "I wouldn't know that type of information even if l wanted to." He screamed. "I am not a forensic examiner."

Neythan remained silent, he just pressed the gun harder against Granick's throat.

"This is not an opened case," Granick screamed again. "I was just helping you. I only wanted to help you."

"Why would you want to help me?"

"I want justice just as much as you want revenge."

"Bullshit. Justice?" Neythan said. "Nobody just does something without an agenda. Not in this world." He put the gun on Granick's forehead. "How about you tell me exactly what you want."

"Ok. I got something." Granick said and forced his hand down to his pocket, he pulled out a card. "I found this in the pockets of the dead guy."

Neythan took the card and wiped off the blood that was on it. He put a focused eye on the card. A restaurant business card with a name on it. "Give me your keys," Neythan said. "You better be out of here when I come back. If we ever cross paths, you are dead." And he headed to the door.

It was already warm outside. The smell of burning sausage drew his attention and he turned his head. Few people stood in the front garden of his neighbor. Two men held Fosters cans and the other one was busy playing in the smoke from the BBQ stand. Two women sat at a distance behind the men, laughing and clapping hands. Another woman came out from the house holding a plate with something on it. Neythan could hear music playing but he didn't recognize the song being played.

He squeezed the key and opened the Ford 2014 hybrid door. With no time, the keys were already in the ignition and the tiers were rolling.

Finding answers. Knowing the truth behind all this was now Neythan's mission. No matter what thought came across his mind. What Jack said kept on playing in his mind. The possibility of his daughter and wife to be still alive only gave him much needed strength. Even though it didn't make sense. He was ready to have a walk in the graves if it meant he would see Tanya running and jumping again, and, feel the warmth of Alisha's body.

Neythan felt the pain from inside. It was like it flowed in his veins. It was torture. Sometimes it felt like the only reason he survived was for him to slowly lose himself to the guilt and the pain which corroded his heart. The more he thought about it, he realized that he would never stop grieving.

What the Doctor had said didn't provide him comfort either. He only hoped the Doctor to be wrong and believed Travis would recover with no uncertainty.

The restaurant proved to be quite a distance. Neythan wanted to get rid of his dark, painful thoughts. He picked up a CD from a pile on the passenger seat. Took it off and picked another one.

He did that five times.

All the CDs seemed similar. They all had religious songs. This was a different sound from Neythan's reggae songs he listened to. But he quit changing. He thought they would all be the same.

The area he drove in seemed general, apart from the fact that it was full of warehouses and industries. A weird place to have a restaurant in, he thought.

There weren't any pedestrians in sight, not even cars driving by.

"In 500 yards. Your destination will be on your right." A computerized voice said.

Neythan pulled the car to the right side of the road. He looked around. The place didn't look like what he expected, to say a restaurant would be there.

Stepped out of the car. When he turned to close the door, he noticed a pink peppa pig doll on the back seat. He didn't give it much thought. The way the place looked, made him focus his attention to everything around him. At his right side, there was a footpath between high walls of buildings. The buildings stretched more than eighty meters wide and were just divided by a meter distance between them. The walls were not painted but plastered. To his left, there was a massive white building, taller than a twenty-story flat. Engine sounds came from that building. He couldn't see the entrance, he figured he was must have been at the back.

Ahead of him, the pattern seemed uniform, enormously tall buildings.

Neythan walked ahead to the footpath and kept on walking. The footpath looked surprisingly clean. It took him about two minutes to walk through to the other side. He got into a road, which seemed to be a close.

Everything was different from the other side of the buildings. They were quite a few corner shops and pubs. The atmosphere was filled with different musical sounds and echoes of people's voices shouting and screaming. But again, there were no people walking on the road.

At the end of the road, he noticed a shop that faced the street. It was quiet, compared to the other shops that were on that road. Neythan noticed few heads of people through the window.

He walked to the shop. Opened the door. The smell of grilled steak made him feel hungry. He approached the counter. Stood with his elbows balanced on the counter.

"What can l help you with Sir?" A lady dressed in a white apron said with a forced smile.

The lady seemed about twenty stone big. Neythan assumed because he was a trainer. He knew a lot about weight. She had blonde hair and numerous red spots on her face. A blister coated her lip. Her hand that touched the counter had dry skin that was coming off. At the end of her fingernails were black with some patches, it wasn't nail polish. Brown long hairs erected all over her arm. Red patches appeared on her upper left cheekbone.

She turned Neythan's sudden feeling of hunger into a thirst of Jack Daniels. "Four shots of JD please," Neythan said.

"Oh. I'm sorry, we don't serve drinks here."

"Why do you have beer on your shelves and in your fridge? Your counter is full of beer pumps." Neythan said. "Why would you not serve beer?"

"It's for staff members only." She said.

"Are you being serious?" Neythan removed his hands from the counter. "The people at the table by the window and two tables at the back, have beers on their table. Are they staff members?"

"Sir. Is there anything else l can help you with?" She raised her voice.

A man wearing an all-black outfit walked toward the counter.

"Yes. Four shots of JD." Neythan said.

The lady didn't reply. She just looked at the man coming towards them.

"Is there a problem here?" The man had an accent.

"Not at all. I just want to be served." Neythan said.

"We don't save people here." The man said.

"No. This man wants JD. I told him it's only for the staff members and he's having a problem with that." The lady intercepted.

"You need to leave the restaurant." The man said.

"Why?"

The man pulled out a gun. "I am not going to repeat myself."

"Is a black man not welcomed in here?" Neythan said and turned to the door.

The man had the gun pointed at Neythan's back, slightly above his waist. He was too close that Neythan could feel the man's cold breath.

The customers seemed not to notice anything. They just kept their heads in their plates.

Neythan scanned his right, then his left side. Not another man was dressed in the same all-black outfit. He smiled, it posed a fair chance to Neythan, despite having a gun attached to his back.

"Turn back to the door." The man said, with his face just a few centimeters from Neythan's.

Neythan fixed his eyes into the man's and the man kept blinking like he had something in his eye.

Neythan reacted fast with an inward swerve of his left hand, gripped the man's wrist, twisted it, just as he moved his body to the right. Neythan's free hand clinched in a reflex and dug into the man's throat. Pulled his hand and released it again. He felt his knuckles sink into the man's eye socket.

The man screamed. Surprised by the sudden attack and pulled the trigger.

Smashing sounds erupted. Broken plates and cups scattered over the floor. A staff lady who carried a tray had fallen just when the gun was fired.

This had now gotten the attention of everyone in the restaurant. And, unfortunately, some wrong people.

Screams of terror, panic, and confusion chorused the air. Neythan gripped the throat. Pushed the man back, his left hand still twisted the man's hand which had the gun.

Neythan slammed the man's hand on the edge of the counter. The gun fell behind. He then felt the man's knee on his groin. Neythan breathed a scream as he stepped back, with both his hands dug between his legs.

The man charged forward, screaming.

Neythan found himself down after he felt the sore of the man's shoe landing hard on his face. He then rolled to his right and felt a brush of air beside his ear when the man's foot missed his face. Neythan rolled back and tangled the man's leg. His left hand held behind the heel, and his armpit rested on top of the man's foot. His right elbow dug against the man's knee.

The man raised his free leg to crush Neythan on the floor.

Neythan reacted faster. He hooked his right leg onto the man's waist, with his heel dug into the man's side, he applied force. The floor slightly shook.

The screams had decreased. People ran in all directions. Some climbed through the windows and some courageously used the door. They screamed and ran for their lives. A woman ducked under the table, behind a pushchair, with a baby wrapped in her arms. An elderly man, who had shade sunglasses on, sat calmly enjoying his meal and seeping an orange juice.

Neythan reached his back. "Stay down." He groaned as he stood up. Kept his eyes on the man.

"Who are you?" The man asked.

"Who's your boss?" Neythan said.

"Put the fucking gun down." A deep voice came from behind Neythan. It had an accent too.

Neythan turned. Four men stood behind him. Only one pointed a gun at him. He placed his gun on the counter.

The man who pointed the gun and the other two wore the same outfit as the man on the ground. The other one looked quite older than the others, early sixties. He had a blue, white striped shirt and a plain black formal trouser. He seemed quite big. His stomach covered his belt. He had grey, short beard, just around his mouth. The man had flashy gold rings on two fingers of his right hand and a toothpick in his left hand.

The man on the floor stood up. "Move." He shoved Neythan forward.

Neythan moved a few steps forward. The men in front of him gave way, including the one who held the gun.

Neythan stood. He felt another push, more forceful than before. He went forward. Stumbled. Regained his balance. He looked down.

A lady was laid on the ground. Blood around her head, flowing down to her feet. Neythan moved his eyes to her head. Her eye was missing, just a clot of blood around the eye socket. It was the lady who had refused to serve him drinks.

The older man picked Neythan's gun from the counter. "Who shot Sheila?"

Neythan raised his head. "He did."

Neythan then saw the smoke from the gun after the sound that cracked his ears. The man's head landed on his feet. Missing an eye.

CHAPTER 6

The water hit his head and flowed down his body. It washed the blood off. His jaw still carried the pain. They were minor cuts, but they still bled.

Granick turned off the shower. Silence came on. It was what he needed. Warm air ran through his nostrils. The mirror he stood faced, sweated. He wiped it with his hand. His reflection faintly stared him back in his eyes.

He breathed evenly, his pulse had not slowed. Things had just changed. Evock could have killed him. Why the sudden change? He thought. Where did he get the information about the victims? Granick asked himself again.

There wasn't much time to ask questions. Only to find answers.

He reached for his white gown and stepped out of the bathroom to his bedroom.

Looked at his police uniform and shook his head. Opened the wardrobe, unhooked a black suit jacket, and threw it on the bed.

In less than three minutes, he had a full black suit on, with a blue shirt and a black striped tie. With odd socks on his feet, looking for his shoes.

He heard the horn from outside. Lifted the curtain and looked. A black car stopped in front of his door. In no time Granick was already locking his front door.

"Police Station please," Granick said and stretched his hand for the seat belt.

"No problem." The driver said.

He dug into his pocket when his phone vibrated. Looked at the phone. It was an unknown number. He didn't hesitate to answer. "Hello?" He said.

He then heard a woman sobbing. "Ray?" She said. "Is that you?"

Granick sighed. "Lorain?"

The woman sounded like she struggled to speak.

"Don't ever call this number again. Ok?" Before she said anything. Granick had already put his phone back in his pocket.

"A bad day huh?" The driver said but kept his eyes on the road.

"Can you pick up the speed please, I don't have time."

"You know what I do when I have a bad day?"

Granick didn't respond.

"I get myself a drink and a canny lass." The driver said with laughter. "That's what you need. Somewhere to offload your frustration." Again, he kept his eyes on the road.

"What's your problem?"

"Sixteen quid." The driver said.

"What?"

"You don't know where you are going?" The driver pulled over. "This is the police station."

"Ok," Granick said and made a deep exhale. He took his wallet out and gave the driver a twenty-pound note. "Thanks."

"What you need is some woman's comfort." The driver took off.

A yard filled with averagely tall brown-bricked buildings. Few cars were parked at the front. Two cuffed men came out of a blue-striped van. One of them had no shirt on and only one shoe on his feet. His hair seemed scruffy or maybe it was his hairstyle. He had dried blood on his face and chest. He shouted the most and Granick couldn't understand anything as the man drooled red saliva.

The other man kept on repeating the same phrase. "I am the victim here."

The two police officers pushed the men inside the building. The police officers seemed tense, they held taser guns in their hands.

Granick followed behind as the doors opened.

"You can pass through." A lady behind the desk said as the door buzzed.

The police officers and their supposed friends passed through.

"Hey, Keisha?" Granick smiled. "How are you doing today?"

"Champion." She said. "I have missed you around here. Where have you been?"

"Just sorting things out, you know."

"Yeah right?" Keisha laughed. "By the way, someone called earlier, um, Lorrain. Yeah, she called asking for your number and 1 gave her."

"What?" Granick said. "Why would you do that?"

"She said she was your wife."

Granick opened a book and went through the pages, scrolled down to the last written line, and signed. "Don't give anyone my number or any information no matter who they claim to be," He slid his pen into the inner pocket of his jacket.

"You never told me about your wife. Why?" Keisha said.

He looked at Keisha for a moment. "I like what you did with your hair."

"Really?" Keisha grinned as she rolled her hair around her long thin finger.

"Is Brian in?" Granick said.

"I saw him this morning"

"Okay. Will see you later."

"As always," Keisha said and opened the door for him.

Everyone looked busy. Some talking on their phones and some staring at their computer screens, some taping on their keyboards. Granick just kept walking towards Brian's office.

"Hello? The door is closed for a reason. You knock first." Brian said.

"I need a favour," Granick whispered.

"Favours cost."

"Fine. Anything, but right now, there's no time." The Detective said.

Brian's office had computers. Camera screens and a lot of wiring Granick didn't even understand what they were for. All he knew was that Brian could find something on that phone.

"Have a look at this and see what you can find. There are mostly numbers, see if you can put names on them." He passed the phone to Brian.

Brian connected the phone on a cable connected to his computer and the tapping began. Granick stood and watched.

Brian raised his head to the side and looked at Granick. "This will take time." And he nodded.

Granick thought that Brian needed space and he left the office.

"Granick!" A voice shouted.

He turned his left shoulder and met his eyes with Chief Superintendent J. B. Daniels, who stood at the door of his office with only his head out. He then gave a node, which Granick interpreted by going to the office.

"Close the door and have a seat," Daniels said.

"Thank you," Granick said and sat.

"I haven't seen you around here for a while. I take it as progress." Daniels said and leaned forward on his desk with his elbows and his fingers intersecting. "You have the location or a name?"

Granick felt cold and warm at the same time. His feet sweated. "There are complications now, Chief."

"What does that mean?"

"Evock suspects me." He faced down.

"How?"

"He's working with someone in our department, I think," Granick said. "He thinks his wife and daughter are still alive."

"How does that make you think he's working with someone?"

"He knew that there was only one person who died at the explosion." He felt his jaw. "Only someone from the inside could have given him that information."

"Seems like you got more problems to deal with." Daniels sat back. "Next time we talk you better have serious news or things are gonna get worse for you."

"Give me more time Chief, I can find it."

"There's no time." Daniels slammed his desk and stood up. "I'm running out of patience, Granick."

He felt the burning stare of Daniels's red big eyes.

Daniels had a roaring sound of a voice. He was tall and big, but muscular. His eyes were always red, nobody knew if he was always angry or high on weed. He had a slightly wrinkled forehead. And a permanent smile, his lips never touched except when he's talking. It made his gapping teeth visibly shone in contrast with his dark skin.

Granick had a dry mouth and a shiver ran through his body. He stood up and slowly walked to the door without saying a word. He didn't turn back but he could still feel the stare of Daniels at the back of his head. He sighed as he closed the door behind him.

Everything seemed like boiling water. To handle it calmly was the best idea, but Granick knew there was no time to plan or approach it cautiously. He had to dive deep into it and deal with everything that comes.

"You got something?"

"You didn't knock. Again?"

"Cut it for a sec. Have you got something?" Granick looked at Brian.

"I told you this might take time. Have some patience." Brian said. "What's up with you anyways?"

"I thought you knew this kind of stuff," Granick said. "What's with the delay?"

"This isn't as easy as eating donuts." Brian stopped what he was doing. "What's your problem?"

Brian was about twenty-two or twenty-three years old. He was skinny, and he always wore tight clothes. Because of his voice and body language, Brian was mistakenly perceived as a girl by some people who didn't know him. And that happened often. He had short black hair that flowed down past his ears and to the eyebrows on his face. His bottom lip was pierced and his nose too.

"Nothing that concerns you," Granick said. "You just do your tricks and give me something."

"Give me till end of the day," Brian said. "I would have cracked whatever is on this phone by then."

"Jesus Christ." He said and wiped his face. "Do it as fast as you can, please."

"Yeah, of course," Brian said cracking his fingers. "Now you have to do something for me."

"What?"

"You remember my sister Lisa?" Brian sat back on his chair.

"Yeah, the one with the sexy voice?" Granick let out a laugh. "How's she?"

Brian gave him a questioned look. "She doesn't sing anymore."

"Why? She was good." Granick said. "I would have bought her album without thinking twice."

"That's not really what I wanna talk about," Brian said. "Her fiancé."

"What about him?" Granick sounded concerned.

"I want you to check him out," Brian said. "I have seen Lisa twice this week and she had a black eye and bruises on her left arm."

Granick only kept his ear open.

"I asked her about it, and she didn't really say anything. She just kept saying I am fine." Brian said. "I think, there's something wrong."

"Have you seen her fiancé lately?"

"Not since the engagement party, that was about seven months ago."

"You must not like this guy." Granick stood up. "I will look into it." He unbuttoned his suit jacket.

"No. Not I will. You are going to. Now." Brian said with a frowned face. "That's the deal, favour for a favour."

"Alright," Granick said. "Make sure nobody knows about the phone and whatever you find on it. And that includes the Chief."

"I will hold on to it," Brian said and faced his computer.

Granick left the office.

He had to find out who Evock was talking to. The Chief was on his toes. He had to speed up whatever he was going to do next. The last thing Granick wanted was to be on opposite sides with Daniels.

The most important thing was to crack the mission Daniels gave him. Everything else was secondary. He had to succeed at all cost.

The answer to all this was Evock.

Things had changed between him and Evock. Granick knew he had to talk with Evock, but how?

He headed to the exit door. Everyone still looked busy like they were working on some Osama bin Laden type of a case.

"You already heading out?" Keisha said.

"Yeah, you coming?" He said and walked towards the desk.

"What?" She stopped what she was doing.

"Was thinking, we could go grab a bite on this lovely afternoon." Granick raised his eyebrows and smiled.

"That would be great," Keisha said. "I was just rapping things up." She cleared the desk. "Busy day today huh?"

"Yeah, I noticed." Granick opened the door for Keisha, and he followed.

The sky was clear. It was calm. Just steady warm air. A perfect summer day.

"Where's your car?" Keisha looked at Granick.

Her eyes glittered with the reflection. It made them to have a beautiful sunflower colour.

"It's a long story." He laughed. "Where did you park?"

"Right here." She said while she dug into her shiny cream and red purse.

They got in the car.

Granick kept on trying to figure out his next step. Maybe if he finds who Evock was talking to, he could get the information he wanted. He also wanted leverage on Evock.

He swore in his mind on the realization that he had missed his opportunity when he was with Evock. He should have asked him, even though it wasn't an easy thing to do.

"I know a nice place just ten minutes from here," Keisha said.

"We go there, then." He said.

"You seem a bit off." Keisha turned her head. "Is everything ok?"

"Aye," Granick said. "Why wouldn't l be when I am with you?"

Keisha smiled.

Keisha was in her late twenties, Granick thought. She was a calm lady with a smile on her face, always. She was taller than an average woman but shorter than Granick. Slim body, but she did carry a huge pair of breasts. She had curvy hips and a bottom that clapped when she walked.

"I didn't know you like Chinese food." He said while he pulled the chair for Keisha.

"Well, I didn't know you could lie to me." Keisha sat down and placed her purse on the chair next to her.

"What are you talking about?"

"What drinks would you like to order?" A waiter interrupted them.

"Just a glass of water please," Keisha said.

The waiter typed something on an I pad. "What about you sir?"

"A pint of fosters will do."

He typed again. "Okay. Your drinks will be here shortly." He left.

"Are you not on duty?" Keisha said.

"Who are you? The Chief?" He smiled. "No, I am working on something else."

Keisha just looked at Granick.

"So, how have you been?" He said while his eyes ran through the menu.

"Except you disappearing on me?" Keisha said. "I have been fine."

"You do look more beautiful every time I see you," Granick said.

Keisha just kept a straight face.

"You know." He forced a cough. "What are you having? Am gonna place the order." He stood up.

"Sure." She said.

Granick placed the order. He knew Keisha had something on her mind, but he didn't want to talk about anything other than something that could help him find the rat in their department. The day wasn't getting any better for him.

"They are taking long with the drinks, right?" He said.

Keisha said nothing.

"I don't know what's going on with you," Granick said and pushed the jar with flowers to the side. "But I want to ask you something."

"What?"

"You remember the Evock case, the one with his family?" He said. "Can you tell me who signed in the evidence?"

"Seriously Ray?" Keisha said. "I thought it was you being nice, asking me to come for a meal."

"Your drinks." The waiter said as he put the drinks on the table.

"Thank you," Granick said and wished the waiter could sit beside them.

"You always come to me when you need something," Keisha said. "Who do you think l am? Jesus?" She had a seep. "I am always there for you and do you appreciate that? No. You just use me and lie to me. I didn't even know you have a wife."

"I don't have a wife. I had a wife." He said. "I didn't tell you because I didn't think I had to."

"Why not? Why would you think that?" Keisha said.

"Because you just---." He didn't finish his sentence.

"Just what?" Keisha said. "Just what Ray? Huh?"

He just looked at her and didn't blink. He could see her chest move as she breath.

Keisha stood up. Grabbed her purse and stormed out of the restaurant.

Damn. Granick thought.

For a moment he remained seated, processing what had just happened. And he followed her. "Keisha wait, please." He shouted.

She kept walking toward the car.

He ran toward Kiesha and stopped in front of her. Leaned against the car door which she was about to open.

They stood facing each other with barely a space between them. He could feel her breasts on his chest as she breath. He looked into her eyes and they still glittered. "God." The word barely came out of his mouth. "You have the most amazing eyes I have ever looked at." He said. "I am sorry."

Keisha breathed out with her mouth. She moved closer to him and put her arms around his waist and laid her head on his chest. "I wish you could just see me the way I see you."

"I do." He said and slightly squeezed her body and kissed her head.

After all the taxi driver was right. He did need a woman's touch.

CHAPTER 7

"Follow me." The old man put a toothpick in his mouth. "No dumb shit or you will end up with no eye." He opened a side door.

The long corridor was as dark as a tomb. Neythan felt the heat that radiated from the walls. He could hear a chorus of splashing waters as they walked, and echoes of dripping water from a distant. The guy behind him made sure Neythan felt the gun on his head. Whether it was a precaution, a reminder, or a warning. Neythan just knew he had to co-operate with these men.

"Damn. This shit." The old man tapped it on his hand. "Does anybody got a torch?"

Nobody responded.

The darkness blinded their eyes. Everyone stayed still. Neythan prayed if only he knew the way around the blacked corridor. But then, he had come for answers, running was not an option no matter the situation.

"I have a lighter." The voice came from the back.

"The Boss didn't say he wants to smoke, Slakky." The guy behind Neythan said.

Everyone laughed. Even Neythan.

"We keep moving." The Boss said.

"Just do something funny." The guy whispered. "I am dying to pull this trigger."

Neythan kept calm and silent. All he wanted now was to get to wherever they were going. He had come for answers. Talking is all he wanted but the situation seemed like they had passed that. The men didn't seem like the talking type either.

They walked in silence. The guy behind Neythan kept on whispering threats. The other two men followed behind and the old man they called The Boss led the way.

They finally stopped. The Boss knocked a door with a distinctive rhythm.

"I killed who?" The voice came from the other side of the door.

"Killing is killing. Dying is dying." The Boss replied.

Neythan heard the release of locks before the light flashed the corridor causing him to close his eyes for some seconds to adjust to the light.

With the light, Neythan realized that it wasn't a corridor but a tunnel. Walls were carpeted with rusty copper pipes. Water leaked from the pipes. They carried hot water, Neythan figured that by the heat that radiated off them which made him sweat.

Neythan went in after The Boss.

A guy stood by the door also wore the all-black outfit. He had a different gun than the guys who came with Neythan. An automatic AK-47.

They went up the stairs. The Boss did the same knock and got asked the same question, which he gave the same answer. They all went inside.

About ten men stood by the walls with automatic rifles in their hands. Two stood by each side of the door and others stood by each corner of the room. There were also two men who were stood behind a chair The Boss sat on. The room was dark, judging by how bright it was outside. All curtains were closed, and the door was also shut when they came in.

"Sit." The Boss said.

Neythan sat down faced directly to The Boss. A black table was between them. A bottle of vodka and small water glasses were on the table.

The Boss placed Neythan's gun on the table. He picked the bottle of vodka. Opened it and smiled. Poured a full glass and placed it in front of Neythan. He poured another one before he placed the bottle down. "This is the Russian glory." The Boss said and sucked the glass, then gave Neythan an eye.

Neythan picked his glass and drained the vodka. He breathed out with his mouth and placed the glass down.

The Boss laughed. "You feel it, huh?" He said.

Neythan just nodded. It was better that way than to honestly express how much he hated vodka or anything alcoholic that isn't whisky. Worse vodka, it has that smell and taste like paraffin.

"Right." The Boss said and twisted the ring on his finger. Put a toothpick in his mouth and started chewing its end. "When a fisherman wants to fish, he goes to where the waters are, same as the hunter, if he wants to hunt, he goes where the forest is." He broke the toothpick and spat out the end that was in his mouth on the floor. "So, you came here for a reason. It's time you start talking."

Neythan reached his pocket. A gun was cocked and pointed to his head.

The Boss raised his hand to the man with the gun.

Neythan threw the card on the desk and looked at The Boss.

The Boss picked the card. Looked at it. "So, you killed another one of my men?"

"I didn't kill anyone," Neythan said. "Whose name is on the card?"

"You are looking at him and it might be the last face you will ever see." The Boss said. "Where's Memphis? I know he didn't just give you this card."

"I was attacked three days ago," Neythan said. "And the person who attacked me used his car. That's how I got this card, from him."

"Where's he?"

"I don't know," Neythan said. "Your man killed my family."

"Neythan?" The Boss said. "That's what you call yourself?"

A rush of heat blew around Neythan's ears. He had not told them his name. It wasn't much a surprise because Memphis had mentioned about the Russians. A look around the room formed a serious realization. One thing he had failed to grasp since he stepped in the first door. These men held the same guns as the ones that fired at him after the court. He had walked right into the pit.

"Where's the money?" The Boss broke his tense silence.

"What money?" Neythan felt his jaw crack after he said that. The back of a gun had landed on it.

The Boss stood up. "Your smart lawyer might have saved you from the police. But here we don't work with the law." He said. "Where's the money?"

"I have no money." He wiped the blood off his lips.

It was too late to react. His hands were pressed hard against the back of the chair. He felt a strong grip around his wrists. His twisted forearms made him very uncomfortable. Neythan tried to free himself but the feeling of a gun at the back of his head calmed him.

The Boss lifted Neythan's t-shirt. "Where's the money?"

"I am telling you man," The scream got to him before he finished his sentence.

The Boss held a flaming lighter on Neythan's chest. He felt his insides shiver. He felt the pain at the tip of his fingers. He screamed. His nipple slowly melted. The flame slowly deepened into his skin. The pain felt like an eating parasite inside his heart. His hands were kept locked. His head pressed back by The Boss, and a gun pointed at him, ready to be fired at the first sign of resistance.

After about nearly two minutes, The Boss clipped his lighter and stepped back. "Where's the money?" He said.

Neythan groaned as he saw the smoke from his chest. His eyes were watery. The pain was still raw as his chest. The guy behind him kept hold of Neythan's hands.

The other men only watched, and the Boss kept chewing on his toothpick.

This was the first time Neythan wished his wife and daughter to be truly dead. If The Boss had them, what would he do to them if he could burn a living man? He wondered.

He had not thought anything through. Neythan didn't expect to end up in this situation. Right then, he realized that Jack was right. It wasn't just about the death of Alisha and Tanya. It was about everything. Everything he got charged for. Winning the case was only the beginning of the nightmare. Thoughts boiled in his head, he knew he had to figure something out if he was to survive and he had to do it fast.

"Let's talk this through man." Neythan struggled to speak. "Who are you?"

"Where's the money?"

"Listen, man," Neythan swallowed air. "When the police got me. They didn't find anything." He said. "Because I didn't have nothing. No money, no shit." His skin felt like it still burned. Pain coated the wound.

"Boss. I think that's the case." A man on the left front side of Neythan said. "If he had the money. The Judge wouldn't have let him walk."

The Boss picked Neythan's gun from the table and sunk a bullet into the man's chest. The man took a couple of involuntary steps backwards out of Neythan's sight.

Neythan then heard a fall and the resting loud sigh. A confirmation of surrender to the underworld.

"Nobody speaks until I tell them to." The Boss said looking around the room.

Neythan's arms felt numb. The man had them twisted and pressed against the back of the chair.

The Boss wasn't going to stop. He was convinced that Neythan had the money and he knew where it was. The question was only what was he going to do to break Neythan? If the guy who was shot in the eye didn't prove what breed of a man The Boss was, the man laid behind Neythan did.

"Where's the money?"

Neythan looked at The Boss. He chose his words carefully, while he watched the Boss reach into his pocket.

The Boss had no patience. He pressed Neythan's head backward, flipped the knife and pierced Neythan's chest.

Neythan felt the knife tore his flesh, slid into his chest till he felt The Boss's thump.

Extreme pain.

Neythan bit his teeth and breathed fast.

The Boss placed his thumb on Neythan's smoked nipple. He pressed hard while twisting the knife till Neythan felt it scratch his ribcage.

"Where's the money?" The Boss shouted while he applied more effort and force.

"I know who has it," Neythan screamed. "I know who has it."

"Who?"

"Raymond Granick." He breathed heavy. "A policeman. Detective ok."

The Boss shrunk his face and pulled out his knife in a slushing motion. Drops of blood dripped from it. "Don't play dumb with me." The Boss said in a low voice. "How can that be?" He pulled a hand-kerchief from the back pocket of his trousers.

There's pain, then there's consciously feeling your flesh being slit from within to the outside with a knife with teeth. It's like being stabbed with a saw and being cut from the inside out. You feel every vein, muscle and meat being hooked, stretched to its breaking point, and then break. That pain, that's the pain that made Neythan feel his blood rush to his head. He felt like a grenade had been clipped inside his skull.

A moment passed till he regained his composure. The pain was still raw. Wind blew into the open hole on his chest. But he understood more than anybody, what the task at hand was. "How do you think the police couldn't find anything?" Neythan gasped. "He was in it."

"Where's he?"

"I know how to find him," Neythan said and sucked breath with his mouth. He felt a little bit afloat. The room, everybody in it and their voices seemed and sounded like he was under water.

"No." The Boss said. "You tell me where he's or we just continue our game."

"Trust me. The last thing you want is to start a fight with the police." Neythan said. "He knows me. If he sees a familiar face, there's no alarm. Let me find him."

The Boss remained silent. He twisted the ring on his finger and looked at Neythan, he didn't blink. He walked back to his chair and rested. Picked up the Russian glory and poured a full glass. Tipped the glass into his mouth, a sigh followed. Put the gun on the table and looked at Neythan again.

Neythan fought with the pain. His body felt wet. His breathing slowly decreased. His eyes felt heavy to keep them open. His hands were kept locked. He had stopped fighting.

The Boss broke his silence. "What makes you think l can believe what you just said?"

"The car," Neythan whispered. "The car I came with is Raymond Granick's car. It's a police car."

The Boss nodded and the man who held Neythan released their grip.

Neythan's hands just dangled. His neck bent at the edge of the chair. He faced the ceiling. His t-shirt wet, it stuck against his body. His chest slowly moved.

"Slakky. Stop the bleeding." A man at the door said. It was the same voice from the tunnel.

"Look at the man. He got to go to the hospital." Slakky said.

"No. We are not doing that."

"Boss, you need this man alive," Slakky said and looked at Neythan. "He can barely breath. Death anytime soon."

"I hate to admit it Boss, but Slakky is right this time." Same man from the door said.

"Okay." The Boss said. "Take Slakky with you." He continued. "You stay only one night in the hospital. If he recovers you bring him back. If he doesn't, you finish him and leave."

"Yes, boss." The man nodded.

Neythan couldn't hear the conversation, only mumbled words. His vision slowly turned blurry. His eyelids became heavier till thick darkness clouded him and his lungs slowly grew tired.

CHAPTER 8

"Morning handsome," Keisha said and pushed the door with her right heel.

Granick turned and pushed the blanket to his waist. He rubbed his eyes to get rid of the morning itch.

"I made you breakfast," Keisha said with a smile on her face.

She wore his blue shirt. The breeze from the opened window blew it backwards. The sun reflected from her orange thighs. The visible print of her nipples on the shirt made him swallow his sour saliva. The seductive shaking of her uncovered bottom made him stretch his hand. The smoothness of her cold skin relaxed him.

"Easy there." Keisha giggled. "The coffee is too hot," And she put down the tray on top of a white drawer beside the bed.

Granick sat. His feet touched the floor. "It's been ages since I had breakfast." He picked up the coffee.

"Aye, I figured that." She said with laughter in her voice. "Luckily, there's a corner shop nearby."

"You would make a good wife," Granick said while he chewed the bacon.

He had never been close to a woman since he separated from his wife. He had only been too sucked into his work. There was something he liked about Keisha. She brought a feeling of home with her presence. With all the coldness around his life, she brought warmth and comfort. She made him forget the tormenting road his life was headed.

Keisha walked to the other side of the bedroom and looked at the pictures on the wall. She unhooked a frame and looked at it for a moment. "Is this your wife?" She said and turned to face Granick.

"Yeah, that was my wife." He said as he seeped his coffee.

"She seems like a nice woman." Keisha walked to the bed.

Granick turned his head. "You clearly don't know her."

"Why?" She said while she took another look at the picture.

"You ask too many questions." He said and laid his head down. "Thanks. I really love your cooking; you should do it more."

"Shut up." She blushed. "Who's the little girl on the picture?" And she threw herself on the bed next to Granick.

"That's Vienna." He said. "My daughter."

Keisha raised her head and looked in Granick's eyes. "You never told me about her."

He didn't say anything.

"Where's she?" She said with a soft voice.

"She's with her nana for the summer holidays," Granick said and rubbed his eyes.

"She's cute," Keisha said. "I hope I meet her one day."

"You will." He nodded.

Keisha stood up. "Gonna head off to work now." She said and reached for her clothes on the side.

"Are you gonna check that thing I asked you to?"

"I am not promising anything," Keisha said while she groaned as she pulled up her black trousers.

"Please, make sure you do that," Granick said. "And another thing." He paused for a moment. "Can you leave your car; I will come and pick you up."

"Seriously?" Keisha said while she faced the mirror putting her earrings on. "Where's your car?"

"Something happened to it, I told you." He said. "I got to go some-where today."

"I hope you know what you're doing Ray," Keisha said. "This doesn't seem like you. Is something going on?" She put her phone in her purse.

"Nothing dangerous."

"Okay." She said. "Take care of my car. I love it more than you."

They both made eye contact. Either of them said anything.

"Do you?" Granick sat up.

"See you later," Keisha said, picked up her purse and the door closed behind her.

Granick just stared at the door.

#

"Come in," Daniels said as he arranged his desk.

A young lady came in. "Morning Chief." She said. "There's some-one here to see you."

"Let them in." He gestured with his hand.

A man in a full navy-blue suit walked in. He seemed firm. His arm muscles suffocated his jacket. He was nearly bald. Middle aged but clean shaved.

Daniels stood up with a welcoming face like he knew the man. Shook his hand and closed the blinds in his office. "What are you doing here?" Daniels whispered.

"What's going on?" The man said. "You should know where the money is by now." He held his hands together on the belt level.

"I told you I will let you know when I know," Daniels shouted with a whisper voice. "You can't just come in here man. This is my workplace."

"You messed up in the first place." The man spoke calmly. "And your guy is taking long. I think it's time we let him know how serious this is."

"No," Daniels said and turned to his chair. "I say we give him more time."

"That's bullshit." The man said. "If we kill the girl, it will give him the motivation he needs because we will be coming after him too."

"I have known him for a while now," Daniels said and rubbed his hands on his bald head. "He's a good cop. Let's give him time."

"You have to be a man Daniels." The man said. "Burn these emotions you got for this guy. We gonna have to press that button if things don't change soon." He left the office.

Daniels rocked his chair back and forth. Chewed his teeth. Even his ears moved by the way he breathed. He stood up the same time as everything on his desk hit the sidewalls.

The waters were rising. He knew that if Granick fails to deliver in time, someone was going to sink.

#

It was just another morning for Keisha behind her desk. Seeing the same faces getting in and out of the police station. She loved her job as a receptionist. It was better than going into the field and dealing with different dark characters of people.

She had done her morning ritual. A steaming cup of black coffee to fuel her for the day. A phone call to Clossfield Care Home to hear how her mother had been the night before. Checked to see if Daniels had left her a list of numbers, she had to call to enquire about whatever she had to. That morning there wasn't a list. A calm day, she thought. She had finished all her paperwork the day before.

Now she was just sat, buzzing the door for the same people repeatedly, wondering what the next case would be. She never gave much thought into it, as she never knew what happens on the outside until the paperwork was dropped on her desk. And she never got used to her job. Always dropped her jaw whenever she read the cases which showed her how cruel and evil the world really is. There truly is another world that exists beyond the mundane. A very dark one. Were there's a clear proof that humans are as much capable of reaching extreme levels evilness as they're of greatness.

She opened the drawer beneath her desk and lifted a bunch of keys. As something she had done countless times, except this time it was for a different reason. She unlocked the door further behind her desk.

The room smelt of paper. It was shelved to the roof. The room had no ceiling. The connected pattern of wooden poles that supported the roof was as visible as the darkness to a blind man.

Brown boxes were stacked in the shelves. A white tape was on the front, written a person's name, day, month, and year. They were in sequence. The boxes with the oldest date where on the top shelves and the recent ones on the bottom shelves.

She ran her eyes through the room, twisting her body in the process. Sighed. She looked again, but slowly. A surprise look clowned her face and went closer to the shelves and started looking again.

She looked again.

As the person who had put most of those boxes in the shelves, she was shocked not to find the box she was looking for. She had unquestioned memory of her placing that box on the shelf and locking the door. She was the only one with the key to that room and that made her question herself. She checked again, box by box and opened them to make sure.

She opened and checked every box dated in the year of 2015 and 2016, and she could not find it. She looked in the other boxes dated years back and she couldn't find a box with Neythan Evock's name on it.

Keisha believed she had put the box on the shelf but couldn't understand how it wasn't there.

She just stood, her teeth gripped the keys. She thought hard but she knew the box should have been there.

She breathed out heavily and got out of the room. Locked the door as usual but the look on her face was far from usual.

Threw the keys back in the drawer and closed it. Logged on into her computer and typed in Neythan Evock case number #502295. And the results said no match found.

Keisha stared at the screen with that look like someone who's trying to remember what they were doing. She didn't understand how the case wasn't in the system, because she emotionally remembered the case were a little girl and her mother died on the scene of an accident. She remembered how she felt when she typed and stored that case.

This is not my job, she thought. But what if it's needed and it can't be found. I must let Daniels know and he will deal with it. I know I stored the files. She thought again.

While paranoia thoughts ate her mind, a person's shadow covered her keyboard. She raised her head and a woman was stood on the other side of her desk.

The woman was shaking. She wore a big grey coat, coated with dirt on the wrists. She had very thin black hair leaving some visible patches on the skull. Her chick bones were pointy that her eyes looked sucked in. Her jawbones were like razor blades and her lips were dry like a dying dehydrated man in the middle of the Sahara Desert.

Keisha's mouth became dry that she forgot to greet the woman.

"Hi." The woman said. She seemed like she struggled to open her mouth. "Can I see Detective Raymond Granick please?"

#

What Keisha might have meant got Granick thinking. He liked her, but to him, their relationship was nothing other than just friends doing each other favours. She had helped him over the years with many things, even when he was still married but then she never knew that. Granick saw her as a trusted friend and that was all to it.

It was one of those disappointing summer days. The midmorning sun torched the ground. From the car, the weather looked on point, Granick thought. When he got out of the car, he realized that the earth's breath wasn't friendly. It made him think he was in January.

The cold earth's breath almost took him off the ground. He couldn't feel his ears in matter of seconds. He kept on going to the door, but he felt the resistance.

He knocked on the door and waited.

Expected time for a response passed and he knocked again and waited.

He gave in all the patience he had and knocked four times and waited. No response. As he turned to return to the car the door was opened.

A young woman stood slightly behind the door in her red, fluffy morning gown. For someone who had just woken up she looked glowing, He thought.

He turned and reached the inner pocket of his jacket. Flashed his badge. "DC Raymond Gran…"

"I know who you are." She interrupted him. "Come in."

Granick stepped in and followed her to the lounge.

"Have a seat." She said.

Granick cleared his throat and sat down. His eyes were all over the room like a lost person. The house was clean and tidy, it smelled fresh. The music was playing. The table in front of them was filled with written papers and a pen.

"My brother looks up to you." She said. "How's he?"

Granick was surprised that she remembered him, and she still sounded the same. It had been at least five years when they saw each other. When she brought Brian for his interview. "He's doing all right," Granick said. "Actually, he's the one who told me to stop by and see how you are doing."

"Why?" She said and reached under the table and pulled out an ashtray with a rolled cigarette.

"He's worried about you."

"Do you smoke?" Lisa picked up the cigarette and lit it. "He has always been worried about me," She blew out the smoke. "Sometimes I think it would have been better if he was the older one."

The smell of the weed made Granick think of the old days when he used to smoke it before he started arresting people who smoked it. "No. I don't." He said. "How's your fiancé?"

"Ben?" She said. "He's all right. You just missed him, he just left for work."

"What does he do?"

"He's a Doctor." She said. "He works with kids."

Granick nodded. "If you don't mind me asking," He said. "Is everything all right between you two?"

Lisa took two quick pulls. "Why wouldn't it be?" She said with smoke coming out of her mouth. "Ben is a very nice guy. He makes me happy and everything is just fine."

"That's good." He nodded again. "Last time I saw you, you were doing music. How's it going?"

Lisa remained silent for a moment. "I stopped." She said. "It was moving slow and too much traveling."

"You were good though." He said. "You have an amazing voice."

Lisa laughed. "Where have you heard me sing?"

"Brian showed me a video of you singing at some concert, carnival probably." He said with a smile. "Can you still dance like you did on that video?"

She laughed again. "I can't believe he still has that video." She said. "It was a long time ago." She lit her joint again. "If you are lucky, maybe you will see me dancing again."

"I would give anything for that." He said with an eye contact.

She just looked back.

Granick sighed. "What are all these papers?"

"I was writing." She said. "Finish this for me." And passed the joint to Granick.

He stubbed it out. "What are you writing?"

"Songs." She said. "You want something to drink? I'm thirst." And she started putting all the papers on the table in one pile.

"I'm all right, thanks." He said. "You still write songs?"

"Yeah," She said. "I stopped singing but I still got the love for music."

She looked happy; Granick concluded. "Ok," He said. "It has always been good seeing you." He then stood up and stretched his trousers.

"Likewise," She said with a two-finger salute gesture.

"I, um, leave-. Will see you." He said and swallowed air.

"I will see you soon," Lisa said and folded her arms.

"Excuse me?"

"Brian's birthday party?" She widened her eyes. "You not coming?"

"Oh, yeah." He coughed a laugh. "Almost forgot that."

#

After walking around his office and cracking his fingers, he finally calmed. He had to. There was no reason to be charging about inside his walls instead of working on things that needed his attention.

Daniels knew all the eyes were on him. He understood that they were people who considered him as the right man for the job. He didn't want to disappoint. And these were top organizations and governments who had expectations on him.

Daniels was supposed to be the crucial bolt that makes the machine run as smooth and efficient as it should. But the current situation didn't prove that. This made everyone involved to turn to Daniels for an explanation on why things didn't go to plan and why nothing was happening.

Daniels knew the whole situation was a time bomb waiting to blow up in his face. And the time was ticking. He knew that soon, the call from the General was going to be firing in. Putting him in an acid spot he had never been in his eighteen-year career.

Everything went according to plan except the person he thought was just a pawn, turned out to be an unpredictable knight piece. Neythan Evock was the person who broke the whole plan Daniels had set in motion.

The money wasn't supposed to go missing.

Daniels had premeditated the whole plan. He knew step by step of how it was going to be executed. And he made sure everyone involved, precisely knew what they had to do by every second to the clock.

But on every job, there's always someone with a different agenda, someone who keeps others in the dark, someone who doesn't care about the next guy, and that was Daniels. And that doesn't usually end well, especially if you include someone like Evock in the plan, that's why Daniels was in this situation. With Daniels, things always had to go his way. He wasn't afraid of stretching the boundaries of the law and humanity to get what he wants. And now, Evock was the blocking wall which had to be knocked down.

Daniels was convinced Evock knew where the money was, but he wanted the whole operation to be in silent mode. No alarms and no news. He had heard enough and had seen how crazy it went, right after the bank robbery and during the trial. Well, even worse after the trial. But this was mostly the victim's relatives and friends, and justice asking citizens.

The Judge had to have twenty-four-seven protection from angry characters who blamed him for letting a murderer go unpunished. And all Daniels was grieving about was the money.

The lawyer wasn't talked about, seemed like he disappeared after the case. Good job if he did because he was the other target from the characters.

Things did settle down when the news reported the death of Evock's family. But some die-hard characters were still out there looking for Evock, Daniels knew it, believed it. Someone had to be, and he was one of them.

To operate in a silent mode, Daniels had Granick deal with it on a low. Granick had proved to be a reliable and trustworthy lawman to Daniels, but in this life, you cannot be so sure, Daniels always thought. He had to have a leash on Granick if Granick was to decide to say something to the wrong people, or decides to back down, well, that wasn't a choice that Granick could make at all and if he wasn't moving with time.

The present situation Daniels was in defined that he had no time and he had to do something. He had to go with a different plan. A plan he called "The J.B Heatwave." This was collateral, merciless, emotionless investigative approach. It was a plan he used only when he had to. It's only focused on a certain goal or answer. Anyone involved must be a piece of a puzzle to the answer he wants. It never ends well for the people who get hit with the heatwave, unless they cooperate. Even if they do, unfortunately, the heatwave burns everyone it gets in contact with. "You walk through a road but make sure you rub off your footprints." Daniels had always said.

Brian walked in.

Daniels raised his head from his folded arms, which were rested on the desk. And he faced the door.

"I am sorry Chief, I knocked several times and you didn't answer." He said looking around the floor which was filled with papers, folders, pens, and the phone.

"What do you want?"

"About that file Chief," Brian said walking towards the desk, jumping things on the floor. "The one you gave me to have a look at."

Daniels jumped up, he felt alive.

CHAPTER 9

The Hospital covered a massive area between Gateshead and New-castle, with about four main entrances, two from each side of the City. Each entrance had two big signs that faced each other, written: Granite Medical Hospital, with the blue NHS colour in the background of the signs.

The directions to every department at the Hospital were labelled but they managed to miss every direction, even the one to the main reception, which was at the right side of the entrance they used. They stopped the car at the Maternity Department and stopped it a meter away from the doors.

"Should we just drop him and leave?"

"Do you fucking think Slakky?" Goddy said and raised the hand break. "Didn't you hear what The Boss said?"

An ambulance with the siren blasting stopped behind them.

"Thank God the ambulance is here," Slakky said with a hyper smile on his face.

"The fuck?" Goddy looked at Slakky with a confused face. "Are you smoking that shit again?" Goddy opened his door. "We are at the hospital, you dumb shit."

The siren silenced but the woman who was being pushed out of the ambulance had carried on. The loudness of her scream made Goddy wonder if it was the siren before or her scream.

"Holy shit." Slakky jumped and covered his mouth with his hands. "What's wrong with her belly?" He closed his door.

"Help me carry this guy inside," Goddy said. "And shut up. Don't say shit, I will do the talking." Goddy opened the back door.

"Is he even alive?"

"Shut up and hold his legs."

They moved Neythan from the car and carried him inside. Their way left a trail of blood. Neythan's golf t-shirt was soaked. His neck and arms looked like they were dipped in blood, it was still wet. He didn't cough or groan. His eyes were closed, and his body was now like he had no bones. This made Goddy hold him by the neck.

When they got inside, a nurse ran toward them, followed by two men, with one pushing a bed.

"Is he still breathing?" One of the men asked and adjusted the bed to the floor level.

Goddy didn't answer.

The two men transferred Neythan from the floor to the bed. They hurried everything they did. They didn't even check Neythan to see if he was alive. Which was the only thing Goddy wanted to know?

"OH hell!" Goddy heard the voice from outside. "The entrance is blocked." The voice shouted again. "Can somebody call a midwife, please? Things have started here." Goddy laughed.

The nurse who came first went outside.

"Could you please remove your car from the entrance?" One of the men said.

"Slakky?" Goddy said. "Go park the car." He handed Slakky the keys even though he wasn't sure if Slakky could drive.

Goddy followed the man who pushed the bed. The corridors were clear but from inside the walls, he heard screams and cries. He also heard cries of babies. He did smell some distinctive disgusting smell like urine mixed with shit and blood. But he held his breath and kept running and taking corners.

The man who pushed the bed was in full throttle, the Usain Bolt type of sprinting. The way he cut corners with the bed testified that he knew his job. He just shouted, "Excuse me? Give way? Mind." But he didn't slow down at any point.

Goddy felt sorry for the elderly woman who had her wheelchair in the middle of the corridor. The man shouted for the woman to move out of the way but Goddy doubted if the elderly woman heard anything. The man showed no signs of slowing down. He increased his speed.

Goddy missed the impact because he was still thinking of how Mr Flash was going to deal with the situation. When he saw the woman's wheelchair tip to the side and the woman's head, bang against the corner of the corridor walls. Her dentures flew out of her mouth to the other side of the corridor. The impact caused her to fall to the right.

The back wheels of Mr Flash's bed caught her legs and tipped the poor lady out of the wheelchair. Her face kissed the floor and the wheelchair landed on her bald head.

"Holy shit," Goddy said, about five meters away from Mr Flash. He struggled to catch up with him.

"I need a doctor please." Mr Flash said after he forced the fire doors to open.

There were no screams in the Critical Department. He only heard the beeping sounds of the machines.

"Bed four." A greying Doctor said when he poked his head out from one of the rooms.

"You can't go past this door now Sir." Mr Flash said with a surprising calmness in his voice and breathing, judging from how he raced against the walls.

Goddy did not want to argue. He anticipated it. He waited outside the door.

He took his phone out and checked his inbox if one of his misses had left a message. No new messages. He sighed. No sadness or pity. Neythan wasn't anything to him, just a guy with the money and a job from The Boss to him.

He had worked with The Boss for fourteen years since he was fifteen years old. The reason which got most guys killed by The Boss was to not follow instructions. Goddy understood that no matter how long he had known The Boss, he was just one mistake away from his grave.

About forty minutes had passed. No sign of Slakky and no update about Neythan. The leather jacket he wore covered the gun under his belt.

#

Her tongue stuck to the roof of her mouth. The cracks on her lips became more painful as time passed. She felt her joints shake involuntarily, and her insides floated like her stomach was filled with air.

At first, she could scream, shout and fight against the ropes that bound her. But now, both the voice and the strength had left her like the hairs of a bald man. She could feel the air freshen the walls of her nostrils, but she wasn't sure if she was still alive. She harnessed all the strength she had left with to open her eyes, but all she saw was darkness. She gave up on trying.

Since she woke up and realized that darkness was over her face and felt the tightness of the rope around her hands, waist, and ankles. She didn't know how long it had been exactly till now.

From when she realized that she could tell the difference between June's day and night by the room temperature. It had been four days since then.

#

"Fucking two hours you took?" He stood up. "Is he alive?"

"Yes." Her voice was loud, but she didn't seem like she shouted. "He lost a lot of blood."

He sucked in a snort. "How long are you gonna keep him in here?"

"We will have to see by the end of the day tomorrow." She said. "He needs rest and a lot of liquids. He is in a bad state."

Goddy looked at the nurse for a moment. "Can I see him?"

"You will Sir. In about an hour. We are just still setting everything up."

"Still setting the fuck?" He put his phone in his pocket. "I want to see him now; I want to know for myself if he is fine." He rubbed his nose. "You seem to be taking your time and the guy is fighting for his life."

"Sir. I can assure you. He is fine." She moved a couple of steps away from Goddy. "We are taking care of him. You will be able to see him shortly."

He just scratched his head.

"Who's the patient to you?"

"Are you fucking serious?" He breathed out heavily with his mouth "Fuck," the word barely came out. "I want to see him."

"Someone will come and let you know shortly. When it's time." She left.

There was now only one thing to do. Kill Neythan.

Goddy paced. He knew he was ready. He had done similar things and even worse than this before. He only had to wait patiently for the nurse to come back and tell him to come.

Slakky appeared in the corridor with his shirt wrapped around his waist.

"What the fuck Slakky?"

"You don't know how many steps I had to climb and the corridors I walked to find this place.?"

"Put your shirt back on man."

"But I am hot." He unwrapped his shirt.

"Some shit you do Slakky?" Goddy shook his head.

"Is the guy alive?"

"Yeah," Goddy said. "I was waiting for you. We have to go see him now." Goddy felt like he had waited enough. Another hour had passed. "Slakky." He said. "You have to relax now." That's all he had to say. Slakky had the nerves of a woman, Goddy didn't want to tell him what he wanted to do.

Goddy opened the fire doors and Slakky wiped the sweat off his face. They both walked to bed four.

Inside the room, there was a man sat on a chair and he typed on his keyboard. The room had no bed.

Goddy frowned his face with his mouth open. He walked inside but the man didn't make a move. "Excuse me?" He said.

The man swung his chair around. Looked up and stroked his long beard. "Yes." He rubbed his ballooned belly.

"There's a man who was admitted in this room." Goddy walked forward. "Where's he?"

"I have just come on shift and the room, well, as you can see." He put his pen down. "It was empty?" Force coughed

"I saw them put him in here."

"Maybe he's been moved to the general care unit." He stroked his beard again. "How critical was he?"

"I spoke with a nurse about an hour ago," Goddy said. "She said he was in a bad state and they were setting everything up for him, or whatever that means."

"What was the name of the nurse?"

Goddy looked at Slakky who picked his nose. "Her badge said, Tracy."

"Are you sure?" The man yawned a sigh.

"Are you fucking with me?" Goddy raised his voice. "I can fucking read."

The man stroked his beard again and cleared his throat. "Sir." He fidgeted in his chair. "I have worked here long enough to know there's no nurse with that name."

Goddy moved his eyes on the man. "Who the fuck are you?" His hand was already moving under his jacket. The man wasn't making sense. Goddy thought the man needed a bullet in his leg.

"How did she look like?" The man said. "Maybe I might be able to tell who she was."

"She had a loud voice and she spoke fast," Goddy said. "She had blonde hair and she seemed to be in her early or mid-twenties."

"I am sorry Sir, there's nobody like that who works here."

Goddy didn't speak. He looked up and noticed one camera at the top corner of the ceiling. "Slakky, close that curtain."

Slakky moved the curtain till it covered the desk the man sat on.

Goddy pulled his gun and pointed it at the man's crotch. "When you walk out of here without your balls, you will know I am not playing."

The man opened his mouth and stammered. "What do you want from me?"

"Where's the guy who was in here?"

"I never saw anyone when I came in."

Goddy picked a pen from the desk and sunk it at the soft spot between the hip and the ribs, on the side of the man.

The man screamed. Goddy shoved the gun in his mouth. "Don't make a sound. Talk."

The man coughed and breathed out saliva through his mouth. He mumbled words.

Goddy removed the gun from the man's mouth.

"If he was moved, I can be able to find where he is in the hospital." He swerved his chair to face the computer. "His name?"

"Neythan," Goddy said.

The man looked up to Goddy. "His full name?"

Goddy faced Slakky who just stood biting his nails.

"Evock," Slakky said with a low voice.

The man typed for a moment. "There's only one person in this hospital with that last name."

"Who?" Goddy bent his body to have a closer look on the screen.

"A boy." The man struggled to move his body and he breathed deep and fast. "He's in a coma. Admitted few days ago."

"What's his name?"

"Travis Evock."

CHAPTER 10

The sea provided a cool breeze. He could hear the unmistakable sounds of people talking, kids screaming and shouting and horns of ships as they moved away from the harbour. Saliva filled his mouth as he fought against the edge to vomit. Since he could remember, he never could stand the smell of fish.

Around noon, Granick parked his car in front of a pub. That's one thing he loved about the Seaham harbour. A small town in the North-East region of England, situated between the great rival football cities, Newcastle, and Sunderland.

He was born in 1980, in a small Yorkshire City, Wakefield. Raised by a Catholic family. His job moved him around the country until he finally settled in Peterlee. He worked in Newcastle, though he hated the big cities. He preferred the less busy small towns.

He stayed in touch with his mother until four years ago when nature called her. It was just after the London 2012 Olympics. He was the only child, his father had died in Iraq, the same year he was born. His mother never remarried. She was a devoted catholic who believed in one marriage.

The pub was already packed on a Tuesday. Mostly were men he could see. They were sat in groups around tables and some found it too long to walk for the beer and sat by the counter.

England flags were flying in the ceiling, from wall to wall. A huge Harry Kane poster wearing the three lion's jersey covered the whole toilet door. Appropriate poster for a guy who had had a great season.

It was just football spirits decorations inside and outside the pub. The men inside spoke about football, but their voices carried anger and frustration.

Granick realised they had to be after the horrific England lose to Iceland the night before. Not only that, but the manager also resigned immediately after the game, before the players left the pitch. The football pundits labelled the defeat to be the worst England performance, not only in the European Championships but in the English football history.

He felt the coldness travel down to his intestines, he leaked the foam off his lips and placed the glass back on the table. He sat by the corner, the whole pub and everyone were in his view.

He leaned back against the wall and rested his head, then he entertained his thoughts. Lisa seemed happy and free. Nothing off about her he had noticed. She became defensive about Ben when Granick asked. For a Detective, that's the open the case moment. Granick left it at that if she wants to talk, she will.

He raised his pint and swallowed. Moved his eyes around and then looked at the same table he had been looking at since he sat down.

Granick believed in thinking. He believed any problem or situation a man finds himself in, thinking is always the way out. But one thing he couldn't figure out was if he was in love with Keisha.

A dark-skinned man from the table Granick had been looking at stood up and walked toward where Granick was.

He stood in front of Granick. His wide eyes looked sideways. He had a very strong odour and his faded jeans had dark patches and his shirt's sleeves were torn. He moved his head more frequently than normal.

"The guy is dead." He said and blinked about five times nonstop.

"What?"

He moved his head again, "The guy's dead."

"I heard what you said," Granick studied the man. "Who? Why are you telling me?"

"I found him this morning." He blinked twice. "I had to tell you."

#

Daniels stopped the car in Windmill Lane, Sheffield. Stretched his hands. Quite a drive from Newcastle. The smell of chip shops filled his car, Firth Park was just down the hill.

He slid the folder under his seat and opened the dashboard, stretched his left hand till he felt his pistol.

All sources had concluded that Evock had no siblings or known friends. The file showed that Layan requested him as the best driver suitable for the heist.

Daniels's four-hour drive was to have a word with whoever lived at Layan's registered address.

He walked to the door. The clouds hid the sun, but the air was warm. He clenched his fist and banged the door four times. He heard someone shout inside.

A young girl opened the door, she couldn't have been older than four years. She looked up at Daniels.

"Is anybody home?" Daniels said.

"Mommy?" She shouted.

Daniels looked to his left where the construction was taking down a church building.

"Yes," She said. "Can I help you?" Her hands were wet and foamy.

"Chief Superintendent J B Daniels." He showed her his badge. "Can I come in please?"

"Sure. This way." She moved from the door to the living room. "Have a seat."

Daniels unbuttoned his suit jacket and sat down with a deep exhale.

The woman sat down opposite to Daniels with the young girl on her lap.

"Uh, this is just a follow-up investigation on the Bank robbery which Layan was involved in." He said. "First, can I just ask your name and your relation to Layan?"

"Chelsea. Chelsea Gravile." She said. "He was my brother."

"Did you know about the heist before it happened?"

"Yes." She said. "He didn't have a choice."

"What do you mean?"

"Some guys in suits came here about a month before the heist." She pulled her dress down to cover her knees. "They gave Layan an ultimatum. He had to do the job to cover his debts, crimes or something."

"What can you say about the guys?" He put his right hand on the arm of the sofa. "Who were they? Anything you noted about them?"

"I can't really say." She said. "Layan never wanted me to meet the people he dealt with." She pulled the girl closer. "So, I didn't really see them, but I heard them speak. They had an accent."

Daniels already knew who those guys were. All he cared about at that moment was the whereabouts of the money. "Your brother, how close was he to Neythan Evock?"

"That cunt," She said. "He killed my brother and the system let him walk." Her eyes turned red.

"Mam, you didn't answer my question."

"They were like brothers." She wiped the top of her nose. "Well, at least that's what I thought."

Daniels cleared his throat. "Did Layan mention anything to you?" He said. "You know, like his plans with the money or where he wanted to put it."

She didn't respond for a moment. "No."

Daniels stood up, shook his hands, and adjusted his tie. He moved towards the woman and he bent over till he sat on his heels with only his toes touching the floor. He exhaled and began stroking the young girl's hair. "Is this your daughter?"

She breathed high. "Yes." She said. "If you don't mind Sir. Can you leave please?"

Daniels scratched his bald head and sniffed. He stood up.

His long fingers locked with his palm around the tiny leg. With force, he pulled his right hand along with her sharp scream. He felt the brush of her hair on his Clarks shoes. The innocent soft skin slipped away from his hand and he turned his head at the moment. Her scream echoed, the back of her head shook the wall before her chin dug into her chest. Her scream silenced while her bones cracked when her legs touched the floor.

The woman could not scream. She was pressed down by her throat against the sofa. She watched her daughter's still body on the floor while she gasped for breath and her eyeballs about to explode.

Daniels relaxed his hand. "Where's the money?" He said very slowly.

Tears filled her eyes and she struggled to breathe as the heavy hand still wrapped her throat.

"Let me go." Her voice spoke tears and pain. "My daughter." She cried aloud.

Daniels's knuckles felt her wet cheek before she splashed blood from her mouth. He sat her up with her face faced down.

She spat blood and two white bones rolled on her carpet.

He pulled back her red hair which forced her to face up. Her eyes looked drowsy and they still poured. Her mourns made her drew blood from her mouth.

"Where's the money?"

"My daughter." She sounded like she was drowning.

Daniels suspected she knew something about the money because when he asked her, she took long to reply, and she scratched her ear, which implied that she lied. "I hope she's alive." He said. "But if you don't tell me what you know about the money, you won't find out."

"My daughter." Words barely escaped her lips.

"You are wasting my time." He placed his long-nailed thump on her eye and pressed. "Wake up and talk."

She screamed a whisper. "Layan never told me nothing ok." She swallowed her blood. "All l know is that he was convinced that Neythan had a plan." She said. "Probably that's why Neythan killed my brother. Neythan should know where the money is, not me or my daughter." She cried. "Please let me go."

"You wasted my time." He bit his teeth and felt his neck veins and muscles harden as the woman kicked her last kicks.

When she finally stopped blinking, he removed his hand from her throat.

He walked to the window and moved the curtain aside, just for his eye to view outside. The machines were still taking down the church. People passed down the road along with teenage boys riding around with BMX's.

He wiped off his hands with the curtain. Pulled his phone out, dialled and waited. "It's Daniels." He said. "I need a cleaner. Windmill Lane."

"I am not around the area." The voice said. "A day from now."

"Get it done," Daniels said. "I will send you the postcode." He hung up.

#

"Raymond is not in today." She focused on her. "Who are you?"

"Lorrain." Her voice was dry. "Lorrain Talesman."

"Oh, we spoke on the phone yesterday." She pealed confused laughter. "I'm Kiesha."

"I remember." Lorrain scratched the back of her head. "When is he in?"

"I am not sure, I am sorry."

"I feel like he's avoiding me."

If Keisha didn't know Granick, she would have asked why. But she knew that Granick never wanted to hear anything about the poor lady. "If you could," Kiesha said. "Can wait till later. Ray will be here to pick me up. "She knew that wasn't a good idea to say that to her. But Keisha thought it would be better for Lorrain to see him despite the possibility of being labelled as Granick's slut.

"I can't do that." She rubbed her nose with the sleeve of her jacket. "I have a hospital appointment later today."

"I am sorry to hear that," Keisha said. "Is everything all right?"

"Yeah." She nodded and coughed.

As it wasn't a busy day. Kiesha had an idea.

If there was anything her life had taught her, it was the ability to notice someone who needs an ear. She had been through horrible events in her life which made her think it would have been better if she had someone to talk to. She cried inside with what she saw in Lorrain. She thought, a sit down with Lorrain was the least she could offer.

#

He flicked his cigarette. This guy must have had one too many to drink, he thought. Truth or not, Granick wanted nothing more on his plate.

He had to find the money. As the situation stood, Evock was the answer. Where to find Evock was the question.

With the flow of nicotine in his blood, it dawned on him that the person who spoke to Evock was not the one who signed in the evidence. Evock's accident case was filed only as a protocol. It wasn't opened for investigation, therefore, no guy from the field could have known anything past the evidence. The only person who could have known that would be the forensic biologist and there was only one in Granick's department.

Granick smiled and took his last pull. He knew it wouldn't be hard to squeeze the information out of Mrs Kyle.

#

"Cold water please," Kiesha said and nodded.

"Any beer would do for me." She whispered. "Thank you."

It was just after mid-day, around lunch, and that surprised Kiesha that Lorrain was already up for a drink. She didn't bother to ask. People drink any time of the day or night, she thought.

"You seem like you really know Ray?"

"Yeah," She said. "I have worked with him for a long time now and he is a good friend."

Lorrain coughed and cleared her throat. "You seem like a nice person." She said. "Thank you."

"No, bother." Kiesha smiled. "How long ago you last saw him?"

"About three or four years ago."

"So why now?" A cold question to ask, Keisha thought.

"Many reasons." She put her hands on the table. "I wanna see my daughter."

"Ray doesn't let you?"

"He doesn't." She said with her eyes red. "I need to see my daughter while I still can."

That made Kiesha think of many things on what Lorrain might have meant by saying that. But most importantly, she wanted to understand the daughter situation. No man should take a mother's right to see her daughter despite their differences. She had known Granick enough to realize he wasn't an emotionless man. Kiesha had a feeling that there was an unsaid story between the two, that goes deeper than mere divorce. "Doesn't your daughter see other family members." She seeped her water. "Like grandparents or aunties whom you are close to?"

"I have never known my parents and I have a sister whom I don't talk with anymore," Lorrain said. "And Ray doesn't have anybody, as far as family is concerned."

Kiesha stared at the water glass and saw her reflection from the ice cubes. She could not make sense out of anything. Granick then might have lied, she thought. Where's Vienna?

CHAPTER 11

He enjoyed the stroke of her soft hands. Looked at her as she looked at it like she wondered. He twitched his toes when her dripping tongue touched its head before her red lips covered it. Very slow she dipped it in her mouth and then out.

Her rhythm made Goddy breath through his mouth. She picked up the pace while her hand stroked circularly. Goddy wrapped her hair around his hand and held the back of her head. This time he rested against the wall while he felt the back of her throat.

He loved how she gagged and looked up with her watery eyes and salivary chin. "Yeah." He said it with a breath. "Do that." He pushed it in while his hand made sure her head won't move back.

The feel of her mouth and how she swallowed and moved it inside got the hold of him. The edge began to mount. Her hand strangled it at the bottom while its head felt the brush of her lips and the warmth of her mouth. She drained it and made a grown man weak and shivery.

A knock. "We don't have all day."

"Shit." He pulled his pants up.

The lady swallowed, licked her lips, then stood up and sat on the edge of the bed. She looked at Goddy. "You know you can stay, right?"

He nodded as he zipped his jeans. "I have to go."

"Stay today please?" She held his hand.

Turned and looked at her with his eyes contracted. "Bitch?" He loosened her grip and opened the door.

The corridor was empty. Goddy just saw one man learned on the stair wall with his elbows and a green monster energy drink can in his hand. He looked down the stairs and his brown hair covered his ears and neck.

Goddy closed the door and Slakky turned.

"I don't wanna die man," Slakky said. "We have to let The Boss know. What you been doing?"

"Been meditating." He approached the stairs. "I needed time to think about how we gonna break it to The Boss." He said. "You know if we tell him that a half-dead man disappeared on our watch, we are good as dead. Right?"

"But we don't know where Neythan is." Slakky seeped his drink.

"Roll me one, will you," Goddy said. "I will talk with The Boss."

#

The wound was still raw. The bleeding had stopped. She placed a folded bandage on it. Removed a plaster from its package and stuck it on her index fingers before she carefully placed it on top of the bandage. She gently pressed the plaster to stick.

She had removed the needles from his veins. She believed he had had enough fluids and his breathing had increased. He had taken in three pints of fluids from the night before till then when she changed the fourth bandage.

She sat on the sofa. Removed her gloves and threw them in the dish with water that was on the carpet. His black jeans were folded beside her. The temptation to go through the pockets kept poking her.

As someone who had worked in healthcare for a considerable time. One of the greatest values she had to have was the respect of confidentiality. But there was a good argument on that because Neythan wasn't a general patient and the situation she was in, could not be bound by health regulations.

She gave in and reached for the jeans. Her hand couldn't feel anything in the back pocket. She went in the side pocket and pulled out a wallet. She opened it. She pulled out his license. The first thing she noticed is that he had a foreign middle name or maybe she just couldn't pronounce it. His address was in Peterlee, Prospect Park. A very nice area, one of the best areas to live in Peterlee. Big bungalow houses and big yards. She was very familiar with that area because it's near the Eden Dene Durham Forest. She had walked in the Dene numerous times. She loved the little river which flows through the Dene to the North Sea on the Seaham beach.

She then pulled out a red card. It was a C E O card of Press Hard Gym in Sunderland. She then opened another layer of the wallet and saw a family picture and a bullet in the same pocket.

He groaned.

#

"Boss, I think we should make a move on the cop tonight."

"I need a competent team for that." The Boss said. "I don't want the police to come sniffing around."

"I got the right guys on standby, Boss." Goddy sniffed in.

"What's with the look Goddy?" The Boss studied Goddy. "Are you not confident about your plan?"

"No Boss." Goddy made a nervous laugh. "I just think we have stayed in this country for too long."

He put a toothpick in his mouth. "I have been thinking about it since this Brexit shit started." The Boss said. "It will affect our distribution passages. It's better to run things from Russia."

"True Boss," Goddy said. "But we need that money first and we need to kick the ball now."

"What did you do with Evock?"

Goddy felt his insides shiver but he tensed his body perfectly. "I took care of him."

"Clean job?"

"As clean as the pillow I used Boss." He maintained eye contact.

The Boss stood up and walked to the corner of the room. Lifted a bottle of vodka from the top of the drawer. He opened it and Goddy passed him a glass. "Find the cop."

#

His eyes felt heavy to open and he felt a force that pulled his body downward. Distant music played. A relaxing smell of perfume tingled his nose. He forced his head to turn and the shadow of a woman looked down on him.

The blurriness faded slowly forming a visible picture of a pretty, blonde lady. Her lips moved but Neythan couldn't make sense of what she said. Her loud voice cracked his ears.

Gradually he regained strength, with that, confusion covered him.

He motioned his hand aimed at her throat but missed. Still felt weak and his false vision made him think that she stood closer to him than she was.

He closed his eyes for a moment and felt his heartbeat. Something is just not right, he thought. He didn't feel any danger, he just couldn't understand.

"Are you thirsty?"

Neythan felt his heartbeat on his throat. He recognized the voice.

His bed was adjusted into a semi-sitting position. He didn't need much work, he just pushed his legs to the side, and he slid to the edge. He realized he had nothing on, just a blue gown wrapped around his waist. The dizziness still troubled him; he supported his head with his elbows on his knees. He took a few heavy breaths. "You got some whisky?" Neythan said between breaths.

He didn't raise his head, but he heard her footsteps. He felt the wrinkles on his tongue and the horrible taste in his mouth irritated him.

Neythan felt a hard tap and he raised his head. Tracy stood closer to him that the back of his head rubbed against her stomach.

It flowed on his tongue and smoothly cracked his dry throat. The shiver massaged his body. The taste blessed his throat and made him remember the reason he loved Jack Daniels. He made a satisfied sigh. "Did you have it in the fridge?"

"Yeah," Tracy said. "The ice takes longer to get it to the right temperature. So, I just keep it in the fridge."

"Thanks."

"How are you feeling?"

"Well, it would be better if I knew how I ended up here." He checked the time on his wrist.

"I took you from the hospital."

"So, they let you kidnap patients now?"

"No," Tracy sat down. "I saved your life."

"Why?"

"I don't know." She blinked. "The man who was with you didn't seem very friendly; he had a gun."

Neythan raised his head and looked at Tracy. "How did he look like?"

"He was slightly taller than me, he had a mohawk haircut with the top bit of his hair dyed red." She said.

"Goddy." The word barely escaped his lips.

"What?"

"Who was he with?"

"By himself." She said. "Didn't see anybody with him."

Nothing made sense. He had a feeling that there was more to this chaos. The first thing was to leave Tracy and have a look at the situation with a different eye. Grief and anger clouded his understanding of everything. He had to get out of his way and read under the words.

He appreciated Tracy; he just couldn't swallow her good deeds. People like her make the most dangerous enemies, he thought. An enemy that comes with a smile is more dangerous than an enemy that you can see coming, he told himself. Right or wrong, his gut told him not to trust her. Even more, he didn't want to tag her along into the dance of sorrow, anger, pain, and death.

"Can you get me another drink please?" Neythan said.

He stood up as she turned her back. He reached for his jeans and his left leg went in after his right leg. He pulled his jeans underneath the gown.

Tracy brought the drink while he fastened his belt.

The glass was empty as soon as it touched his lips. His legs felt heavy, so was his arms. The black, suede shoes were in front of him. He bent his back to reach for his shoes. "Fuck." His chest had landed on his left knee. The pain was real.

"I can help you with that."

"No." He slid his foot in the shoe. "I'm fine."

The music still played, low volume. Tracy sat on the sofa, in tight white jeans and her hair was tied back, like before. She had cute, small ears without earrings. Smooth neck but firm upper body. Her shoulders and biceps proved that she knew something about working out.

Neythan put on his navy blue, no colour jacket on. He couldn't zip it up. The pain was real.

"Thanks," He said. "I guess."

"It's my job remember?" She looked at him.

"Am gonna go now." He caressed his knees.

"I wouldn't suggest that." She said. "You need some rest."

"I have had enough rest." He stood up. "What I need to do now is to go."

"Go where?"

"What?"

"Where are you going?" Tracy stood up and walked to Neythan. "The guy who brought you. Who's he?" She looked into his eyes. "What happened to you?"

"Listen." He held on her shoulders. "I appreciate what you have done for me. I honestly do, but these questions, I can't answer."

"Don't you think I deserve to know what happened to you at least." She said.

"The moment you know anything about this." He said. "Your life is in danger."

"Let me get this straight." She started walking around the room. "You rob a bank, kill people and hide the money." She said. "Now people are coming for you?"

Neythan reached his back. Pointed the gun at Tracy. "Who the fuck are you?"

"Seriously?" She said with no sign of fear in her eyes. "Anybody who watches Sky News could come up with this theory." She said. "You forgot; your trial was the most talked-about news."

He shot a soundbar that played the music. "I don't like games. I am putting the next one in your neck." He walked over to her. "Who. The. Fuck. Are. You?"

She went silent, her hands shivered. She looked at the gun and stood up. "Unless somebody trust somebody, the earth is gonna be left with nothing."

Neythan laughed. "I know that quote." He put his gun under his belt.

"You scared me there." She said.

With a serious face. "Oh, I wasn't playing."

She made a nervous laugh.

"You seem to have balls and you are smart." He said. "Let me ask you a question?"

"What?"

"If I have something you want, and you have something I need, and you know I would do anything to get it." He continued. "Would you go through the trouble of looking for me and torturing me and then trying to save me?"

"No," She said. "I would do an old school. You either give me what I want, or I will destroy what you need which I have."

He remained silent for a minute. "Okay, we going Sheffield."

CHAPTER 12

He closed his Bible and placed it gently inside a drawer beside his bed. Stood up. Took off his white t-shirt and threw it in the washing basket beside the wall. Placed his rosary necklace on top of the drawer beside his watch.

Kiesha was taking a shower. Granick switched on the TV and Joyce Meyer preached. He loved her teachings. They were more philosophical than religious. Granick was interested in studies and teachings about life and the manipulation of nature to one's advantage. At that moment he was trying to understand more about the law of attraction after he watched a movie called The Secret.

He was a man who questioned life and searched for the meaning behind every human's existence on earth. He had no regrets, for a man who had been divorced nearly five years earlier.

His life revolved around Vienna, the only person in the world he would cross every line for her safety and wellbeing. The only thing he never wanted for her daughter was to become like her mother.

Darkness had crippled into his life about six months earlier. His detective instinct tangled the order of his and Vienna's life. Granick came up with a theory that the heist had to be an inside job and the police had to be involved. He had said that there was no way, common people or even professional thieves could take out a huge sophisticated and overly secured bank like TNR Reserve Bank that clean, undetected, all systems down and not a single camera spotted them.

This theory couldn't go out to the public especially when the system was gripping Neythan Evock by the balls in the Crown Court. Granick had made it worse when he confessed his theory on national TV. His exact words were, "I think this whole case was rushed and it is very questionable. I mean, here the police arrested a man but there was no evidence of the money, and he didn't have any weapons on him. The question that nobody can answer is, who made the call to the police? Nobody. The police just turned up and found the suspect parked, out of the car like he waited for someone. This is suspicious to me."

What he had said did not just piss off Daniels, there were some other people he had to meet after the press conference. It also made Daniels suspect that Granick knew more than he had said. The worst-case was he knew what he shouldn't.

J B Daniels and two men in suits had visited Granick at his house, in the middle of the night after his conference. After the two men tortured Granick, trying to get what he knew. He had to find the money and keep his mouth shut. And that was also the last night he saw Vienna.

Finding the money meant finding Vienna to Granick.

Keisha walked in. Granick was sat on the bed in his blue shorts.

Smile on her face as usual. "What are you looking at?"

Granick smiled, then stood up. "You're the reason, why I refused to be a Priest." He laughed. She gave back the laugh. His hands caressed her curvy hips, moved his hands up slowly with a firm pressed touch. His lips felt her neck and she smelled like a morning fresh breeze by the sea. Very relaxing.

His tongue touched her neck and he felt her grip on his back. He kissed her gently. He felt the towel drop on his feet. He held her waist while she had his bottom lip in her mouth. Her breathing got higher and her grip became firmer. Granick moved his hands, he grabbed the base of her ass and then opened the chicks while he pulled Kiesha closer to him.

She pushed him, and he fell on the bed. He watched her as she slowly put her left knee on the bed then the other, putting his waist between her knees.

He met her eyes while he felt her hard nipple with his tongue. His hand was already between her legs.

She breathed out with her mouth and her eyes closed. She took a pillow and covered Granick's face.

#

It was the seventh time he had played the CCTV video footage. This was after he had checked to see if the footage was dubbed or fake. It wasn't. The only disappointing issue was that it wasn't clear enough and the recording angle didn't capture everything. It didn't clearly capture the person who had fired the gun. But it did prove that the person fired from inside the bank.

He decided to hide the CD. It wasn't his fight. He only had to focus on his upcoming birthday.

#

00:03 am was the time. Keisha breathed peacefully on Granick's chest. She had the quilt over her shoulders and her left leg rested on his thighs. An odd sound from downstairs had woke him.

He tensed his face to concentrate on the sound. Nothing happened. He threw his head back on his pillow and kissed Kiesha's forehead. She didn't move.

He started thinking as he always does. This time he began with a little prayer and ended with, "In Jesus's name I pray, Amen." Somehow, he had felt he needed a prayer. He had to ask God for more time. It had been almost a week since Evock had been released from custody. In that period, he failed to maintain a relationship with Evock and failed to locate the money.

Every day that went by without getting the money was a countdown to his daughter's death. But did the money really exist?

It sounded like footsteps came up the stairs. He wasn't sure, and he didn't suspect anything. Silence, only the sound of Kiesha's breathing in her deep sleep. A loud friction sound, like a rubber, had rubbed off against his wooden floor made Granick jump off the bed. Kiesha awoke.

He walked slowly towards the bedroom door. On his toes like the floor was hot. His heartbeat was rising. Stretched his left hand till his fingers wrapped the handle. He held his breath to have a sharp hearing. Slowly he pulled the handle down. It clicked. Nothing else he heard. He pulled the door slowly and the light from the corridor escaped through the tiny space into his bedroom.

The rays of the light became wider until the door touched his left leg's toes. He let go of the handle and stepped his right foot forward. His left leg followed. He stepped into the light.

A hard metal landed on top of his nose with a force that made him feel a heatwave inside his nostrils. Gravity pulled him, but he didn't give in. He only made three steps backwards before he heard the click of a cocked gun.

Kiesha crouched on the pillow, the sheet wrapped around her. She pushed against the headboard. Her head was almost between her knees. The way she shivered made the headboard tap against the wall. She sniffed but she didn't scream.

The man chewed something in his mouth. He kept smiling with his gun pointed at Granick. He walked toward Granick. He raised his hand with the back of his gun aimed at the same spot. This time Granick saw it coming.

Granick swerved his head to his right. His fist clenched. He motioned it, right underneath the guy's raised hand. Aimed between the bicep and triceps muscles. His knuckles felt the man's bone. The blow paralyzed the guy's arm. The gun fell. Granick's forehead then connected with the guy's teeth, with a force that put the guy to sleep.

"We need to go." Granick's said. "Now." He shouted and picked up the gun.

He rushed to the corridor, then to the stairs. A bullet hit the wall light beside him. He ducked down and crawled back. "Get back." He shouted and returned fire. He fired a good number of bullets until the gun stalled. He dug down and ran across the stairway to the bathroom, while bullets drilled the walls. He pushed in a tile underneath, side of the tub. The tile fell inside, and he put his left hand inside.

The sink was already damaged. The mirror was still on the wall, but he couldn't see his reflection. Cracks and bullet holes. The floor was sticky. Shampoo, bleach, shower gel, mouth wash liquid and other toiletry liquids flowed on the floor.

"Hold your fire." The voice came from downstairs before the guns stopped firing. "You, go check."

Granick took his hand from underneath the tub. He froze and listened to the rhythm of the footsteps that came up the stairs. The shadow of a man covered the door of the bathroom. He waited.

Granick jumped from behind the door and squeezed the trigger. The sound cracked his ears and the kick jerked him backwards. He saw a man's hand ripped off and splat against the wall. The body flew down the stairs with blood spraying on the wall.

He now stood by the stairs. Clear view downstairs. He took another man's head off before the body knocked the main door down. He had now gotten the hang on the kick from his ruthless shotgun. He cocked it again before he put a hole through his black leather sofa.

He checked the kitchen. Nobody there. He came back to the living room. No sound, just the shotgun boiling off the smoke. He looked behind the sofa and saw a body laid on the floor with half of its stomach blown off. Just a few ribs poked out and some intestines filled the hollow stomach. Dark brown liquid flowed down from his remains.

Granick just looked at the hole on his sofa and shook his head. He heard wheels spin and ran outside just to see a red car make a right turn. He thought about jumping in the car and give the man a chase but then, he remembered Kiesha.

Granick walked back inside. On his doorstep, he could feel his feet squashing human meat on the ground. On his right, a man's body rested on his white cracked door. The neck of the dead body still pumped out blood. He couldn't see the head nearby and figured it must have been its remains that he stood upon.

Nothing scratched his mind except the thought of checking to see if Kiesha was alive. He hoped that no bullet had found its way to her. He jumped across another dead body at the bottom of the stairs and ran up the stairs. Blood on the wall and the voices across the streets had increased. He knew it wasn't long till someone dialled 999. Granick wanted to make sure he would be long gone by the time the police show up.

He slipped in front of his bathroom. It was the loose, bloody shoulder he had stepped on. Straightened his knee and walked towards the bedroom. He opened the door and Keisha came charged toward him with an iron. She struck with her right hand aimed at Granick's face. She screamed. Granick raised his left hand and gripped her wrist in the air. Pulled her toward him and locked her by the waist with his right arm. He looked down into her eyes, they were closed, her mouth wide open breathing out a roar of a scream. "Kiesha." He shouted and shook her. "It's me. It's me, babe."

She stopped the scream, but he could feel the vibration of her hands on his back. She just laid her head on his chest and Granick flattened her hair on the back of her head. He did that for about two minutes. When he felt that she had caught her breath, "We have to go now." He said. "Did you hear what I said?" He moved away from her. "Put on some clothes, a gown or something."

Granick opened the drawer and pulled out black sweatpants and unhooked an Arsenal t-shirt, jersey. Keisha was stood, her hands folded covering her breasts. She trampled like she had loose joints.

Granick looked at Kiesha while he put his shoes on. He wanted to say something, but he kept his mouth shut. He walked straight into the bathroom. Granick's bedroom had an ensuite. With a shower place and a huge round tub by the corner. Behind the door, he kept his gowns hanged. He unhooked one.

He put a blue, feathery gown around Kiesha and tied it around her waist. She had to be covered at least, there were people outside. Possibly the police.

There wasn't much time to move with Keisha's pace. Granick understood the complications it would bring if the police found him there. He just swept Keisha off her feet into his arms. His right hand supported the back of her knees and his left hand supported her back.

He walked out of the bedroom into the corridor. This time he paid attention to the loose hand on the floor. Step after step, he was at the bottom of the stairs and out into the street.

It was dim. There were no streetlights. He had always despised that fact but that night he was grateful. Few people stood outside their doors looking. Some had even crossed the road to get closer. He wondered if they weren't scared of guns.

Granick opened the passenger door and helped Keisha in. It was Kiesha's car. A white Nissan Juke. He got in and took off towards A19.

He sped through Durham Way road and then took Kinsley rd. He slowed down at the roundabout before he headed North on the A19. For about twenty minutes he stepped the accelerator. He clocked between 120 and 125mp/hr.

He didn't talk with Keisha. He wanted to give her some time to shake off whatever that held her. She barely blinked, she just faced forward.

Nothing of worthy he noticed about the men. Maybe if he had had time he could have searched through their pockets. I guess someone will have to fill me in, he thought.

Left, he took the exit towards Washington. Sped through roundabouts, crossed red lights on the right side of Gateshead Bus Station. Kept straight. The road was clear. No sign of any vehicle ahead or behind him. He took a left after a mini-roundabout. That turn took him into residential areas. He had to slow down to about 60mph. Right, into a small road behind the houses.

Only his headlights torched the road. All the lights in the houses were off. Few parked cars on the side of the road. Blue bins were placed on the front of each gate. Slowly he came to a stop. Looked on his interior mirror, nothing appeared behind him. Turned off the engine. Took a deep breath and looked at Keisha. Her hands were between her legs. Her eyes wide open and her shoulders shook.

He stepped out of the car. No moon or stars in the sky. Weak wind blew across his face as he walked to the passenger door.

"Come on." Granick held Kiesha by the hand as she came out.

He kicked the wooden gate wide open and let Keisha pass first. They walked to the door and Granick climbed a slab, then knocked.

The ground was clean. It was a small back yard with plastered concrete on the ground. No lawn. A bin placed by the corner, under a window seal. A rope crossed from the wall of the house to the wall that supported the gate. He waited patiently because he saw a light turn on after he knocked the second time.

A young guy opened the door. He had a towel wrapped around his waist and he rubbed his arms. "Yes?" He said and poked his head out to look behind Granick.

"Is Brian here?"

"Yeah." He opened the door and moved away.

Granick held Keisha by her waist, close to him. They passed another door and walked into the living room. Maybe. It was a weird-looking space. Where they stood, there was a shiny, thick wooden table with four black chairs on each side. Further, that's where the sofas, a small table and a TV was. Granick couldn't clearly see that side because the light was off.

"Holy shit," Brian said while he came down the stairs. "The hell happened to you?"

"What?"

"You got blood all over your mouth."

Granick tried to wipe it off, but it had dried up already. "Listen." He said. "Can Kiesha find somewhere to lie down. It's been a hell of a night."

"Oh, I didn't see you there Kiesha," Brian said and looked behind Granick, where Kiesha was stood. "I didn't know that you two were..." He laughed.

"Brian?"

"Oh, right." Brian nodded. "I will show her."

Granick thought about taking Kiesha himself, he didn't. He wanted her to shift her zone. He was starting to get worried.

The house was warm. Not smelly, something that could be expected from a young man who lives by himself. It was tidy. Only a faint smell of smoke, nothing else. Nothing on the table. A big picture of a reindeer was on the wall behind Granick.

Granick pulled a chair and sat. Comfortable, he thought. Brian rhythmed down the stairs.

"You mind if I smoke?"

Brian said nothing and reached the top of the fridge in the kitchen. Walked back to the table with an ashtray in his hand. "What's up with Kiesha?" He sat down opposite to Granick.

"She's all right." He said. "Just a little bit shook up?"

"What happened? What's going on?" Brian yawned. "There's a lighter in the ashtray."

"Who's the lad that came to the door?" Granick lit his cigarette.

"Him?" Brian said. "Don't worry, Kiesha will be fine. She's in a spare room."

"Him?" Granick raised his eyebrows.

"Oh, he's in my bed."

"What?" Granick flicked his cigarette.

"What?" Brian laughed. "He's just a friend."

"I am not saying nothing." Granick laughed and felt his nose. It was swollen.

"What happened to you?" He fixed his eyes on Granick. "Do you even know what time it is."

"Right now, time is the least of my worries."

"Did you get jumped by some Newcastle fans like," Brian said. "Around here, if you walk around with a football jersey that is not black and white you will be problems."

"No." He had a puff. "But they lost the derby today." Granick smiled smoke out of his mouth.

"Fuck off." He chorused his words. "We will be back in the Premier League next season though."

"Will see."

"We can bet on it."

"I knew it," Granick said. "As soon as we started about football. I knew it was gonna end up with betting." Another long pull. "How much you lost last season?"

"Shut up." He said. "What did Lisa say?"

Granick stubbed the cigarette out. "She didn't say anything."

"What do you mean?"

"She said everything was fine."

"I think she's scared of that bustard me."

"She seemed happy to me, or maybe it was the weed she was smoking?"

"Weed?" Brian left his mouth open. "See?"

"What?"

"She never used to," Brian said. "Probably the bastard is causing her to."

"Are you saying people can't start new habits?"

"Not Lisa."

"Listen to me," Granick adjusted himself. "There's nothing we can do unless she says it herself. That is if there's something actually happening."

"Obviously there's." Brian put his elbows on the table. "Come on Ray. Don't tell me you didn't notice anything. You have always been able to tell if someone is lying."

Granick knew that there was something wrong, surely. He noticed how Lisa became defensive about Ben. But he didn't want to agree with Brian, as that could make Brian do something stupid. Who wouldn't? If they knew that their sister was being abused that way.

"Brian." He looked at Brian's face. "Lisa is fine. She's old enough to know that she should report abuse like that." He felt his nose again. "She will talk if there is something wrong."

Brian sighed. "You're shite mate. Pass me a tab."

Granick pushed the Richmond box.

"I hope you're right." Brian picked the lighter from the table.

"What did you find on that phone?"

"I have been wanting to talk to you about that, but you haven't been coming to work."

"Yeah, yeah, yeah. What?"

"I found a lot more than just the numbers." He smoked with the side of his mouth. "Which makes me have a lot of questions." He licked his lip. "How did you get your hands on the phone?"

"What do you mean?"

"The owner of the phone hasn't been seen since about the same time you gave me the phone."

"How's that?"

"Well, most people haven't heard from him. His coach too."

"His coach?"

"Yes," Brian said. "He played pool. Semi-pro?"

"How do you know all this?"

"I called them."

"What?" Granick raised his voice. "Jesus fucking Christ. Fuck you did that for?"

"Calm your tits man." Brian posed his hand. "I lied about who I was, you know I am untraceable."

"Brian, this is not a game." His voice carried a different tone.

"I figured that out when I started digging, which makes me wonder how you got involved in this?"

"Stop with the questions," Granick said. "What did you find out?"

"I think this is somehow connected to the bank robbery that happened last year," Brian said. "You know, with that Neythan guy."

"What makes you say that?"

"Well, they were two people who died during the robbery." He rubbed his eyes. "One of them, the guard." He blew smoke. "The guard was the brother of the owner of the phone."

"I know that." Granick pushed the ashtray. "Tell me about what you found on the phone for Christ's sake."

"Just listen." He stubbed his cigarette. "There's more to this than the fucking phone."

Granick felt his nose again.

"Memphis works for a Russian Boss." Brian scratched his chick. "Or worked, I don't know if the guy is still alive."

"Yeah, go on."

"Blanco Petrovich," Brian said. "That's the name of the Russian Boss."

Granick frowned his face. He remembered the name. It was the same name that was on the business card he gave Evock. "I know the name." He said. "He's a chef or he owns a restaurant."

"No," Brian waved his hand. "If he does, that means restaurants are not the only thing he owns." He licked his lip. "He supplies girls to brothels around the country, owns a few strip clubs too."

"Shit." He breathed the word out of his mouth. "What did Memphis do?"

"He was an accountant," Brian said. "The numbers you saw on the phone were actually the names of the accounts."

"What?"

"You know when you save a contact in your phone right?" He paused. "Yeah. The contact number was the bank account and the name of the contact was the phone number of the owner of the account."

Granick didn't blink.

"You want me to repeat that again?"

"I get it," Granick said. "I am not that daft, man." He laughed.

A faint dimmed daylight shone through the curtains. Granick's nose was still swollen. Blood stained his lips and his short beard around his left chick and chin. Granick had a long face, but thin. Short beard that covered his chicks, chin and around his lips. He had a slightly big pointy nose, but it fitted perfectly with his face. He wasn't sure about the colour of his eyes, the colour always changed. He was two and a half inches shy of six foot. Fit but not muscularly built.

"Stop touching your nose," Brian said. "Ok. There were four accounts. From different countries though." He reached the box. "One from Romania, two from Russian and the other one from Poland."

"So, how is this connected to the bank robbery?"

"I haven't figured that out yet." Brian lit a cigarette. "What I think is," He paused. "Because nobody really knows how many people were involved in the bank robbery and who were those people. I can't really tell." He blew out smoke. "The guard worked for the Russian Boss was involved. That means the Russian Boss was involved. The fact that nobody knows where the money is, is actually the real problem."

"Problem?"

"Ray, you are looking at a lot of money here." Licked his lip. "That job to be pulled off as clean as that. There had to be a lot of work that was put in and a lot of people involved." Brian coughed. "But things went shit. People died, and the money went missing." He paused. "This calls for war. Because there are people who will be after the money or after revenge. It seems like something went wrong."

Granick looked at the brown surface of the table. His face reflected. He noticed the bruise on the top of his nose. He froze for a moment trying to take in what Brian said. He agreed with what Brian said but at that moment his mind was trying to understand who came to his house.

"Are you sleeping?" Brian said.

Granick didn't respond. He just kept focused on his thoughts. The only scenario that proved sense to him was, it had to be the Russian Boss. The motive could only be what Evock said to the Russian Boss. Granick believed that Evock had made his way to the restaurant. Granick wasn't sure of how the trip went. Did Evock tell them I killed

Memphis, or I had the money? Granick thought. Either motive, revenge, or the money, they were going to come after him again. Granick didn't argue with that logic.

He had to stay alive, keep moving and find the money. Granick had played a plan in his mind and the end game always leads him to Evock. He had to speak with Mrs Kyle and follow the chain from there. But he still needed leverage on Evock.

He raised his head. "This is not a game Brian," Granick said. "I want you to stop looking into this."

"What?"

"Check on Kiesha till I come back."

CHAPTER 13

The bottle between his legs. Tracy shifted the gears as she passed through Meadowhall. It felt like home to Neythan. It had been almost thirteen years he had been in Sheffield. The noise, the busy roads, the stagecoach and first buses, the hills and a smell that said, "Welcome home."

His ears felt like heat blew past them. His body felt strong. He felt awake but there was no denying that the whisky also did its job. Just a few sips were left at the base of the bottle.

Guilt and blame couldn't leave him. He found it better when he fills his stomach with Jack Daniels. Not that it chased the guilt away, but it made him focus and made him move forward. Exactly what he needed to do.

He didn't believe, it couldn't make sense to him that Alisha and Tanya were alive. He hoped they were. A part of him wanted to believe, the same part that wanted to believe the Doctor who told him about his mother's death lied. Neythan still remembered it like it was yesterday. He still remembered how the Lady Doctor came to where he was sat and went on her knees till she sat on her heels. She talked about how his mother had gone far away and he might not be able to see her again. Neythan was old enough to read between the lines and grasp the reality.

He took a seep. "Can you turn off the siren now."

She pressed a button and the siren silenced.

To his knowledge, Neythan had never been in the front of an ambulance. It smelled of sharp chemicals. He couldn't tell if it was the chemicals or the whisky that tingled the middle of his brain. Boxes of medication were under his feet and in the side pocket of the doors. Tracy popped some mints.

"Just park here." Neythan didn't want to announce his arrival. He wasn't sure if he would be welcomed with smiles or a bullet in the head. Either way, he wouldn't blame them. According to the police, he had killed Layan.

They walked a few steps till they turned right onto Windmill Lane. He felt the heat on his neck and the windscreen of oncoming cars torched his eyes. The familiar smell of kebab and chips blew him like wind.

He looked to his left and stopped. He thought he was on the wrong road until he saw a sign on the wall of a house with the name: Windmill Lane. This is the right road, he thought.

What had confused him was the Church. It wasn't there. The Church was big enough to stand out, especially the cross that was at the top. He could now see the Sheffield Town Centre below his shoulder.

He brought his mind to the right side of the road where the houses were. The door he wanted was three gates down. At the third gate, a black van parked.

Tracy adjusted her hair to make it tighter. They walked forward, didn't speak.

Neythan felt the heat off the van. It had an advertisement about Sky Broadband painted on it. A short ladder was tied at the top. Neythan led the way. He walked forward. The gate was open, but the door was closed so were the curtains. His gun dug into his hip.

He knocked. "Come behind me," Neythan whispered. "I'm not sure how this is gonna play out."

He knocked again.

"I don't think they can hear you," Tracy said. "The music is too loud."

"Can you see anything through the window?"

"No." She nodded.

"The Sky guy just been in." He turned his head back to face Tracy. "Maybe they will turn the music off soon."

"How do you know the guy has just been?"

"I felt the heat off the bonnet." He whispered. "The engine is still warm."

"It's fucking burning out here." She moved her head forward and backwards while she said that. "Of cause the van is gonna be warm."

Neythan tut. "You obviously can never understand what I am talking about."

"Whatever." She said.

Neythan knocked hard, with the bottom of his palm.

Nobody in the streets. Maybe it was because of the sun, Neythan thought.

Tracy scratched the back of Neythan's shoulder. "The curtain moved." She said.

"There's someone in then," Neythan said.

"Obviously there's someone in. You slish." She punched him on his back. "The music is playing, remember?"

"Okay, smart…" He paused for a moment. "Couldn't find a shit name for you." They both laughed.

About three minutes had passed since Tracy said she had seen the curtain move. The door had not been answered.

Neythan pushed the handle down slowly. "It's locked." He said.

"What do you wanna do?"

Neythan kicked the door with the front of his foot. Four times.

Tracy picked up a brick she stepped on. The force made the brick push through the double-glazed window. The sound wasn't louder than the music. Other pieces fell on the lawn and most of them fell inside.

"Shit," Neythan said and felt his fingertip on the trigger.

Tracy moved back, away from the broken glasses.

Neythan two-stepped towards the window. Stretched his right arm. He grabbed the thick curtain. Pulled it outside and his right foot crushed glass pieces on the window seal. He dug his head to avoid contact with the remaining teeth of glasses at the top. His left leg followed.

He had a quick scan of the room and jumped further away from the two black bags in the middle of the carpet. A vibrated soundwave attacked his ears. The smell of bleach and other chemicals he couldn't identify cut through his nostrils.

He looked around. The brown sofa by the kitchen door looked wet and rubbed as it had just been cleaned. The bags on the floor were thin but long, different lengths. He fixed his eyes on the bags. At the corner of his eye, a man appeared.

The man held a cleaning white container and an orange stuff on the other hand. A green, short-sleeved golf t-shirt covered his body to the waist. It had a sky logo. Thick yellow gloves covered his forearms to the elbow. Black cargo pocketed trousers. The shoes were covered with shower hats.

The man dropped what he held as he raised his hands.

Neythan's eye and gun were fixed on the man. "Who are you?" He shouted.

Neythan couldn't hear what the man said. He thought the man had said "What?" But he wasn't sure. Neythan was no expect in sign language.

The second Neythan turned his eye to the Tv, wondering how he could turn the music off. The hard saw of the shoe landed on his straightened elbow. The shock sent numbness and vibrations to his fingers. The gun hit the bulb case on the ceiling. Pieces of shattered glass rained at the same time he felt knuckles flatten his right ear against his skull. He made a step back as he released his right hand into the air. At that time knuckles landed on his exposed rib cage. He fell on his knee.

A knee to his face sent Neythan flat on his back. His head made echoing sounds inside. Neythan bent his leg and released his heel to the man's knee. He felt the knee ball move and saw the man's mouth wide open. The volume was too loud to hear the scream.

Neythan then rolled to his left side where the man was now laid and sunk his elbow into the man's diaphragm. He folded his back while his right knee broke the laid man's ribs. His right hand on the throat and his left hand to the eye. Liquid splashed from the man's eye before the blood followed.

Tracy turned the music off.

Heavy breaths and blood dripped from his mouth. "Close the curtain," Neythan said.

Tracy managed to make the remaining half of the curtain to cover the whole window.

"I have never been caught off guard." Neythan wiped his mouth. "You ain't no Sky employee. Who the fuck are you?"

The man coughed and said nothing.

"What are you doing here?"

The man groaned. Blood and thick white discharge drew from his eye socket.

Neythan stood up. His ear still screamed, and his head still made echoed sounds inside. His left arm was weak.

He grabbed the back of the man's colour and pulled with his right arm. He fought against the pain on his right side of his ribcage as he dragged the man to the kitchen.

Neythan left the man laid on the tiled kitchen floor.

"What are you doing?" Tracy asked.

"Trying to talk with him."

"How?"

He stared in the sink for a moment. A look of shock clowned his face.

"What?" Tracy said and walked to the sink to have a look.

"The spoon," Neythan said and looked at Tracy.

"What about the spoon?"

The tail of the spoon was put in the drainage, leaving only the head out.

"It's a lookout tip," Neythan said. "We used to do this. That's how we told each other that the police had been in." He looked at the man on the floor. "Usually if the police were looking or asking related specific questions." He shook his left hand and clenched and released his fist. Trying to get rid of the numbness. "This means Chelsea wasn't living by herself. She left this for someone." He continued. "Oh shit." He stepped to the man. "Where is Chelsea?"

The man said nothing.

"Okay. Fuck this." Neythan said and started opening the cupboards. He then bent down and opened the ones at the bottom and lifted an olive cooking oil bottle. He reached the side of the sink and grabbed the white electric kettle. Poured the cooking oil to about half of the kettle and placed the kettle on the plug and switched it on. "Someone has been here." He scratched his short black hair. "Looks like I wasn't the only one with that in mind."

"Who do you think?" Tracy said with a calm voice.

"He's gonna tell us." Neythan just looked at her and then looked to the kettle. The bubbles had started. He lifted it. The kettle made the sound like the rush of a sea. The weak smoke and the strong smell of burned cooking oil filled the air.

He stood faced down. The kettle in his right hand and the man groaned on the floor. Neythan bent over and titled the kettle. The mouth of the kettle aimed at the man's face. "Where's Chelsea?"

The man tried to move but he couldn't. "I don't know who that is."

"What are you doing here?"

"Was just doing my job." The man said.

"What job?"

The man remained silent.

The man then broke his silence with an ear cracking scream. The oil boiled and cooked his eyeball. His eye socket emitted smoke. The oil sunk in as it melted the eyeball. Some oil drops had spilt over the side of his bald head. Red patches like pimples formed instantly and where the oil flowed, it took the skin off with it.

"Shut up," Neythan shouted. "You will taste it on your tongue if you don't shut your mouth."

The man bit his teeth and kept making sounds like an engine being raved.

"What are you doing here?"

"I am cleaner." He breathed through his teeth. "I make evidence disappear."

"Which evidence?" Neythan wiped his mouth.

"There are two dead bodies in here." The man said. "A woman and a young girl."

"What? Where? Who?" Neythan said and stood upright.

"The bags."

Neythan made a long stride to skip over the man and took a few steps toward the bags. His right knee touched the carpet while his right hand pulled the zip.

He fell to a sitting position. Tears poured from his eyes. His lips shook, and he pressed his head hard with both hands. His heart beat faster with a cold feel.

It had been over a decade since he had seen Chelsea, but he was more than sure that it was her corpse that laid before his eyes. Drew of spit dripped from his mouth as he cried. He hated himself and despised himself. In his eyes and his heart, he believed he caused it.

It wasn't the first time he wished he was dead or wished it was him who had died instead of Alisha, Tanya, or Chelsea. Innocent people paid the price for his sins. The desire to look in the eyes of the person who killed them take their last breath gave Neythan strength.

Neythan stood up and picked up his gun from behind the TV. Walked to the kitchen and pulled the trigger.

The bullet tore apart the man's bone, just below the knee.

"Who killed Chelsea?" He shouted with tears in his eyes.

The man took heavy fast breaths through his mouth. He forced himself to stop screaming. "I didn't kill her."

Another bullet went through the man's shoe. "I said who?"

"Daniels." The man said while he struggled to breath. "His name is Daniels. He's a Chief of Police. Newcastle."

Neythan looked at Tracy who leaned against the sink.

"Who are you?" Neythan said.

"I am a cleaner."

"Who do you work for?"

"Nobody." The man said through his breath.

Neythan turned his head up to look at Tracy.

"You hear that?" Tracy said.

"Yeah. We got to go."

The sound got louder with every second that passed.

Neythan aimed his gun at the man, at the right side of the chest. "It will keep you alive long enough to feel yourself drown in your own blood but fast enough for you to die before the police get here." He pulled the trigger.

Neythan straightened his body. "Let's move."

"They are here," Tracy shouted from the window.

"Shit." He said. "Follow me."

Earlier, Neythan had observed the back garden and it would have taken a blind man to miss the fallen fence right next to the footpath.

CHAPTER 14

He had been in McDonald's; the queue was too long for his patience. He had now crossed the road and went further down. Subway.

Decent queue. Not too busy and it wasn't a big shop. With less time, he was the next to be served.

"What can I get for you today?" Her white teeth shun as her lips formed a smile. Dark skinned. Small piercing on her nose. Her hair flowed down to her shoulders, it had ginger, blonde and black colour. Small nose and long eyelashes.

Daniels liked her and smiled back. "Can I have a foot-long please."

"Which bread?"

"Any." He said. "If you can make the chicken spicy. I would appreciate that."

"You want the cheese melted?" She cut the bread open with a small knife.

Daniels reached his pocket. "Hello." He moved away from the queue.

The response took long. "Hello?" Daniels said again.

"Evock was here." The voice said.

Daniels heard coughs between the words. "What do you mean?"

"He's coming for you." Groaned sounds and heavy breaths followed. "He was with…" The voice trailed off.

"Was with who?" Daniels raised his voice. "Hello?" No answer. Daniels heard the phone being moved.

"Hello, Chief." A different voice. "He's gone."

"What do you mean?"

"He was tortured and had a bullet in his chest, leg and foot." The voice said. "He asked me to call you soon as we turned up."

"Is there anything else in the house?"

"Yes, Chief." He paused. "Two other bodies. They seem to have been cleaned. They are bagged."

"Listen," Daniels said. "What's your name and who else are you with?"

"Officer Kevin Quinn and my partner Marry."

"Nothing goes out ok," Daniels said. "Neythan Evock is still my case and we know he was there." He continued. "I will send my guys to collect the evidence and the bodies."

"Chief, this is a sensitive situation." Officer Quinn said. "The victim is a SIB operative of the Royal Military Police. The army has to be informed immediately."

"I will contact the Military myself and I would appreciate if you keep that information to yourself," Daniels said. "Give his id to my guys when they get there."

"Understood. Chief."

Daniels hung up the phone and walked toward the counter. "Hey." He said. "I am sorry I got to go now." He reached inside his jacket. "Would you let me finish this apology tonight if you're free?" And he slid his card underneath her palm on the counter. He headed out of the shop.

#

A half-full bowl of nuts was placed on the table. Bottle of Vodka beside it. Two full glasses with ice rested on the bottom was in their hands. A pistol on the table, next to The Boss's right hand. His left fingers held the cigar which burnt slowly, and the smoke escaped from it into the air like a flying snake.

"I think my consciousness is catching up with me as I get older."

"What do you mean Boss?" Goddy unzipped his leather jacket.

"I have lived this life without care of who I burn." The Boss said. "It was always about the money and respect you know. I never thought about what kind of business, with me, it has always been about how much money coming in."

Goddy raised his glass and kept his ear focused on his boss's voice.

"When we get this money. I am done with human trafficking." Sucked his cigar for a good thirteen seconds or so. "It's better to sell drugs or guns, at least the people who buy them would have made a choice."

Goddy coughed. Spilt some drops of vodka on the table. "Boss." He said. "You have spent twenty-three years building this empire. You have links in four countries. All of them bow to you. You have nothing to do now, everything is always in motion." Cleared his throat. "What's stressing you now? You know I am here if you need help with anything."

"It's about peace." Lifted his glass and filled his mouth. "I can't find peace when I sleep. I have robbed these young girls of their lives and their dreams." He said. "The ones who have died over the years because they couldn't handle the drug. I can feel their souls staring at me every time I close my eyes before I sleep you know." He put a toothpick in his mouth.

"Boss, what's got into you?" Goddy said. "We are giving these girls a good life. We are giving them sex and money. What's more to life than that?"

The door was budged open. The sound of music and voices of people faintly filled the room. Slakky stepped in. His hands shook, knees trembled. Sweat dropped on his shoes off his nose and chin.

"Where's the cop?" The Boss said.

Slakky waited till he caught his breath. "He killed them all." His voice came out dry.

"How did you survive?" The Boss smoked his cigar. "Come, have a sit." He lifted a glass and poured some vodka.

Slakky moved slowly toward the table. He sniffed and pulled the chair from underneath the table.

"Have a drink." The Boss extended his hand. He looked at Goddy.

"Boss. He, he, he just started shooting back." Slakky said.

"There wasn't supposed to be a shootout." The Boss opened a little bottle he pulled out from his pocket. Pulled a toothpick with his nails and placed it on his tongue. "You were supposed to go in clean and catch him off guard."

"That's what we did Boss." He nodded.

"It doesn't seem that way." He said. "Why did he spare you?"

"I escaped Boss."

"So, you ran away?" The Boss slammed his glass on the table.

"No Boss." Slakky couldn't keep a stable hold on his glass. The shiver in his hands spilt the vodka and the glass sounded like it bounced off the table.

"What do we say about cowards Slakky?"

"Boss, the situation was…"

"Answer me." The Boss interrupted him.

"Cowards we burn," Slakky said. His lips shook, and his face looked like he had just come out of the shower.

"Goddy pick up the gun." The Boss puffed. "Aim just at the side of his neck. With his last breath, he will understand how the guys felt."

Goddy's heart raced. He knew there's no questioning an order. His eyes locked with Slakky's. He had known Slakky for a long time and been through enough experiences to love him as a brother.

Tears flowed down Slakky's cheeks. His lips shivered. The look on his face begged for mercy. He did not say a word.

Goddy's palm felt warmer than usual as he wrapped it around the pistol. It was hard but that was the life. No emotions should interfere with business or orders. The trigger felt heavy, his arm was unsteady, and his eyes could not hold back the tears.

"I am sorry," Goddy whispered as tears dropped from his eyes. Another look at Slakky was all he could do before the blood gushed.

Goddy threw the gun on the floor and jumped towards Slakky. Blood sprayed over the table and to the wall. His knees touched the ground, his right hand pressed against the wound. Goddy could feel the tingle on his palm as the blood pumped with pressure against it.

Slakky's body jerked. He gasped for breath as he choked on his own blood. He held tight on Goddy's hand that pressured the wound. His eyes blinked non-stop. He opened his mouth as if he wanted to say something. He choked, coughed up blood. His body tensed.

"Don't fight it Slakky." Goddy looked down on him. "Just relax your nerves."

Slakky closed his eyes but he kept chocking and his whole body still jerked. His blood filled the floor. It covered where Goddy knelt.

The blood stopped escaping between Goddy's fingers and Slakky stopped chocking. Goddy felt Slakky's grip loosen and watched his hand splash the blood on the floor.

A feeling of heat travelled through Goddy's body. Tears fell. His heart felt like a harmer was landing onto it. He kissed Slakky's forehead and sobbed. He opened his palms and dipped them in the blood on the floor. He washed his hands with the blood. "With your blood, I wash my hands." He said. "And for your forgiveness, my tears have asked." He looked at Slakky's body. Tears still poured. "Rest in peace and watch over me."

"You have to find the cop and get that money."

Goddy said nothing. He looked at Slakky's body and looked at the gun on the floor. His fingers twitched.

#

Sad weather. Dark clouds covered the sky. The wind that carried the smell of rain blew into his lungs. His mind calculated the situation. The main aim was to recover the Xenner, but nobody would have to know about that. Not even the media, the police, the intelligence, the army or even Evock.

This was the type of situation he was prepared for but hoped it would not come. Never really believed in hope. Premeditated and calculated actions to solve any problem was his best strength.

He walked into the police station with a lot of conversations debating in his troubled mind. It seemed like a normal day to everyone else.

He opened the conference room door.

"Afternoon Chief." Everyone chorused and then sat down after Daniels did.

Daniels looked at the people in the Conference room. Of the five people in there he only recognized four faces. There was a new face.

He was sure he had never seen it before. Middle-aged man with ginger curled hair. He wore glasses and his shirt was misbuttoned at the colour.

"Chief." Sarah broke the silence. "We can't get hold of DC Granick."

"Why do you need him?"

"We found four dead bodies at his house last night." She said. "A call came in the early hours of the morning."

"From who?"

"It was an emergency call from a few neighbours reporting the same incident." She looked at Daniels. "The case was passed on to us this morning. The officers who responded to the call said Granick wasn't at home when they got there."

"You tried contacting him?"

"Yes, Chief." Sarah nodded. "His mobile is going straight to voice mail. We need him here for questioning Chief."

Daniels didn't respond.

"I need your clearance Chief." She said. "We have to bring him in. By now he must have reported to us or been in Chief."

"That's not necessary Detective," Daniels said. "I will deal with that. We have a bigger pot to cook." He coughed. "Neythan Evock."

Nobody responded.

"Right." Daniels exhaled deeply. He looked at the new guy for a moment and then to Detective Inspector Sarah Willows.

"Oh, I do apologize about that Chief." She laughed under her breath. "That's DCI McCunt from the South Yorkshire branch."

McCunt stood up and extend his hand to Daniels. "Pleasure to be working with you Chief."

"Mine too." Daniels stammered. "I didn't catch your name right."

"It happens often," McCunt said. "It's McCunt. Scott McCunt."

"You serious?" Daniels smiled. "Your name is My Cunt?"

"Yes, Chief."

"My-Cunt?" He said very slowly.

"No Chief." He said. "Mc-Cunt. Irish."

"I see," Daniels said. "Would you leave us alone please." He looked around to everyone.

McCunt stood up.

"Not you," Daniels said. "I want to have a conversation with the DCI in private."

The chairs moved as Sarah and her team stood up. They walked out.

Daniels made sure the door was shut. "Why are you here Detective?"

"I need Evock for questioning Chief."

"Evock is my mine. This is my investigation."

"I am aware of that and I respect that Chief." McCunt sat down. "But what brings me here is the death of the woman and the little girl. Evock was the last person to be seen at the crime scene."

"Evock killed the woman and the girl. There's no questioning needed."

"I don't buy that Chief."

"How?"

"That's why I need to speak to him."

"Do you know where he is?"

"No. Not right now." McCunt said. "But I am sure I can get him Chief."

"How?"

"We both know Evock killed a military operative Chief." He said. "We put that out there. We declare him a terrorist. He becomes the public and the media's enemy." He coughed. "We will have him within five hours from now."

Daniels shook his head. "We are not doing that."

"That's the best move we can make Chief," McCunt said. "We need to use the public to our advantage."

"How old are you DCI?"

"Thirty-two."

"Exactly," Daniels said. "You haven't lived long enough to understand what it means to portray the system's confidence and strength to the public." He balanced his hands on the table. "Do you understand the weight of this situation? How do you think the public is going to react when they know that the system let a terrorist walk away?"

McCunt didn't respond.

"This situation must be contained," Daniels said. "Evock cannot know we are coming after him."

"I think he already knows Chief," McCunt said. "When the police broke in, he was still there."

"So how did they lose him?"

"The SIB operative required immediate attention."

"That must be the most fucked up shit I ever heard." Daniels stood up straight.

McCunt scratched his head and shifted in his chair. "What's your plan Chief?" He said. "Evock is still out there, probably out of Sheffield by now."

"Alert every police in the country. We need a stop and search in every motorway and small exits out of Yorkshire." Daniels said. "That means everyone in Yorkshire should be on their fucking toes. Big cities, small towns. Everyone."

"Only one request Chief," McCunt said. "I would want to see the file from Evock's previous investigation. I want to get a feel of this guy."

"That case is closed." Daniels turned away. "Focus on finding him."

"That's why I need to see his file Chief."

"I think we are done here, don't you think?" Daniels said.

They just looked at each other.

#

Granick stepped out of the car. Locked it as he looked around trying to locate Mrs Kyle's house. Detached houses but very similar in shape and colour. Dark cream.

A lady stood faced the door. She scrubbed it and held a bucket in the other hand. It had to be her, he told himself. Short woman, short black hair, a few extra pounds.

He approached her, and she turned when he opened her gate.

"Detective." She said with a smile.

"Good day Mrs Kyle." He didn't move a muscle on his face.

"Is everything well, Detective?"

Granick silenced for a moment and then looked at her. "Where's Neythan Evock?"

"Excuse me?" She stopped scrubbing.

"Where's Evock?"

"What is this?" She frowned her face with a node back.

"I know you examined the evidence from the accident, and you moved the results outside," Granick said. "Both of these counts are enough to make you spend your retirement and your last days behind bars."

She didn't respond.

"I'm gonna repeat my question." Granick moved closer to her ear. "Where. Is. Neythan. Evock?"

"I don't know where he is?"

Her eyes looked innocent. It was true. She didn't know. Granick was good at reading people if they told the truth or a lie. "So, who did you give the information to?"

"My son."

"Who's your son?"

"Jack."

"Jack who?"

"Jackstein."

"Fuck. Shit. Shit." Granick spat the words. "He was Evock's lawyer. Wasn't he?"

She nodded in agreement.

"Call him," Granick said.

He waited as Mrs Kyle reached in her bra and pulled out her phone. He watched as she dialled and closed her ear with the phone. Granick then grabbed the phone off her.

Two more rings, the phone was answered. "Hello?"

"If you want to see your mother alive in the next hour bring me Neythan Evock."

"What? Who's this?"

"If Neythan Evock is not here in the next hour," Granick said. "I am gonna be the guy who killed your mother."

"Listen you fucking cunt," Jack said. "If you touch my mother, I am gonna feed you your fucking balls."

"Countdown starts now."

"You are fucking dead for threatening my mother." He hung up the phone.

CHAPTER 15

The lift stopped on the sixth floor. Neythan stepped out after Tracy. They walked the corridor past several doors till they got to room number 672. Neythan inserted the key card he held in his hand into the door. He opened the door when the key flashed a green light.

Tidy room. A small TV on the wall. One small chair under a desk. Fair sized mirror on the wall beside a wall wardrobe with empty hangers. Two plastic cups and a small tray with salt, sugar, and ketchup sachets on top of the desk. White electric cattle, with two white mugs beside it. A big towel rolled nicely on top of the bed. Fair sized bed for a Travelodge Hotel.

Neythan sat on the bed while Tracy checked the toilet and the shower room.

He laid on his back and put his hands beneath his head. His right ribcage still carried the pain. He closed his eyes and took in a heavy breath. He kept seeing Chelsea's corpse. They grew up together even though she was younger than him and Layan. The image of Chelsea kept flashing in his closed eyes. How beautiful and peaceful she looked. He tried to interpret the image that way than embracing the truth that she was dead. That truth felt like he had a knife stuck in his stomach twisting his intestines. He blamed himself.

He screamed and jumped to his feet. His eyes red but he fought hard against the urge.

Tracy took one of the plastic cups and went into the bathroom. She waited for a couple of seconds while the water splashed against the bottom of the sink.

"Here." She said. "Have some water."

Neythan didn't make a slight movement.

She put the cup on top of the drawer beside the bed. Then put her arms around Neythan and laid her head beneath his chest. "I don't really know what to say." She said with a calm tone. "I am truly sorry about your friend."

Her touch eased his tensed body. Calmness travelled through him internally. He stretched his right hand and held Tracy's back, his fingers relaxed on her left side ribcage. He held tighter.

She looked up. His brown eyes locked with her eyes.

He saw honesty in her watery eyes. Her pink lips shivered. Her eyelashes waved when she blinked. Her face looked like a genius work of art. Her beauty was close to perfection. Neythan agreed. The visible smoothness and brightness on her skin made Neythan's eyes to smile.

He slightly bent his neck to the right. Lowered his head with his eyes fixed on her lips. She just kept her head tilted up.

He tested the saltness of her tears. Another lip movement sent a hiccup to his manhood. Soft lips she had. They exchanged saliva. It wasn't long before Tracy started sucking on Neythan's tongue. He just left it deep in her mouth. His right hand slid under her white jeans. Her ass felt cool and smooth. He grabbed it and shook it. His left hand caressed her small breasts. He unbuttoned her jeans.

#

McCunt looked at the steam that rose from his cup. Too hot but he picked it up. The best way to drink coffee is when you feel the heat before it touches your tongue. "Yeah." He nodded with a groan before he sat the cup down.

He stared at the steam again. The best part of drinking coffee was watching the steam until it dies out. A very unusual reason but that's why he loved drinking coffee. In those moments was when he played everything in his mind. He was a very intellectual man.

It could only take a very hard working and intelligent individual to hold the position he had at his age. Five years earlier MI5 had approached him, but he refused their request.

In the present moment, his confidence had been shaken. The trail of his previous case had gone cold. What frustrated him was the nature of the case. He was going after Sparott, a man who kidnapped, raped, and killed girls as young as twelve years old. The man had killed five victims and the oldest victim was a sixteen and a half years old girl.

Even though he hadn't entirely given up, he wasn't going to allow the same thing to happen with Neythan Evock. He knew the most crucial thing was to keep Evock on his toes. To not give him time to rest or assess the situation he's in. And he needed the file from his previous case. There was one specific picture McCunt wanted.

Another sip. The door opened. He turned, and Sarah approached.

"What is it?" He said.

"We have a location on Evock's cell phone."

"Where?" He sat upright.

"Travelodge." She said. "Less than two minutes away from Meadowhall Centre."

"Alert the Sheffield Police."

"Already done it."

"Good job," McCunt said. "Every exit out of Sheffield has to be blocked."

"It is in place." She said. "Are you going to update the Chief, or should I?"

"Just focus on the job," McCunt said. "We need Evock in custody now."

"Clear." She said and turned to the door.

"One more thing." McCunt stood up. "Daniels mentioned that you would give me the file from Evock's previous investigation."

"Did he?" Sarah turned back. "I will look in the storage."

"Thanks," McCunt said. "I would appreciate it. If you do it now, please."

#

His body stuck against the sheets. His face steamed. He watched Tracy as she jumped off the bed and stepped to the window. She moved her naked body with confidence. Neythan fixed his eyes on her back and scanned her from the head down. Slim. Smooth skin, no scars, or scratches. She was sexy as any man would say but not the type of Neythan. Her ass was small and not finely shaped. Her hips were flat, not curvy.

She turned around and jumped on the bed and laid on Neythan's chest.

Neythan ran his fingers down her spine. She rubbed his abs. He looked down to her smiley face. "Why you smiling?" He said and put his hand between her warm thighs.

"I have always been curious, but now I know." She said.

"Know what?"

"You know what I mean." She looked at Neythan. "Your chest is bleeding." She said. "We need to change the bandage."

"Shit," Neythan said.

Tracy reached her bag which was on the bed. Took another bandage and wet wipes. She put them beside Neythan.

Neythan just winced when she removed the bandage. She took the wet wipes and gently cleaned the wound. "It's closing up." She said. "I think you got hit there."

"Yeah, I might have," Neythan said.

"You do realize this nipple is not gonna grow back right?"

"I know." He said while he watched her small hand carefully run the wet wipe over his wound.

"You are a strong man and a good fighter too." She said. "What do you do."

"I am a personal trainer." He said. "I also train self-defence to women."

"Why women?" She opened a new bandage.

"Let's just say, one good trained woman is one less victim of domestic violence," Neythan said. "You should come to my Gym and see what I am about."

"I will." She said. "Do you enjoy what you do."

"Of course."

"So, how did you end up in this mess?" Tracy pressed the bandage against his chest.

"Loyalty."

"What do you mean?"

"Helping a friend."

"Still don't get what you mean." She looked at him.

"An old friend needed help," Neythan said. "His life was on the line, I did what he would have done for me."

"So, you robbed a bank?"

"No."

"Layan's body was in the van the police found you with." She said. "And Layan's blood was also present at the bank. That puts you at the bank."

"I was there but I didn't rob anything," Neythan said. "How are you so informed?"

"I watch the news."

Neythan just frowned his face.

"Don't you think you can stop all this if you give up the money?"

"What?" Neythan wrinkled his forehead.

"Where's the money?" Tracy said.

"You finished with that bandage?"

"Yeah, almost." She said. "Am just asking."

Neythan's phone rang. He moved away from Tracy and stretched his hand to reach his jeans on the floor. He took his phone from his pocket. Looked on the caller id. Jack. "Hello?" Neythan said.

"There's a problem and there's no time my friend." Jack said. "Where are you?"

"What do you mean?"

"How fast can you get to Durham?"

There was a loud knock at the door. "Hold on," Neythan said and approached the door. He looked through the pupil. Two armed policemen stood in his sight. "I will call you back." He hung up the phone.

"Get dressed. Quick." He said as he put his shoes on. "The police are here."

Third knock. "Open the door."

His t-shirt over his head and the gun in his hand. "Get down." He looked at Tracy.

The door opened. About five policemen entered the room with their guns aimed at him. "Put the gun down." The policeman at the front said. "You are coming with us."

"Why?"

"You are under arrest for the murder of Chelsea Gravile and Bella Gravile, and the murder of a Royal Army personnel."

CHAPTER 16

"We don't need Granick anymore," Vichk said.

"It's in our best interest if he gets to Evock first," Daniels said and glanced at the rearview mirror.

"He knows too much already," Vichk said. "And he's not reliable."

"We need him," Daniels said. "You are not going to touch him."

"Open your eyes man." Vichk faced Daniels. "It's time we start eliminating rotten fruits. Things are already going south. The police are involved now, and we also need to start considering that Evock might know about the Xenner."

"Get your head together. We are still on top of this." He checked the mirror again. "Nobody knows about the Xenner."

"All I am saying is Granick needs to go," Vichk said. "I am just weighing the options here."

"There's only one option left."

"Which is?"

"The heatwave." Daniels cleared his throat.

Vichk smiled and remained silent.

"Evock is coming for me, well, if he manages to avoid the police," Daniels said. "The Heatwave is not going to give him no choice but to surrender the money to me."

"What if he refuses?"

Daniels turned his head and looked into Vichk's eyes. "Nobody refuses to family."

#

The urge woke her up. Her stomach tightened. Threw the blanket with her hand and her feet were already on the floor. Past the door, turned left. Pushed the door behind her. Her face in the sink. Gushed her insides through the mouth. It had a sweet taste and a horrible smell that made her continue vomiting.

Her heart beat fast. She breathed heavy. Opened the tap. The cold water ran over her fingers. Splashed some water on her face. Held her palms together and sucked in a gulp of water to wash her mouth. She did that four times before she stood upright.

Brian must be cooking something, she thought. Tightened the gown and went down the stairs.

"Was wondering what time you were gonna wake up?" Brian smiled and closed the oven.

"Where's Ray?" Kiesha said and stood with her arms folded.

"Are you alright?"

"I said where's Ray?" She raised her voice.

"I don't know," Brian said and took off the oven gloves. "He said he will be back soon."

"What's going on Brian?" She walked toward the kitchen. "Why did Ray come to you? Why were there people trying to kill him? Who were those people? Why did he kill them?" Tears escaped from her eyes. "He didn't even seem affected by the fact that he had just killed people." She couldn't stop her tears. "What's going on Brian?"

For a moment, Brian froze. Then he walked forward and put his arms around Kiesha. "Everything is alright. You're safe here."

Keisha sobbed on Brian's shoulder. "It's like I don't even know who Ray is anymore."

"He cares about you. You have nothing to worry about."

"I am worried." Kiesha said.

"Ray is a good guy and a good friend." Brian said. "Trust me, you have no…"

"I am pregnant." Kiesha interrupted.

"Really?" Brian moved back to look in Kiesha's eyes. "Congratulations. Does, does Ray know?"

"No." She shook her head.

"Is it his?"

"Of course, it is." She wiped her tears.

"Sorry. I mean, I didn't even know that you two were, you know." He smiled. "Yeah, sit down here." He pulled a chair. "I will make you a cupper."

"Coffee please." She sniffed. "Black, no sugar."

"I cannot stand coffee me." He switched on the kettle. Took a white mug from the sink. Wiped it with a paper towel. Opened a tin and dipped a teaspoon. Poured the coffee into the mug. The water had already boiled.

"Here." He said and sat across Kiesha. "So, have you told anyone else?"

"No. Just you." She held the mug with both hands.

"Really. I am the first person you told." He said with a laughter. "That's the best birthday gift."

"Oh, Happy Birthday."

"Thank you." Brian waved his hand.

Silence. Awkward eye contact.

"Why haven't you told Ray?" Brian said.

"I'm scared." She said. "I don't know how he would react."

"I bet he would be thrilled."

"I don't think so."

"Why?"

"Can I ask you a question and can you give me an honest answer?"

"Yeah, sure." Brian leaned forward.

"What happened to Ray's marriage?" She sipped the coffee.

Brian cleared his throat and leaked his lips. "The truth?"

"Yeah." She nodded.

"You want me, to tell you, the truth?" He raised his eyebrows and scratched his neck.

"Brian," She focused on him. "Just tell me. Please."

"She uh, ok. She's an alcoholic." He said. "Ray tried to help her. He paid a lot of money for her rehab, shrinks and other people he thought could help. She didn't stop drinking. She was always pissed, always." Brian scratched his arm. "The night she was pissed and, smoking in the house and lit the house on fire was the time Ray called it quits."

"Was the house burnt down?" Keisha asked.

"It wasn't really about the house." He said. "She left their daughter inside when she got out and didn't even call emergency."

"Really?" She said.

"The firefighters said they found her sat outside with a bottle of cider and a cigarette in her hand. She couldn't even form a sentence."

"Was the daughter safe?"

"Yeah, they got there while the fire was still in one room." He said. "Thanks to the neighbour."

"Wasn't she arrested?"

"No." He said. "Ray refused to let that happen. He only wanted her away from him and their daughter."

"Now I understand why he hates her so much." Kiesha shook her head. "I would as well."

"I don't blame him." He said.

"I think she's dying."

"Who?"

"Ray's wife, ex-wife, I mean."

"What do you mean?" Brian frowned his face.

"She came to work yesterday, looking for Ray." She said. "She didn't look well, she wanted to see her daughter."

"Ray would never let that happen." Brian clapped his hands.

"Where's she?" Kiesha said. "The daughter."

"You should ask Ray." Brian stood up. "I don't know." He walked to the kitchen and opened the oven.

"What are you cooking in there?" Kiesha said.

"Ribs and chicken."

"Are there people coming like?"

"Just my sister and her fiancé," Brian said. "And Ray too. He will be here later."

#

Based on her assumption. It had been five or six days, bound on the chair. No light and nothing had gone in her stomach. No Tanya or the knowledge of her safety or where she was.

Her lungs felt tired of sucking in the air. Her intestines felt like there was fire travelling inside them. Her head felt lighter than air. The veil on her face was still there. The room smelt of sweat and urine.

The thoughts about where Tanya was never left her mind, but the answer never came. She only hoped her son was safe and wished Neythan would somehow know that she was still alive. She knew it was next to impossible for him to know that, but she knew for definite that if somehow, he knew, he would find her.

She refused her mind to wonder about anything other than Tanya.

Light shown through the veil. Sharp sounded footsteps approached her. Her eyes felt heavy to open. Her hands and legs felt numb. Her heartbeat remained steady. A shadow blocked the light and she opened her eyes to the walls of the veil.

Slowly the veil brushed her neck then her cheeks, ears and passed her eyes. She blinked fast trying to wet her eyes and form a true picture from the blurry form of the body which stood before her.

It was a man. Definitely. She blinked again. Dark skinned, she agreed with her vision.

The man bent down with a glass of water in his hand. He slowly motioned it to Alisha's mouth. The edge of the cup touched her crusty lips. Her jaws cracked as she tried to open her mouth. The water toucher her tongue and then moistened her dry throat. She felt it travel through her intestines till it settled in her stomach. The water was sweet. Grains of sugar brushed the surface of her tongue.

She drank slowly and carefully. She didn't want a single drop to escape her lips. The last drop went down her throat and she looked up.

Her vision was now clear. She could see the man's big teeth and his bald head which reflected the light. Hugely built and very intimidating red, wide eyes.

Her strength renewed by every second that passed. Gradually.

"Where's my daughter?" She said as loud as she could. It was only a whisper.

The man didn't reply. He crouched in front of Alisha and looked into her eyes.

"Please?" She pleaded earnestly.

"You will see her." He said and scratched his bald head. "When you tell me what I want to know."

"What?" She said. Tears mounted in the back of her eyes. "Is she ok? Where's she please?"

"Where did Neythan put the money?" The man said.

"What?"

"Your husband." He said. "Where did he put the money?"

"What money?"

"The money from the bank."

"I don't know." She said. "He didn't rob the bank."

"Do you want to see your daughter?"

"Now please." She said.

"So, think very hard and tell me where the money is." He stood up. "Where's the money? Who did he give it to or where did he put it?"

"I don't know honestly." She begged. "I have no idea and I have never heard him talking about that money."

The man turned. "You obviously don't care about your daughter." He swung his right hand.

Pain exploded on Alisha's right cheek and ear. The force and the weight of the man's fist took Alisha and her chair to the floor.

"You are gonna die in here." He said and turned to the door.

CHAPTER 17

"What?" Neythan stepped back. "I didn't kill Chelsea."

"You have the right to remain silent, anything you do say, can, and will be used against you in the court of law." The policeman said and pulled cuffs off his waist.

"Uh, Boss." One of the policemen from the back said. "There's supposed to be a woman in here. He left the crime scene with a woman."

"Where's she?" The policeman with the cuffs said. "Turn around?"

Neythan turned and faced the window. The blinds were down. Moving vehicles and trains produced a chorus that relaxed his nerves. "I came here alone."

"See?" Neythan felt the cuffs tighten around his wrists. "Now you are just playing with my intelligence, don't you think?" The policeman stepped in front of Neythan. "I wouldn't think that cute handbag on the bed is yours."

Neythan remained silent but maintained eye conduct.

"Where's she?"

"Who?" Neythan said.

The policeman walked toward the bed. Scanned the room as he walked. Picked up the handbag and looked at Neythan who didn't twitch. For a moment, the policeman just stared in the handbag. Then proceeded to search it. "Hmm, a wallet?" He turned his head to Neythan. "Let's see if we can't find an id." He nodded his head. He pulled the wallet from the handbag, but it escaped his grasp and bounced off the edge of the bed onto the floor. "Sugar." He said and bent his back.

A shuffling sound made Neythan turn his head, but he missed what had happened. He only saw the policeman laid on the floor, coughing uncontrollably with both his hands on his throat.

Tracy pushed from underneath the bed with the gun aimed at the policeman on the floor. "Don't move or I will blow his old skull open," Tracy shouted to the other policemen who now had their guns aimed at her. "Stand up and unlock the cuffs."

Neythan read Tracy. That's the number one rule of survival Neythan had depended upon in his previous past. When danger or war clouds, you must see if the man beside you is ready to fight or run as your back is in their hands. Closely, he looked at her. She had no nerves. No fear in her eyes. She held the gun with confidence and intimidation like someone with experience. Not only the experience of holding a gun but of using it to neutralise danger.

Tracy attached the gun onto the back of the old policeman's skull. "Where are the keys?"

"Lady," He said. "I don't know who you are, but this man is a murderer. He didn't just only kill civilians but a Royal Army Policeman." He swallowed saliva. "You don't know what you are doing."

Tracy cocked the gun.

The room smelt of danger. Guns were still aimed at Neythan. Some at Tracy. He looked at everyman's face. They were all focused, he believed their hearts knocked fast and loud in their chest.

He wondered if there were others in the corridor. He knew it wasn't going to be easy to make it out alive or to not leave other policemen in the world of the dead. He didn't want to do that. He only wanted Daniels. Whoever the man was, Neythan wanted to chew his heart. He had a feeling that Daniels was the answer to all the questions he had. Are Alisha and Tanya alive? If they are, where are they and who has them? He had to get out. Not with the police but as a freeman on a mission.

He stared at the policeman's wrinkled face. A courageous man, Neythan thought. The cuffs loosened.

"It's not over." The old policeman said and took back his cuffs.

Neythan picked up his gun. "I don't wanna hurt nobody." He checked his magazine. It was full. "Daniels killed the woman and the child. As for the shithead? Why don't you figure out the fuck he was doing there?" He walked toward the door. "Tell your boneheads to put the guns down or I will make them."

The old man nodded.

"Let's go," Neythan said and grabbed the room key from one of the policemen.

Tracy picked up the other key from the desk and picked up her wallet from the floor. She kept the gun aimed at the old man. "You are coming with us." She said and held her bag. "If any of you poke your heads out. The old man is history." She pushed him forward. "Move."

Neythan opened the door and the policeman stepped out first then Tracy, then him. He closed the door. "We gotta use the stairs and the fire exit door."

"The stairs are down this way," Tracy said.

"This is only gonna buy us a couple of minutes. Every second has to count."

Tracy poked the old man's head with a gun. "Is there anybody else outside?"

He groaned. "No, but it's a matter of time till an army of them show up." The old man said. "May I remind you. You have a Detective Inspector as a hostage. This is a shoot on-site situation." He glanced back at Tracy. "Young lady, you can walk away now. Don't let this cold-hearted animal drag you to hell." He glanced at Tracy again. "Say you do make it out of here somehow. He's going to kill you because that's what he does. Point that gun at him, I am the head of this case, I will let you walk free."

"Shut up." Tracy said. "You don't know shit you are talking about."

"Hey, if you keep talking, I am gonna rum that disfigured head of yours into the walls," Neythan said. "One staircase left."

"What's the plan?" Tracy said.

Neythan didn't respond as they descended the stairs. "Right." He said. "Give me your cuffs."

The policeman pulled his cuffs and handed them to Neythan.

Neythan cuffed the old man's left arm and dragged him to the poll by the stairway and cuffed him against it. He searched the policeman's pockets and pulled out his phone. He dropped it on the dusty, cemented floor. Stepped hard on it, three times.

"Now. We run." He said and pushed the emergency exit door. The sound erupted as quick as they left.

#

Granick checked his watch. Twenty-seven minutes had passed since the phone call with the Lawyer. All he needed was Evock. There wasn't much time left. Vichk had sent him a video message, where the Russian shaved his daughter's hair with a knife. Forty-eight hours to deliver Evock and the money, or just the money, the Russian had said.

He had known Mrs Kyle for almost half a decade. He kept thinking if he could discipline his conscience and suffocate the breath out of her if the Lawyer fails to turn up with Evock. He didn't know himself anymore. He didn't know what he could or couldn't do. Life had changed, so was his values. One thing he knew for sure was he loved Vienna and he would do anything to get her back. The whole situation had changed the core of him. His humanity had departed. Granick couldn't understand if the truth is worth anything good in this world anymore. His daughter was in this situation because he had stood for the truth. He spoke up against the system. If the system which has sworn to protect and preserve justice is the one inflicting pain, then there's no humanity left in the world.

Granick had already made up his mind. After he gets his daughter back. He would resign from the police force.

"I have always thought that you were a saint." Mrs Kyle said.

Granick raised his head. "Just keep your mouth shut."

"What happened to your nose?" She said again.

"Didn't you hear what I just said?"

"Why does it matter anyway." She frowned her face. "You are going to kill me, aren't you?"

"Well, you better pray your son shows up."

"What makes you so sure that he would know where Evock is or if Evock would agree to come?"

"That's why I said you better start praying."

"What I did might be against the law, but it was the most humane thing to do." She said. "I wasn't going to let a man grieve for his family when it is alive."

"Even death is the most humane thing," Granick said and checked his watch.

"You can arrest me. Why would you want to kill me?"

"Because killing seems to be the only form of justice these days." He said. "Just stop talking. Won't you?"

#

He turned back, and Tracy was on his heels. Ten minutes away from the Hotel. There were now in Wincobank. Running up the hills. No tail behind them. Just heavy breaths and a burning throat. They headed to the ambulance. Five minutes away.

"Let's take this footpath," Neythan said. "It's a short cut and away from the busy roads."

"Can we slow down for a moment." Tracy struggled to speak while she rested her hands on her knees.

"We walk then. We are not stopping." He said while he walked backwards faced at Tracy. "I have to make it back today."

Mid-morning. The sun was present but not as hot as it was the day before. A weak wind helped them regain. The ambulance was close to the crime scene but out of view and on a different road. It wasn't bad.

They passed through a field. Few teenagers played cricket. Nobody behind them.

His thoughts went back to the old policeman. What he had said. If the cleaner was a Royal Army Police, why was he disposing the bodies? Why is the Army involved in this? He couldn't answer the questions but one thing he knew for sure was Daniels knew what was going on.

Jack was right, he thought. Something must be going on. Neythan then reached his pocket and pulled out his phone and called Jack.

"Hello?" The phone was answered in one ring.

"Yeah, what you saying?" Neythan said.

"Where are you? What the hell is happening?"

"I am in shit. Been framed, Police is on to me." He said and checked on Tracy who followed behind him. "What did you mean there's a problem?"

"Where are you?" Jack said. "Need to see you in like, thirty minutes. Something is going on my friend."

"Now you talking like you wanna set me up," Neythan said. "What's going on? Tell me, the fuck is the problem?"

"Listen, my friend. We can't talk about this on the phone." Jack said. "Meet me at the place of life in thirty minutes."

"Two hours tops," Neythan said. "Can't get there in thirty minutes."

"Shit," Jack said. "Ok. Quick as you can please."

"Bless. See you soon."

"Wait. Neythan?"

"Yeah?"

"If the Police are after you. You got to lose that phone now."

The phone went dead. Neythan looked at Tracy. "Give me your phone."

"Why?"

"We have to get rid of it."

She reached inside her handbag and gave the phone to Neythan.

Neythan threw them in the hedge beside them.

"You should have destroyed them," Tracy said.

"This buys us time. If they are tracking us. They will come here. Now with more people. When they realise we are long gone. We would be long gone for sure."

"Makes sense," Tracy said. "There is the ambulance."

"Don't see nobody near it."

"Yeah. Run." Tracy said and took off toward the ambulance.

CHAPTER 18

"These fucking mofos." McCunt slammed the table. "How did they lose him?" He stood up.

"We don't know how they lost him, Detective." Sarah said.

"Put the old man on the phone."

"Who? Sorry." She looked at McCunt.

"DI John Andrews." He inhaled heavily. "Put him on the phone."

Sarah put the call on speaker. The phone went straight to voicemail.

"This is just bollocks," McCunt said as he paced the room. "Who contacted you? Put them on the phone."

After three rings. "Hello?"

"Yes, who's this?" McCunt said.

"It's Officer Kevin Quinn."

"Ok Officer." He said. "You're speaking to DCI McCunt. Yorkshire."

The Officer breathed a suppressed laughter. "My pleasure Sir."

"Likewise," McCunt said. "What happened down there?"

"Evock got away Sir."

"How?"

"He had an accomplice. A female. Maybe military by her looks." Quinn said. "They took DI Andrews with them."

"How did you let this happen, Officer?" McCunt realized that it was a pointless question to ask. Evock was already on the run and this time he would be aware. He now knew what was after him.

"The accomplice managed to take DI Andrews's weapon." He said. "We had to comply, we had to let them go. She had DI Andrews on gunpoint. Protocol Sir,"

"So, do we know where Evock or Andrews is?"

"Not yet Sir," Quinn said. "We are checking the building and reviewing the CCTV"

"Alright," McCunt said. "Keep me posted. Report directly to me."

"Understood, Sir."

"Good."

"Uh, before you go, Sir," Quinn said. "Evock said something before he left."

"What did he say?"

"He said he didn't kill the woman and the child. Daniels did."

"What?" McCunt's voice came out sharp. "How sure are you about this Officer?"

"Absolutely Sir." Quinn said. "There's another thing Sir."

"Go on." McCunt sat down.

"I was the first person to arrive at the crime scene. The man was still alive. The SIB Operative." Quinn said. "The first thing he asked me to do was to call Daniels. He died while on the phone with Daniels." He coughed. "Another thing was the other two victims. They were bagged and cleaned. The SIB had gloves on and traces of bleach on his cargos. He was undercover as well, as a Sky guy."

McCunt remained silent.

"Daniels requested all the evidence and refused to report the death of the SIB to the Army." Quinn continued. "The only reason I am telling you this Sir, is for you to pass your judgement correctly. I came face to face with Evock and I can say, based on my experience, he wasn't lying. He also could have killed us all if he wanted to."

"He also might have already killed Andrews."

#

Forty-seven minutes had passed. His heart raced. Was he ready to put a bullet into the innocent old lady's head? He was ready to do whatever it takes to get Vienna back. It was no longer about right and wrong but about what are you willing to risk, to get what you want. A cold-hearted killer with his daughter in his arms didn't seem that bad at all to Granick.

"Just ten minutes left." Mrs Kyle said. "Why don't you just get it over with."

She wasn't making it easy for Granick. He looked at her. She was on the verge of tears.

"Why are you doing this?" She said again.

Granick just stared at his watch.

"You must be protecting lives, not taking them." Her hands shook.

Weak sun lit the earth. Chilled breeze relaxed Granick's neck. Was it really? Kill for your own. Was it how the world around him had become? Vienna.

"I am going to close my eyes and pray." She said while she closed her eyes.

Granick watched her lips as they moved slowly. He reached for his gun. Then the phone rang. He picked it up. "Not much time left Mr Lawyer."

"Is my mother alright?"

"She won't be in the next six minutes."

"I need two hours," Jack said. "I will bring you Neythan."

"I thought I made myself clear."

"This isn't an easy thing." He said. "I am doing my best. I am asking you to understand. I will bring him in two hours from now."

"I will call you in two hours telling you where we gonna meet." Granick hung up the phone. "Stand up. You are coming with me." He stood up and grabbed her arm.

#

They had managed to pass the roadblock to get into M1 motorway. The ambulance proved to be a crucial asset. With the siren blasting, the police gave way. Getting away from Sheffield wasn't hard. Neythan's mind was already trying to figure out how he would open Daniels's chest and squash the man's heart with his palm.

Thoughts paced, fought, and argued inside his skull. In the middle of all that, almost two weeks had passed. The Doctor hadn't called. It was time he had to visit the Hospital. Even though the Doctor had said they could be some implications on Travis, if he was to survive, but the Doctor had said he would wake up. That's all Neythan wanted. He wanted to hear Travis talk. He hoped, wished, and prayed.

"Do you trust this guy?" Tracy said.

"Who? Jack?"

Tracy nodded.

"Yeah." Neythan said. "About the only person I could trust right now."

"Did he tell you what's going on?"

"No." He said. "Must be something serious because he sounded a bit shaky. That's ain't like him."

"Why didn't he tell you?" Tracy said. "I don't think we should just go meet him not knowing what's exactly going on. We might walk straight into an ambush."

"Jack wouldn't do that," Neythan said and checked the review mirror. "I know him."

"Does he know where the money is?"

"What?" Neythan turned his head to look at Tracy. "What money? What you talking about?" He said with a different tone.

"Come on, you know for sure what I'm talking about." She said. "Where's the money Neythan? At this point, that money is the only thing that's gonna stop all this."

"There's no money anywhere." Neythan said and accelerated. "Why are you so concerned about the money?"

"I am concerned about you." Tracy said. "Do you want people to keep dying because of you? Open your eyes and start thinking straight. Why are you on the run? Why are you framed? Why is your family dead? Huh?" She looked at him. "This is because of the money. You need to give up the money. Where's it?" She raised her voice.

Neythan remained silent. His eyes on the road. Tracy's words were like a needle in the eye. "Everybody is gonna die. Everyone." He said. "Everyone who's involved, who was ever involved and who will be involved." His throat tightened. "They poked the wrong beehive."

#

"Can I have a coffee please?" McCunt said. "Three sugars."

A junior officer left the conference room.

Large room. A long table in the middle with about twelve chairs on each side. A massive whiteboard by the wall behind McCunt. Third floor, good view of the southside of the City Centre. The curtains were closed, so was the windows. Classic Daniel O'Donnell played in the speakers. Low volume but very relaxing as McCunt thought. He loved classic music. Sixties, fifties, and seventies. Anything urban and present, he considered it cancerous. There was something about classic songs that drew him. The instruments and voices injected his imagination. The message of the songs and the sound was like the answer to life. He believed every question about life anybody could have is answered in the classic songs. They fed his imagination and creativity. The very thing he needed.

He looked at DI Sarah Willows. "Did you get the file?"

She went through her folder and pulled out a file with a grey hardcover. She handed it to McCunt. "I don't get why he would've wanted me to give the file which wasn't in the storage."

He extended his hand. "Where was it?"

"In his office. Locked away."

"Oh. I see." McCunt nodded. "Thanks."

"What do you think Detective?" Sarah said. "Do you think Chief would do something like that?"

"Don't worry about that. Let's just focus on finding Evock. Ok?"

"Yes, Detective." She stood up and walked to the door.

McCunt looked at the file for nearly two minutes before he opened it. A picture of Evock was at the top right corner:

Name: Neythan T Evock.

Date of Birth: Seventeenth of March Nineteen Eighty-one.

Mother: Deceased.

Father: Unknown.

No siblings on record.

Spouse: Alisha Evock.

Children: Travis Evock and Tanya Evock.

Occupation: Personal Trainer.

Criminal History: None recorded.

The face in the picture wasn't about innocent. The afro hair was neatly cut, the sides shorter than the top. Light brown skin. Broad shoulders. The white t-shirt firmly shaped his curved shoulder muscles and the division between his chest stretched.

The door opened and McCunt turned. "Thanks love."

He had a seep before he placed the mug beside the file. Not much information was in the file that wasn't in the News at the time. The whole case was an insult to McCunt's intelligence. The only piece of information that proved a challenge was the fact that not a single CCTV camera caught anything during the robbery. It was, of course, one of the most secured banks in England if not the most secured. NTR Headquarters was in the heart of Newcastle. He had to visit the Bank.

McCunt didn't want to make Sarah think that he believed what Officer Quinn had said. He had come to Newcastle for answers which he knew where hidden beneath the floor of the Police Department. From the moment he stepped foot in the station, a smell of corrupt and deceit had greeted him with disgust.

His mind remained focused on getting Evock. A man who had proved smarter than the criminals, the judge and the detectives who worked on the Bank Robbery case. Was Evock a murderer? Not the kind of man who would do things without a motive. What was his code? McCunt believed everyman has a code and knowing that code is getting into the head of the man. A man's code dictates what he's willing to die for and protect.

McCunt stood up and headed to the door.

Walked the corridor and opened the door on his left. Sarah and her team were heads-in their computers. He walked to Sarah. "Where are we?"

"We have a location." She said. "Evock is still in Sheffield."

"Forget that," McCunt said. "He's gone. There's no way he would stay in one place now. He ditched his phone."

"We already have units en route to the location."

"Call them off. Let them focus on the roads and exits."

Her phone rang. "Hello?" She said. "Yeah…roger. Double the security in the roads." She said again. "Understood?" She hung up.

She seemed drained. Her lips were dry. Her eyes were a bit swollen. "He's gone." She said.

"We will get him. He's coming to us." McCunt said.

"What do you mean?"

"Which Hospital is his son in?"

"Granite." She said. "About twenty minutes from here."

"I want you to take one of your men and go to the Hospital," McCunt said. "Call me when he turns up."

CHAPTER 19

Fresh breezy dried his throat. He felt it. He needed a shot of Jack Daniels. He took off the white gown, then closed the ambulance door. Further forward, that deep bend of the road made his insides move. The mental picture of Travis's unresponsive body laid there. His son's skull open and covered with blood. It's an image which will haunt him for the rest of his life. Anger boiled inside his head, guilt and blame consumed his heart. The universe had saved him, but it brought undeserved pain to his family. That, he couldn't find peace with.

"Where's he?" Tracy said.

Neythan closed his eyes hard that he felt his eyelashes dug into his eyeballs. A deep breath gave him the momentum to descent past the gravel and into the trees. No cars passed by, same as that God-forsaken day. His heartbeat raised as he descended. Flashbacks of the car rolling and hitting the trees cracked his mind. A deep pain struck his heart. The kind of pain which one can't explain but can feel every bit of its voltage in the middle of the heart.

He raised his head and looked forward. A man stood with a phone in his hand. He wore black suit trousers, a white golf t-shirt, and brown shoes. Neythan recognised him but the blackened soil reminded him of the harsh truth. He had stepped on top of the soil where the remains of his daughter and wife's particles laid. The car had been removed. The smell of wet ashes and burned particles filled his lungs. He fell on his knees and his eyes couldn't contain his tears.

The pain was unbearable. What was worse was that he felt it deep inside his soul that he had to do something, but he couldn't know what he had to do. His lips shivered. The guilty, blame and need for revenge felt like a curse he couldn't cast away or overcome. He felt it. He knew it. It was his fault.

He dug his fingers into the wet, ash darkened soil. He clinched into a fist as he took the cursed soil with it. He raised his hands to his chest level. Opened his palms and stared at the blackened soil with his watery eyes. He hoped the soil might have a clue of what he had to do next. A feeling of strength ran along his spine and a self-promise sat in his heart. If they were alive, he was going to find them. Faith, action, and determination had always been the foundation of his way of life.

The sound of a phone ringing made Neythan raise his head.

"Hello?" Jack said and paused. "Yeah. But is she ...""? He paused again. "Where?" He said. "Ok. We will be there." He scratched the back of his head. "Make sure my...shit?" The phone must have cut off.

#

A refreshing scent. The smell of polished wooden benches brought back his childhood memories. The memories of his mother taking him to Catholic Cathedrals. The stained glasses with pictures of Jesus, Mary and John the Baptist brought in a rainbowed ray of sunlight into the church. The walls were filled with statues of Jesus's crucifixion.

He knelt with one leg and bowed his head, then stood up and walked towards the cross. He turned to his right and approached a shelf filled with candles, some lit and some not. He took the lighter from his pocket and lit a candle. Bowed his head, closed his eyes and prayed in his heart.

He gestured the cross and said, "Amen."

He glanced to his left and realised the green light on the confession room light was on. Proceeded to the door. He opened the door. He saw red cushioned stools. Too small for siting. The wooden wall next to the stools had a small opening which was squared. Through the holes, he could see the Priest sat on the other side.

He cleared his throat and rested his knees on the stool. "Bless me, Father, for I have sinned."

"When was your last confession?" The Priest said.

"It's been long, Father. Too long." Granick said. "Before I started shaving."

"What is your name Son? What do you want the Lord to forgive you for?"

"My name is Raymond Granick, Detective." He cleared his throat. "I want the Lord to forgive me. I have killed Father."

The Priest remained silent for a moment. "Men kill for many reasons. What was your reason?"

"To protect myself and my family Father."

"Would you kill again?"

"Only if you don't listen and do what I tell you," Granick said.

"What do you mean Son?"

"Father, I have a loaded gun in my hand." He said. "I want you to stay in there, lock your door, turn the entrance lights off and remain silent till I knock on the door." Granick stood up. "It's for own good Father. Just pray for both of us." He walked out and closed the door behind him.

His footsteps echoed in the empty cathedral. He fixed his eyes at the door. He knew they would enter at any moment. He cocked his gun and waited. A deep breath opened his ears to pick up any slight movement and sound.

The door opened. He hid behind the statue of Jesus. He had choruses of voices. The footsteps got closer by every deep breath he took. It wasn't one person. He heard a loud woman's voice. Who is that? Granick wondered.

He applied a firm grip on his gun. Slid his index finger on the trigger and waited. The footsteps got closer. One last deep breath. He jumped out with his gun aimed at them. "That's close enough. Stop." He said.

"Fuck." The man Granick recognised to be Evock, yelled. "You again? I am gonna kill you."

"You know him?" The young lady asked.

"Where's my mother?" The other man said. It must have been the lawyer, Granick thought.

Granick pulled out his phone. "Don't move." He typed and put the phone back in his pocket. "I have sent you the address. That's where she is."

The Lawyer checked his phone. "It's not over." He said. "If she's hurt in any way. I am coming for you." He took off towards the exit.

"The fuck you want man?" Evock said.

Granick stared at the man. It was Evock. Still had an angry attitude. It was understandable for a man who had gone through what he went through. "Who's the lady?" He said.

"Nobody." Evock said. "What do you want?"

"You and I, need to talk and understand each other," Granick said. "We can help each other. But first, I need to know who she is and if she needs to be alive."

"You can talk. I am listening but don't threaten her." Evock walked forward. "She needs to be alive more than you."

Granick raised his gun at Evock. "Don't get any closer."

"Are you gonna talk or you gonna keep pointing that gun at me?"

"I need to know who she is." Granick looked at the young lady. "I don't trust her. She looks like a police officer."

"Really?" Evock said. "You gonna talk about trust? You?" He walked forward again. "Trust is nobody's fucking concern right now. You gotta start talking or put that fucking gun down and let me get out of here."

"You take one more step, I am going to shoot her," Granick said. "Evock, I have been a police officer for over ten years. I know how someone in authority carries themselves. Who is this lady?"

"I am a nurse at Granite Hospital." She said and scratched her ear.

Granick believed that she lied. He had always believed that if a person answers a lie, they always make an awkward body movement. That belief had never failed him in all the years he had been a police officer. Like his boss, Daniels had said, "When you ask someone a question, don't focus on their answer but observe their body language, and if its someone you know, also pay attention to the tone of their voice."

He looked at Evock who stared at him with piercing eyes. He realised there wasn't time to waist. "Do you trust her?" He put his gun down.

"Yes, she saved my life."

"Ok, that's good enough for me," Granick said and felt his nose, it was getting better but still a bit swollen. "You were right Evock."

"About what?"

"About your wife and daughter." He cleared his throat. "They are still alive."

"What?" Evock whispered and extended his right arm to feel the bench behind him before he sat down.

Granick just looked at him.

"Are you sure man?"

"Yes," Granick said. "I know who has them."

"Who?"

"This is why I am saying we can help each other." Granick stepped closer to Evock. "We are in a similar situation and we have a common goal. To get our loved ones back."

"Who has them?"

"Listen. They have my daughter and the only way I can get her back is if I bring you to them." Granick cleared his throat and watched Evock in case he made any sudden movements. "This is a win-win for both of us. You get to see who has your wife and daughter and I get my daughter back."

"What do they want with him?" The lady said.

"The money. They want the money." Granick said.

"Why didn't you say that before?" Evock said.

"Because that wasn't the deal before." He said. "I didn't need to bring you in. I only had to find where you put the money, but your lawyer messed that up."

"What if you still want the money?"

"Yeah, I think that's all you want." The lady said. "You are just making up this story."

Granick looked at the lady, then to Evock. "Do you have any idea of what I had to do to find you?" He said. "I don't need the money. I just want my daughter back." Granick sat down facing Evock. He still had his finger on the trigger. "The money, on the other hand, it's your leverage. You can use that to trade it for your wife and daughter."

"Neythan." The lady said and put her arm on Evock's shoulder. "I think this guy is in this. Listen to him. Trade? He just wants the money. If your wife and daughter are alive. He must be the one with them. All he's doing right now is proposing a trade."

Evock raised his head to look at the lady and then at Granick. "Take me to where my wife and daughter are."

"I can't do that because I don't know where they are," Granick said. "I only know who has them, and I have already told you how this is gonna work."

"I promise you one thing," Evock said and rubbed his ribcage. "If you are part of this whole shit, I am gonna pull your tongue out, your teeth, your eyeballs, and squeeze your balls with my hand until you hear them pop and slice your throat with a blunt knife."

"Fair enough," Granick said, he believed that Evock might do what he just said. "I am gonna set that in motion. Right now, you must come with me. Every police in the country are looking for you. I know a place where there are not gonna come looking."

"Where's that?" The lady said.

"A friend's house," Granick said and turned to the confession room.

#

Just after four in the afternoon. Good time as the banks close at five. The City Centre was as busy as someone would expect on a Saturday. People rubbed shoulders as they minded their business. Young girls in much revealing attires, McCunt thought. It seemed as if dressed almost naked was a way to thank the sun during the summer. He could notice a few men turn their heads to get a good look at the girls' backsides. It wasn't until he noticed himself focused on a woman bent over trying to adjust her baby in a pushchair. He shook his head trying to lose that focus but there was no denying that the glistering, shining, shapely rounded ass could catch any man's attention. The yellow shorts which only covered half her buttocks and showed the visible print of her pussy made it hard for him to not take a second look.

A force pressed against his shoe. "Sorry." The man who had just passed him said. McCunt just nodded. He understood things like that were bound to happen in a crowded place. He raised his head and started to scan the area. The NTR Reserve Bank was surrounded by clothing shops. In his view, he could see Next and River Island on both sides. Further ahead he noticed Barclays and Halifax banks. Coffee shops, a Chinese Buffet and a few more shops were around the area. He checked the outside cameras of the shops around the bank which could capture the entrance of the bank. Quite a few there were, McCunt nodded in acceptance.

How can all these cameras fail to record at the time of the robbery? There was no explanation to that question, McCunt had agreed but that's what he had come to understand. He walked towards the entrance of the Bank. The door was open, he just walked in. Few people were on the cash machines and some were talking with the Bank staff.

A young lady approached him. She had a red tie and white shirt, black skirt, and black shoes. She gave McCunt a smile that made him wonder how it would be like to kiss her. "Hi?" She said. "What can I do for you today?" Fashioned a warm smile.

"I would like to see the manager, please."

"Did you have an appointment?"

"No." McCunt reached the inside of his pocket. "I am DCI Scott McCunt."

"Oh, ok." She said. "I will let him know. Could you just give me a sec?"

"Yeah. Sure." McCunt said. He watched as she walked to the elevator. Her golden hair bounced on her back. I could marry her, he told himself.

He checked his phone. No update about Neythan Evock. He knew Evock would be trying to get back. If he knew about Daniels like what Officer Quin had said, then he could also be coming after Daniels. Men like Evock are not the kind of men who let their transgressors walk free. The kind of torture Evock did on the SIB Operative showed the heights he's willing to get to. But what exactly is Evock after? McCunt asked himself. It was the last piece to the puzzle he needed. McCunt knew that Daniels was corrupt. He believed what Officer Quinn had said. He just couldn't figure out what Daniels and Evock had in common. Why did they both go to the same place? What information was Daniels after and, also, what information was Evock after that made him burn a breathing Royal Army Personnel?

"Hello?"

The voice interrupted his questions. McCunt believed that to come up with an answer, first, you must have the right question. "Hey, you the manager?" McCunt said.

"Yes." He said and extended his hand. "What can I do for you?"

"Is there someplace private we could talk?"

"Yes of course." The manager said and turned. "Follow me."

McCunt followed behind the Manager. They took the stairs down. He could hear keyboards, and a few people speaking on the phones. They walked past a few doors and corridors. Finally, the manager opened the door and McCunt followed. He sat down after the Manager pointed to the chair.

"What brought you here Detective?"

"I just have a few questions to ask," McCunt said and adjusted in his chair. "How's the security around here?"

"We have confidence in it." The Manager said and sat back.

"Camera-wise, I can agree. Saw that almost every angle in the building is in view of at least one camera." McCunt said. "But I didn't notice any guards at the door or on our way down here."

"Because a lot has changed since the robbery Detective." He said. "Our guards dress like customers now and they are always armed."

"How could a Bank like this be robbed so clean?"

"I don't get it either Detective." He burped. "All I can say is, the people behind it had incredible technical skills. They overrode everything, the cameras, the passwords, face, palm, and fingerprint recognition. Everything. The sensor alarms, everything. Everything electronic was overridden. They were able to shut down the whole system."

"How's this possible?"

"It's not possible but they managed to do it." He scratched between his fingers. "They could have emptied the bank if they wanted."

"Who do you think could have that kind of skills?"

"It's not just that. These people knew the interior. Where hidden vaults are, where classified vaults are. They knew everything."

"So, you don't think this was an inside job?"

"Obviously it was." He said. "The lad you died, um the guard. They needed him to open the entrance door. Which is the only manual door which requires a key." He continued. "Apart from that, they didn't need an inside man because there's no one person who knows everything about this bank or who can open every door in here."

"Was it one of the classified vaults that were robbed?" McCunt said.

"No, they took the money?" He coughed. "But they could have taken anything if they wanted to."

"What things do you store in those vaults?"

"They are classified for a reason Detective." He said. "Besides, I wouldn't know. All I know is, there might be some government and army stuff in there, but I wouldn't know exactly what it is."

"So, how sure was the bank that only the money was missing?" McCunt said.

"According to the system, nothing else was missing except the seven million."

"But how could they rely on the same system which was compromised?"

"I wouldn't know Detective." The Manager said. "All we are focused on now is strengthening our security."

"Would you say three people could have pulled it off?"

"No way Detective." The Manager smiled. "No way that's possible. That's why Evock walked free because the jury could see how it didn't make sense." He said. "I am no Detective, but I think the police knows exactly what happened."

"Why would you say that?"

"How where they able to catch Evock miles away from the bank? No cameras were working. What are the odds that they could guess where he was and not anybody else who was involved? It can't be that Evock guy pulled the job by himself."

I know that McCunt thought. It wasn't much help from the Bank. The job was too sophisticated for people without the right set of skills. McCunt realised he had been looking at it the wrong way. The right way was to find out the motive behind the bank robbery and who was involved. Everyone.

CHAPTER 20

Food and plates filled the table. Kiesha had also helped with the cooking and the preparation. Beer was in the fridge. Hard liquor was everywhere in the kitchen. Brian drank Rose wine. It was going to be a long night of drinking. He preferred to start with the red wine before the martini and then the Sambuca shots. That's what he had planned but he knew when the alcohol got hold of him, he would drink anything close to him until he passes out. After all, it was his twenty-fourth birthday. He had the right to drink to the boarder-line of life and death.

About six in the evening. It was still bright outside, as it turns to be during summertime. His sister would arrive at any time as she had promised. Kiesha had just come out of the shower but still with her gown from last night. She had no clothes and Brian's trousers and shorts couldn't fit her.

Brian poured his red wine and nodded his head to an Ed Sheeran song which played in his loudspeakers. Granick will turn up, he believed it.

He checked his phone. Nothing. What's delaying them? He thought. Has that bustard done something to my sister? He thought again. Questions played in his head that he didn't realise the knock on the door. He just heard voices after Kiesha ran and opened the door. Brian walked from the kitchen.

"There is the birthday boy," Lisa said with a loud smile. "Happy Birthday Lil bro." She wrapped him with her arms.

A warm feeling of happiness comforted Brian. He was much happier for Lisa though. It was about the first time he had seen her with a smile on her face in a long time. "Thanks." He said. "So, so glad you came."

He looked to the side. Kiesha rested her back against the wall with her arms folded. He felt sad for her as he was sure that she had thought it would be Granick who had knocked. Beside Kiesha, there he was. The man Brian despised the most. Ben. Almost a year he hadn't seen the man. "Come on in," Brian said. "Make yourself at home."

"Wait," Lisa said. "I got you something." She turned her head. "Ben?"

"Oh, yeah," Ben moved forward and extended the carrier bag which contained something to Brian.

"Thank you," Brian said and took the carrier bag.

"Open it," Lisa said with laughter in her voice.

"Ok." He said and placed it on the table. Opened it and disappointment spelt his face. "A Harry Potter book. Really?" He faced Lisa.

"No, that's my mine. I am reading it but open it." She said with a smile.

Brian picked up the book and opened it. Papers that looked like receipts fell out. He picked them from the table and had a close look. He ran his eyes through them and then let out a scream and skipped up and down like the floor had become a trampoline. He ran towards Lisa and hugged her tight. Couldn't stop screaming. "Thank you, thank you, thank you." He said and kissed her on the chick. "Uhm I can't believe you did this." He said with his heart pumping fast and his knees shaking. "You are the best. Thank you so much." He kissed the papers.

Lisa laughed. "You have always said you wanted to go to Thailand, didn't you?"

"You are the best sister ever Lisa," Brian said and fanned himself with his hand while taking in heavy breaths.

"Glad you like it." She said. "Ben bought the tickets."

He hated the man, but he wasn't going to refuse the gift. "Thanks, Ben," Brian said and shook his hand.

"You are welcome," Ben said with a smile which seemed forced.

Brian took in a heavy breath and rubbed his hands on his thighs. "Almost forgot." He looked at Kiesha. "Kiesha, this is my sister Lisa, whom I was talking about, and her fiancé, Ben." He said and then looked at Lisa. "That's Kiesha. I work with her."

Lisa extended her arm. "Nice to meet you Kiesha."

"Nice to meet you too." She said in a low voice.

"Alright," Brian clapped his hands. "Let everybody sit down."

Lisa sat down next to Ben. Kiesha sat opposite them. Brian went to the kitchen and poured some wine into his glass. He came back and sat beside Kiesha. "Ben, there's beer in the fridge." He said. "You can help yourself."

Lisa watched Ben as he stood up. She took a bite and chewed. "These wings are so good." She said while chewing. "No way Brian cooked this."

Brian laughed. "Shut up. You know I cook better than you."

"I thought we settled that argument a long time ago when you blew up the oven." She let out a laugh.

Kiesha laughed also. "Did you really?"

"She's lying," Brian said with a smile. "She's the one who put a teen of beans in the microwave."

"I was eight then," Lisa said. "We can't start talking about the embarrassing things you did when you were younger." She put some lettuce on her plate.

"I wanna hear this," Kiesha said and budged Brian's shoulder with her elbow.

"Shall I?" Lisa looked at Brian.

"If you are ready to be exposed as well." Brian chuckled.

"You got nothing on me." Lisa motioned a dishing spoon on Brian's face. "Let me tell you, this one time yeah," She looked at Kiesha. "I walked in on Brian in my room. Faced the wardrobe mirror trying on my dresses. He had my make up on and his mouth and eyebrows were covered with my red lipstick." She laughed. "What did you do Brian, after that?"

He sipped his wine. "I ran into the bathroom and locked myself in there for nearly two hours."

"He was so scared," Lisa said. "I had to talk to him until he opened the door. He came out crying and said don't tell Dad or anyone."

"And you never did," Brian said.

"I told nobody till now." She put a fork filled with rice in her mouth. "You are all grown up now and you are happy. Am happy for you, wish Dad could see how wonderful you turned out to be."

"Well, he wanted nothing to do with me after I told him I was gay," Brian said.

"I think you should forgive him and give him a chance Brian," Lisa said. "It would be great for all of us to seat down. I hate him too for what he did to you and I would never talk to him until you are ready to."

"Not while I am alive. No." Brian shook his head.

Ben was already on his third Stella. He never said a word. He just chewed the steak and the pork ribs while emptying the bottles. Kiesha silenced. Maybe the conversation made her uncomfortable.

"Anyways," Lisa said. "It's your birthday. Let's not talk about him." She put more ribs in her plate. "Is Ray coming?"

Ben gave Lisa an eye which Brian noticed. "Yes, he is coming," Brian said. "He told me he came by your house the other day."

"Did he now?" Ben said and turned his heard to Lisa. "And you were gonna tell me about this when?"

"I forgot about it," Lisa said. "He came by and left. Didn't stay long."

"What did he want?" Ben placed his bottle on the table.

"Was just checking on me." Lisa stopped chewing.

"Why?" His facial expression began to change.

"Lisa," Brian said. "I got some Martini for you. Come have a look." He stood up.

Lisa stood up. Brian could see Ben grinding his teeth. He hoped if Granick would just come and break Ben's neck. He didn't like Ben and now he could see why.

They walked into the kitchen and Brian closed the door. "What was that all about?" He whispered.

"Nothing," Lisa said in a whisper. "He was just asking?"

"Like that?"

"You the one who started it," Lisa said. "Why did you have to say something like that?"

"So now it's my fault because that bastard got issues?"

"Let's go back before he starts thinking of something else."

"You are afraid of him, aren't you?" Brian said and opened a bottle of white martini. "Why are you with him, Lisa?"

"Come on, pour the martini." She said.

"Fuck," Brian said pouring the martini. "You shouldn't have brought him here."

Lisa took the glass and opened the door. She left.

Brian rested his back on the counter above the washer. He stared at the wine. Had a sip. I hate this bastard, he thought. He opened a bottle of Sambuca beside him and took three shots. He sighed, then sipped his wine. Switched the kettle on. Made a coffee and walked out.

"Here." He said to Kiesha. "Are you alright? You been quiet."

"Yeah. Just worried." She said and held the mug.

"Is something going on?" Lisa leaned on the table.

"No. Everything is fine." Brian said.

"Wait." Lisa raised her hand. "Can you turn the volume down. I think I heard a knock."

Brian stood up and headed to the door. He opened it. "Man, what took you so long?"

"Just got held up." He said. "How is Kiesha?"

"She's alright," Brian said. "Come in."

"Guys," Granick shouted. "It's clear." He stepped inside. "I got some friends if you don't mind."

Brian opened his arms. "No problem." He said. "Better to be more people. Wanna have a good time."

"Happy Birthday," Granick said. "Sorry, couldn't get time to get you something."

"It's ok," Brian said. "As long as you know am waiting for that present though." He laughed.

"Yeah."

A man and a lady walked to the door. "Come in," Brian said and walked to the lounge.

Kiesha turned, jumped out of the chair, and ran to Granick who put her in his arms. "Glad to see you all waked up," Granick said. "Was worried about you last night."

"Why did you just leave." She said. "Never do that again." She kissed him on the lips'

"Yeah." He said and released her from the hug. "Has Brian been treating alright?"

"She was safe." Brian smiled.

"I know," Granick said and faced forward to the table. "Lisa. I didn't see you there." He walked toward her and put her in his arms. He smiled and looked at her. "How are you?" He looked into her eyes.

"I am good." She said with a smile. "Was wondering when you were gonna turn up."

"I wasn't gonna miss Brian's party."

"Yeah," She said and looked at Ben. "Ray, that's Ben. My fiancé. Am not sure if you have met him before."

"No, I haven't," Granick said and extended his hand to Ben. "It's nice to finally meet you, Sir." He bowed his head with a smile.

"Likewise," Ben said.

Granick walked back to the man and the young lady. The lady couldn't have been much older than Brian if she was at all. Brian thought.

"These are my friends. Don and Tracy." Granick said.

"Nice to meet you." Everyone chorused.

"Nice to meet you all." The lady said. The man didn't say anything.

"You are a star, Brian," Granick said and picked up a plate. "Was wondering where I was gonna get something to eat."

"I know how to take care of my guests."

"You seem familiar," Ben said. "Have we met before?"

"Me?" Tracy said.

"No," Ben said. "Him." He pointed to the man.

"No," He said. "I don't think so. I am an old friend of Ray. Am not from around here." He rubbed his ribcage. "This is a nice house you got here young man. How do you know Ray?"

"Thanks," Brian said. "I work with him."

"Oh, so you are police as well?" He said.

"Yes."

"Who else is the police?" He said and looked at Granick.

"I am," Kiesha said.

"That's good." He laughed. "We know we are safe tonight."

"So, how do you know Ray?" Brian said.

"I have known him long before he became police." He said. "Have you got some JD. I am thirst." He laughed.

"Yes, in the kitchen. On the side." Brian said and sat down.

"Thanks." He said. "Ray, could you give me a hand please."

Granick and the man went to the kitchen. They closed the door.

Kiesha looked at Tracy. "Have a seat."

"Thank you." She said and sat down.

"What do you do?" Lisa said.

"I am a nurse."

"That's nice," Kiesha said. "Get something to eat."

"I am fine. Thank you."

"A drink?" Brian said.

"Please," Tracy said. "I wouldn't say no to a drink." She smiled.

"What do you drink?"

"I will drink what she's drinking." She pointed at Lisa.

Brian walked to the kitchen. He opened the door and heard the man say, "Yeah, but I didn't know you were making me walk into a fucking police station." Before they silenced after they realised he had walked in.

"You got the fosters in the fridge?" Granick said.

"Of course," Brian said and picked up the martini bottle. He opened the cupboard and took a wine glass. "I got to talk to you about Ben," Brian said.

"Brian, let that go, mate," Granick said. "We talked about this."

"This time I know what I am talking about."

"Listen, we will talk about it ok," Granick said. "Right now, I got to make a phone call." He pulled the phone out of his pocket. "Close the door behind you."

Brian walked out.

#

The blanket covered the bottom waist of his naked body. His hands rested under his head. He watched her while she put on her red thong slowly. The glim of the night light worshipped her spotless dark skin. She turned around with a smile and pushed her head through the red dress. It brushed her swollen youthful nipples as she stretched it over her hips to her thighs. It fitted perfectly like she was born wearing it. Her shape was that of a goddess. Her beauty could make the gods fight.

Daniels swallowed saliva. "Didn't think you were gonna bring me my order."

She smiled. "Well, you left without it."

"You are something else." He said.

"You paid me very well." She slid her heels on.

"You can come by tomorrow after work."

"I will let you know." She stood up and picked her handbag. She looked at him, smiled and the door swallowed her.

Daniels still played the sound of her moaning in his head. One young girl had made him rethink his decision of not marrying. She was a perfect being, Daniels thought. He might have fallen in love, but for an old man who had never believed in love, he was unable to tell if it was or not. But he was sure, she had touched his soul.

He pulled the blanket to his chest. His phone rang. He reached the drawer beside his bed. He looked at the caller id. Mrs Kyle? What does she want? He asked himself. Hesitated and then answered. "Mrs Kyle?"

"Granick." The voice said.

"Granick?" Daniels sat up. "Where are you and how come you using Mrs Kyle's phone?"

"You told me to find who leaked the information," Granick said. "I didn't just find who did, I got Evock."

"What?" Daniels said. "Are you serious?"

No response on the phone. "Bring him to me," Daniels said again.

"That's not the deal," Granick said. "Tomorrow night. Ten O'clock. Bring my daughter with you."

"Where?" Daniels said.

The call ended. He redialed the number. It went straight to voicemail. "Shit."

He went through his contacts and dialled Vichk's number.

"Hello?" The phone was answered in two rings.

"Granick just called," Daniels said. "He got Evock."

"Are you sure about this?"

"No, but he has set up a meeting."

"Where?"

"Ten O'clock tomorrow night." He said. "He didn't tell me where."

"That's understandable," Vichk said. "What do you think?"

"Play along," Daniels said. "If he's playing. We will kill the daughter."

"Then we shouldn't bring the daughter then."

"Yeah, but you are not coming."

"What are you talking about?"

"I have a plan B if this doesn't work out," Daniels said. "You ever heard of Blanco Petrovich?"

"The Russian Boss?"

"Yeah." Daniels nodded his head. "Granick killed his men last night. They must be after the money too. That means we got something in common."

"Why would they be after the money?"

"The guard who died was his man and I had promised them a cut after the heist but Evock fucked that up," Daniels said. "Listen. You need to tell him that we got Evock's family and he's coming with the money. We need his men for back up." He continued. "We don't know what Granick or Evock is planning. One thing I know now is to not underestimate Evock."

"But you can't go there alone."

"They can't do anything to me," Daniels said. "I am the only one who knows where their family is."

"So, what's your plan for tomorrow?"

"Just do what I told you," Daniels said. "You need to get Petrovich's men to the farmhouse. If you don't hear from me by midnight tomorrow, kill the daughters and torture the wife till she talks or dies."

#

"Sing another one," Granick shouted, and everybody cheered in support.

Lisa had a shot which was already on the table. Brian could see that his sister was now possessed with the alcohol. So as everyone in the room. "No, I have sung three songs already." She said and burped. "Brian put some music on. I wanna dance."

Brian connected his phone to the tv. It wasn't advanced technology for him as he knew more than the professionals as far as technology and computers are involved. He went on YouTube and gave Lisa the phone. "You put what you want." The light from the phone's screen hurt his eyes.

She played a song which Brian didn't know but he liked it. She danced while everybody watched. She was as good a dancer as she was at singing. What she was better at than the other was debatable. She could move her waist and her feet in an accord like good music.

Granick cheered, then stood up. He joined Lisa. They danced, jumped, laughed, and clapped hands together. Tracy also stood up and started to throw hands in the air. Everybody was happy except for Ben.

Brian took a slice of cake. He thanked God that they had sung him Happy Birthday before they got their heads poisoned by the alcohol. His birthday wish was good for him. He didn't know if God liked it. He had wished for Ben to die.

It was now past midnight. Kiesha dossed on the sofa. She was the only one who didn't drink with the others. Brian wondered if Granick had noticed that and if he did, what reason had Kiesha given him.

Brian put his glass down and joined the people dancing. He wasn't a good dancer, but he was having a good time. He bumped on Granick who then dropped his can. Granick didn't seem bothered, he just picked it up and had a sip.

The song finished. Everyone stopped dancing. Granick and Lisa had lost their balance.

"Play another one," Tracy shouted.

"Another one will come on," Lisa said and stumbled forward. "Let me go to the loo before I piss my sen."

Everybody laughed.

Another song played. Brian knew it and sang along, "I took a pill in Ibiza…" Nodded his head to the beat. He reached for his glass, it was empty.

Granick held Kiesha's hand and pulled her up. "It's our Brian's birthday babe. Let's dance."

"I am tired, Ray. Wanna go to bed." She laid on his chest.

"In a minute babe."

Brian walked to the kitchen. He ran his eyes in the kitchen. All the martinis had finished. There was still some whisky bottles, vodka, rum, and gin. He picked up a half-full bottle of Sambuca and put it on his lips. The minty sweetness tingled his throat.

The door was opened. "Still got some JD?"

"Yeah," Brian said. "You finished a litre already. You wanna die?"

He laughed. "I will be alright."

Brian turned to the door and extended his hand for the handle to open it.

"Stop."

Brian turned to face Granick's friend.

"Have you found out who killed Layan yet?"

"No, not yet," Brian said.

"The fuck you mean not yet?" He said. "It's more than six months after he died and you telling me not yet?"

"Neythan?" Brian said. "You think I don't wanna find the son of a bitch who killed my brother?" He whispered while stood closer to Neythan. "Your camera didn't have a clear view of the inside. The shot was fired from inside the bank. I have been using reflections to try and capture the image. I am close."

"Yeah, the camera was on the dashboard," Neythan said. "I thought it was on a good angle. That's the best I could do anyway. Couldn't put it outside because they could have spotted it." He opened the Jack Daniels bottle. "Did you at least manage to see an image, even vague or blurry?"

"Yeah," Brian said. "It was a woman, but the image is not yet clean to make sure. I am not able to see the colour of her skin or her hair or the right shape of the bloody body."

"A woman?" He said. "You sure?"

"You know I am never wrong on these things."

"Good," Neythan said. "Listen. Tomorrow might be the day. Get ready and do exactly what I told you. There's no room for mistake, I don't want you to get hurt or worse."

"What about Travis?"

"Don't worry about that," Neythan said. "You just worry about the…" Neythan did finish what he wanted to say. The door was opened.

"Don," Granick said. "Your girl is going crazy here."

They walked out of the kitchen with bottles in their hands.

Tracy was on the floor doing push-ups. Kiesha was counting and she was in the sixties. "I tried to compete with her, I gave up." Granick shook his head.

"Let me show her what real men do," Neythan said and took off his jacket. "How many she did?"

"On eighty now," Kiesha said while she counted.

"Impressive but not better than me," Neythan said and got in position. "Brian, start counting when she stops." He started. Up and down. Up and down.

For a man who had finished a litre of whisky by himself, he still had respectable strength. Brian thought and watched. Tracy stopped at one hundred and twenty-three. He was impressed as well as shocked. He could barely do thirty push-ups and a girl, a nurse, pushes through hundred after alcohol like it's nothing.

The music played. Tracy laid flat on her stomach. Kiesha went on the floor to check on Tracy.

Brian was now on sixty and Neythan was still going strong. He sipped Sambuca while still focused on Neythan. Brian decided it was time he joined the gym. Drunkard up people were twice than he could ever do sober.

Neythan stopped in position and looked up.

"Why did you stop?" Brian said. "Just five more to a century."

"I thought I heard a scream," Neythan said.

"No," Tracy said. "He's just trying to find a way to rest. Put him back by ten Brian."

"Eighty-five now," Brian said. "Let's go."

"Cool," Neythan said and started. He went fast like he had a spring in his hands.

"How many did you do Ray?" Brian said.

"Don't even ask mate," Granick said and laughed.

"He barely did twenty." Kiesha laughed.

"She's lying," Granick said.

Neythan had clocked hundred and was still going. Tracy had stood up and sat on Neythan's back. He didn't stop.

Brian thought he heard a scream. He listened again. The scream came from upstairs. "Lisa?" He shouted as he dropped the bottle in his hand while his legs tried to run faster than his heavy heard. He slipped on the stairs. He didn't stop. He used his hands to balance. He ran to the top of the stairs. Only the toilet door was closed. He budged it with his shoulder with a force that threw him right onto the toilet seat. The door wasn't closed shut. His armpit landed on the edge of the seat that his elbow sung into the chamber's water. The adrenaline ignored that impact. He sprung up. Ben had Lisa's head pinned in the sink. Her dress pulled over her waist. Brian didn't think. He motioned his left fist. It landed on the wall. He heard his fingers crack, but it wasn't louder than the slap that landed on his right cheek.

He found himself in the tub. Ben stood faced down on him. Lisa pushed Ben and he staggered until he fell outside the door. Brian stood up. Tears in his eyes. Every part of his body shivered. He pulled off the shower pipe and charged toward Ben who was getting up on his feet. Brian swung the head of the shower. It missed Ben's head. Brian stumbled, and his neck fell into Ben's palm. The grip was tight that Brian felt the blood run into his eyes. He couldn't remove the hand. The grip loosened after Brian's toes dug into Ben's groin.

The kick wasn't enough to put Ben down. A blow to the back of the head sent Brian down the stairs.

"The fuck is going on?" Somebody shouted.

Brian heard footsteps coming towards him. He felt like he was floating. He couldn't feel any pain, he couldn't move his body. He saw Neythan's face in the air.

"Brian, what's going on?" Neythan said. "Did you fall? Are you ok?" He slapped Brian on his cheek. "Brian?" Neythan grabbed Brian by his armpits and lifted him.

Granick got hold of Brian. Brian just looked up the stairs. Lisa still screamed.

"What the fuck?" Neythan said and climbed the stairs.

Lisa tried to run down the stairs. Ben grabbed her hair. Her scream echoed.

Ben stood by the top of the stairs. Lisa on her knees while she screamed trying to get off. Neythan climbed the stairs.

Ben pulled Lisa up and pushed her backwards. He now stood with his eyes fixed down on Neythan who still climbed the stairs. He tried to connect Neythan's head with his kick while he still held the high ground, but he only found the air. Neythan jumped forward and stood by the corner. They faced each other.

Ben motioned his right hand straight to Neythan's face. Neythan moved his head to the side while allowing Ben's hand pass between his raised forearms. Neythan closed his forearms together with a force that broke Ben's elbow. Ben couldn't scream as Neythan's fist landed on his jaw.

Ben laid flat. Neythan's heel created another sound on Ben's knee cap. Neythan then squeezed Ben's throat with his heel.

Brian had regained his strength.

Granick ran up the stairs. "That's enough." He said. "You don't wanna kill him."

"People like him deserve to die," Neythan said.

"No," Granick said.

Neythan didn't respond.

"Evock. Stop." Granick shouted with a gun in his hand.

"You are ready to kill me not dickheads like him?" Neythan said and lifted his leg.

Brian was nearly up the stairs. His sister sat by the wall crying. Her head hid between her knees. He walked towards where Ben was laid. He looked down and spat on Ben's bloody face.

Lisa stood up and walked toward Granick. She stopped beside him and snatched the gun from his hand. "Evock?" She said. "Neythan Evock?" She pointed the gun at Neythan. "You killed my brother."

"No," Brian shouted and ran in front of Neythan. He heard the gunshot the same time he felt the heat on his chest while looking at the ceiling. He felt like he sunk into the floor before he started coughing blood. Neythan's head was above him. It was blurry, and he couldn't hear anything. He felt Neythan's warm hand on his cheek and a wet drop from Neythan's face hit his eye, but he couldn't blink. He felt paralysed. He felt the need to breathe and vomit at the same time. He coughed more blood. "Neythan." He said. He only hoped Neythan could hear him as he couldn't hear himself. "The CD is," He coughed. "In the…" Blood bubbled out of his mouth. "Bible under my bed." He could feel himself suffocating. "The thing." He let out a hard cough that shook his body. "It's still in the same…" That's all his strength could allow him to say. He tasted his blood. He felt a strong force that pulled the insides of his head down. Powerful than dizziness. He closed his eyes.

CHAPTER 21

Early morning. Seven-thirty. Still wide awake. As it had been for a week since Slakky died. Goddy couldn't find peace with himself. He was sure Slakky would've forgiven him, but Goddy hadn't forgiven himself. Before Slakky took his last breath, Goddy saw a vulnerable and honest man in Slakky's eyes.

He had never had a problem of sending people to the underworld. It had never disturbed his peace or his sleep. But Slakky wasn't the same as everyone else who walked on earth. Slakky was a friend. Their bond was beyond friendship. Goddy had sworn in his heart that he would protect Slakky to his last breath. A sworn promise was the holy grail loyalty amongst the brotherhood. But, by his hand, the hand which had sworn to protect, took Slakky's life.

Slakky's body had been shipped to Russia. Goddy couldn't get himself together to attend the funeral. He didn't know what to say to Slakky's family. The death of Slakky was a painful and heavy burden to his family. It was a big family and they all depended on Slakky. Small children, children in school and the mother who's in care for a disease which doctors can eventually treat but they need a down payment. Slakky would've come up with the money had he not died.

Goddy had thought about it countless times. Since he couldn't sleep. He spent most of the time in his head. He had concluded one thing. The money. Fuck The Boss. Goddy wanted the money all to himself. He was ready. He believed Slakky would protect him. He was going to do it alone. He knew more than much on how to get things done. Fifteen years he had lived under the shadow of his Boss. Fifteen years of lessons. It was time for him to take his own path and become his own Boss. He was willing to die. The money was enough to help Slakky's family and for him to start something of his own.

It wasn't an easy mission for one man. But he had one thing he knew would make Evock give up the money.

#

The rushing sound of the waves had always been the best music of nature. Neythan stared at the violent waves which tried hard enough to reach his shoes. He wondered how peaceful it would feel to go further in the sea that he couldn't see the shore. Only surrounded by waters. It must be peaceful, he thought. Away from all the hurt, pain, regret, blame and misery which surrounded him with long, dirty claws that scratched his skin deep to the bones.

"There she is." Tracy pointed to someone who approached them from their right side.

The morning sun wrestled with his eyes that he couldn't form a positive image on her. It was Lisa. He was sure. She was the only person who knew where he would be that morning.

Tears never departed his eyes. They would stop and then visit again. His eyes itched. He had not slept but he wasn't tired. The strong smell of the waters and the salty air was like caffeine to him.

"Brian oh Brian." He said to the waters. "Even faced with death you still had the composure and the intelligence to speak a secrete the right way." He looked at the mist above the waters. "You are so much like Layan. Wish I had known you long enough. Rest in peace." Tears began to flow again. "I will find who killed Layan. I promise you that." He wiped the tears with his arm and bowed his head.

Neythan turned away from the sea and Lisa fell into his arms. She sobbed and snorted. He felt the wetness on his chest. "I am sorry," Neythan said. "I have no words, but I understand how you feeling."

"Should l give you two some space?" Tracy said.

Neythan nodded and Tracy headed to a pub nearby.

Neythan understood the weight of the situation that was on Lisa. He had to think that he was the right person to comfort her. He felt obligated. The least he could do was to tell Lisa the truth as well as take care of her. Even that wasn't enough until he found the people responsible for the death of Layan. "Lisa." He said and gently removed her from his chest. "Look at the sea."

She still sobbed but she did.

"If a huge wave comes and sweeps us off our feet." He looked at her. "Would you blame it? Or it was us who stood in its way?"

"But that doesn't change the fact that I killed our Brian." She wiped her nose with the sleeve of her jacket. "My brother. I killed my brother. How am I supposed to live with that?" She cried.

"It wasn't your fault." Neythan looked into her eyes. "It. Wasn't. Your. Fault. OK?"

She didn't respond. She just looked at him with sorrowful, teary eyes.

"Listen," Neythan said. "I am here for you." He wiped his eyes. "Did you tell the police exactly what I told you to say?"

"Yes." She said.

"Good." Neythan nodded and held her shoulders.

"You saw the video, right?"

She nodded.

Neythan turned back to face the sea. The waves still tried to get to his shoes. "I didn't kill Layan." He said. "The police made everyone think I did but they didn't have any convincing evidence. That's why I won the case." He looked at her. "Brian was looking into that video to see who killed Layan."

"How do you know Brian?" Lisa said. "I mean, I know you and Layan were friends and all but me and Brian weren't that close to Layan."

"Layan wasn't just a friend," Neythan said. "He was like a brother. We grew up together and we went through a lot. He saved my life a couple of times too." He let out sad laughter. "I left Sheffield to come up here about thirteen years ago." He continued. "I cut contact with everyone I knew, I wanted to change my life because at that time I had a family." He rubbed his burnt chest. "About six or seven months ago, Layan wanted to track me down. That's how I knew Brian, he's the one who found me."

"What did Layan want from you?"

"I owed Layan my life. He needed a favour."

"Favour for what?" Lisa said.

"I don't know what kind of deals he was into, but he owed a lot of money to the wrong people," Neythan said. "He came to me with a job he said it meant life and death to him. I had no choice but to help him."

"A job?" Lisa said. "To rob the Bank?"

"Yeah." He said. "He said everything was planned. Everything was in place. All I had to do was drive." He looked at Lisa. "Right there is where I failed to see something wasn't right."

"What do you mean?"

"I guess the real reason Layan came to me was for me to help him get away from those people," Neythan said. "He knew I was good at reading situations and understanding hidden agendas." He looked at the sea. "He must have known there was no way we were gonna get out of there alive."

"Who are the people?"

"I don't know yet." He turned his head to Lisa. "That's why I want to know who killed Layan. That's where I will start?"

"So, what was Brian owning about?"

"That's why I said I failed to understand Layan's reason," Neythan said. "I had my plan to get away or for him to getaway. Too sad mine was after the job. He must have wanted to get away before the job. I think he knew what these were capable of." The wind dried his eyes. "I had to get someone in my plan and that was Brian. Someone they didn't know or expect would have a connection with me and Layan." He continued. "I had to get to the meeting point without the money. The plan almost worked out perfectly but then Layan died, and I got arrested."

"So, Brian had the money all this time?" Lisa said.

"Neythan," Tracy shouted while running toward them. "We have to go. There's police everywhere."

#

"That's too much sugar Ray," Kiesha said. "What's wrong with you?"

Granick stirred his coffee. "It's just sugar. It did nothing wrong to you." He said. "What's gotten into you?"

"Try to spend six hours being asked the same questions and each time giving the same lies."

"So, what did the police say?"

"Ben is in custody, but he still can't talk," Kiesha said. "His mouth is swelled up. Teeth sticking through his lips."

"I agree with Evock on this one." He put his cup down. "There was no way Lisa was gonna go down for this. She's suffering enough as it is, and I wasn't gonna go down either coz it was my gun that was used." He looked at his watch. Nine thirty. "Ben was fighting Brian and I tried to stop him. He took my gun and shot Brian before I beat him up. That's what happened."

"But why did you have to bring Evock to the party Ray?" Kiesha said.

"I didn't know," Granick said. "I didn't know Evock and Brian knew each other or that Brian and Lisa were related to one of the victims."

"I am tired, and I am drained," Kiesha said. "Can't deal with this right now. I wanna go see my mum and you are driving me there."

"I don't think that's a good idea right now babe," Granick said. "We will go on a different day."

"I want to go now." She stood up. "I haven't seen her in a long time. Wanna see if she is ok."

"Jesus." He breathed the word while he stood up. Few people were in the Coffee Shop. Bright day but he couldn't wait for the night to come. That's the night he will have Vienna in his arms. He was done. The sudden death of Brian was like a heartbeat. It was time he got his daughter, leave the police force, and get away from Evock and Daniels. Take Kiesha and Vienna to someplace safe and lead a normal family life. No deaths. No guns. No blackmail. No dirty cops. Just a safe family life with his two girls. He now knew and believed that he loved Kiesha. Life is too short. The night before was a hurtful example.

"Watch your speed, Ray."

"Babe, you need to relax." He said. "Calm down. Everything is and will be fine."

"Ray, Brian died." She cried. "He died. Why God?"

"I know babe," Granick said. "He was a good lad."

Kiesha sobbed.

Granick turned his head. "Do you want me to turn around and drop you home."

"No." She sniffed. "Keep going."

The roads were clear on a Sunday morning. Kiesha gave him the directions. He thought about Brian. How a young and honest man can meet an untimely and cruel death. He thought about the life he wanted. A life that doesn't create enemies. A life far away from the law and the criminals. A life where he can grow old and see his daughter get married. Being a grandfather. Happy thoughts. Happy life.

"Turn left here." She said. "That's the Care Home."

Granick turned and parked the car near the entrance. Big Care Home. About three floors.

He opened the first door and the second was locked.

"Press the buzzer," Kiesha said.

Granick pressed the buzzer. Two offices faced the entrance where they stood. The door made a sound and Kiesha pushed it open.

On the right side, just after the entrance, was a small table with a book which Kiesha signed.

She then moved from the book and walked forward before she turned right. There was a door going to the staircase. She put in a code and opened the door. She went through, and Granick followed. They went down the stairs and passed through opened fire doors. They walked the corridor. They passed a room with a pool table, then a big lounge, and a staff room before they passed the kitchen. The smell of gravy and Yorkshire puddings. He wouldn't mistake the smell of Sunday dinner. The one thing he loved about Sundays.

They passed through another fire doors, and Kiesha turned.

A woman in her forties approached them. She wore a white zipped shirt. Black trousers and black shoes. She greeted them with a smile.

"I am here to see my mum," Kiesha said.

"She's in her room."

The Assistant seemed to know Kiesha well. She talked about how it had been long since she had seen Kiesha around.

Kiesha knocked before she opened. Granick followed.

A woman sat in a chair faced the window like something was amusing outside.

"Hi, mum," Kiesha said.

The woman turned around and looked at Kiesha like she didn't recognize her. "Ahh, our Kiki." She said and held Kiesha's head and pulled it towards her, then kissed on her forehead.

There was a strong resemblance between Kiesha and her mother. The eyes looked the same. The eyes that make a person feel comfortable when you look at them. She was just an older version of Kiesha. She had a clean, short haircut. Grey hair with fragments of blackness at its roots. She had a necklace with a cross. The cross reminded him of his mother. They could have been religious friends, Granick thought.

"How are you, mum?" Kiesha said and sat on the bed.

Granick just stared at the TV. The Olympics were on. Rio 2016. The analysts were all hyped up about Usain Bolt winning the hundred metres gold for the third time in a row.

"I have been all right love." She said and then looked at Granick. "Who's this lovely gentleman?"

"That's Raymond, mum," Kiesha said. "He's a friend."

"Oh." The mother said. "I see."

The room smelt of air fresheners and it was tidy. Sculptures of animals and cities were on the window seal and some next to the TV. She must have travelled in her days, he thought. Pictures covered the wall behind the TV. Some old, which were black and white, and some new, in colour. One picture got his attention that he walked to the wall to have a closer look. It was Kiesha, Granick thought. She looked like Kiesha at least. A young girl, in a hospital bed with a baby in her arms.

Kiesha and her mother talked and laughed behind him. He stretched his hand and unhooked the picture. He looked at it again. That looks like Kiesha, he said to himself. He focused on the picture again.

Granick walked back from the wall with the picture in his hand. "Kiesha?" He said. "Who is this?" He motioned the picture to her.

"What?" She said. "Sit down beside me." She patted the bed. "That's why I wanted you to come. To know a part of my history I never talk about and don't feel comfortable talking about."

"What are you saying Kiesha?" Granick looked into her eyes.

"That's me." She said.

"I didn't know you have a kid," Granick said and wondered why she never mentioned it.

"That's because she died not long after that picture was taken," Kiesha said with tears flowing down her cheeks. "She was born with two holes in her heart. The doctors couldn't do anything."

Granick held her hand. "I am sorry to hear that." He said. "I didn't know."

"Her father was a man who raped me when I was only fourteen, coming from school in the winter." Kiesha sniffed.

Granick put her in his arms, and she cried. "I am so sorry babe." He rubbed his hand on her back. "You are a strong woman babe. I can't believe you went through all this. We will deal with this together. I love you." Granick felt the tightening of her grip around his waist.

"Don't cry, darling." The mother said and tapped Kiesha's back.

Kiesha raised her head. "I know mum." She said. "I love you, mum."

"Could you get us a cup of tea Kiki." She said.

"Ok." Kiesha stood up and walked out.

The mother looked at Granick in silence and then said, "Our Kiki loves you." She looked on her fingers. "Would you take care of her? She's a very vulnerable child."

"I most certainly would," Granick said. "With pleasure."

A ring that had a stone. Black stone. Granick wasn't sure if it was a diamond or not. Is what she removed from her finger. "This ring has been in my family for generations." She said. "My mother gave it to my husband like I am doing to you right now." She put it in Granick's hand. "Make sure you give it to our Kiki the right way."

Granick hastened his hand into his pocket when Kiesha walked in. "What's going on?" Kiesha said and put the cup of tea on a table next to her mother.

"Nothing love," She said. "Raymond here is a true gentleman."

"What did you do with my mum, Ray?" Kiesha nudged Granick's shoulder with a smile on her face.

"Nothing." He laughed. "We were just talking."

"Mum," Kiesha said. "The lasses who work here said you are not taking your medication."

"I am tired, love." She said. "If the Lord wants to take me. I am ready. Let his will be done."

"Don't talk like that mum."

"Gonna go to the toilet," Granick whispered in Kiesha's ear, then stood up and walked outside the door. He walked the corridor up to the room he had seen the pool table in. He closed the door after he entered and took the phone from his pocket. He dialled and waited.

"Hello." The voice said.

"Cathedral. Downtown." Granick said. "Bring my daughter."

CHAPTER 22

The hours of the day had quickly disappeared like the smoke from his mouth. A spliff of weed calmed his thoughts in the gaze of the golden sky. The sun was retiring and Goddy hoped if it could also retire with his thoughts of loss.

Muscles relaxed. Eyelids became slightly heavy to stay in their natural position. Through the window, the view was stimulant. It was like nature had perfected the art of saying goodbye. The sunset satisfied his eyes. Steady wind which carried the smell of rain comforted his uncovered chest.

It was time. In a couple of hours, the darkness would cover the earth. By dawn he would have the money or Evock's son would be dead. He was ready to go all in. The close falling night was going to be a rain of lava on most people.

Another puff and the phone rang under his gun on the window seal. The Boss's number. Ten minutes to eight was the time.

#

Neythan stepped out of Chettars pub. He needed some air to breathe or maybe he had had a little too much of the whisky he had been drinking since the morning after he had left Lisa in her house. He had given Lisa specific instructions for the following morning. He had also vowed to himself that he would not see the dawn without his wife and daughter in his arms. Not when the man who has them will stand before his eyes in two hours. He knew what to do. He knew people were going to die. No mercy, no reasoning, not when they left Travis in a comma. Not when they made him mourn and emotionally torture himself for people who still had breath. They had poked the wrong beehive. Chosen the wrong person to play with and the wrong game to play. They had awoken a demon since buried by the birth of Travis. A demon which was developed and poisoned in the harsh streets of Sheffield. Not to a twelve-year-old who knew nothing but survival. Whose default state was to kill. Who had no family and no friends but the comfort of terror, blood violence and killing in the cold winters'. That was the wrong man to take away the one thing most dear to him. The one thing he would kill for. His family. The man must be foolish to stand before me if he's the one with my family and who has caused harm to them, Neythan thought to himself.

The darkness was shy but slowly grew thicker. He looked to the sky. No stars, just sad, dark clouds ready to cry. Moments like these are when he wondered what his father would advise him to do. It's the moments which hurt him the most. As a man who grew up without a father, the emotional anger towards the absence of much-needed inspiration, advice, and teachings, forms a thick line of separation from the world around and a deep self-reliance belief filled with destructive anger, loneliness, and severe lack of trust with a total absence of love and care.

He never knew him. He could be alive or dead but Neythan believed a worse father would be the one who fails to protect his family than the one who's dead or abandons it.

A touch on his back disrupted his sad thoughts. He turned his head and she stood by his side. The lights everywhere. From buildings to moving cars.

"What are you thinking?" She said.

He sighed. Close to an angel she was. She had taken on a battle she didn't need to. She had saved his life. Twice. Showed care for his wounds and weak body. Tracy. "Are you alright?" Neythan asked. He looked at her. He wanted to thank her but that couldn't come out of his mouth. People like her are like a shooting star. Not always would you see them in your life and when you do, not long they stay in sight. It was time for her to go. She had done enough. More than enough, but Neythan did not want to see another person die. Not the ones close to him. He had seen enough deaths and had mourned enough.

"Yeah." She tilted her head up to look at him. "The police guy will be here shortly I think."

"Anytime from now," Neythan said.

"You seem a bit unbalanced," Tracy said. "Looks like the wind can carry you any minute."

"I will be fine," Neythan said. "I am not looking to have any conversations tonight."

"Do you trust this guy?" Tracy zipped her black jacket. "I know a lot has happened, but have you stopped to think about this? We don't even know who we are going to meet tonight. It could be one person, it could be twenty."

"I am done with thinking." He said. "If he's lying, I will kill him. I told him that."

"What if he kills you first?"

"He would have killed me already if he wanted to kill me," Neythan said. "It's not him I am worried about."

"He didn't kill you because you haven't given him the money," Tracy said.

Neythan looked at her. "Nobody is getting no money."

"Where's the money Neythan?" She stared into his eyes. "We can stop this now if you give me the money."

"What?" Neythan contracted his eyes.

"If you give up the money, I mean." She chuckled.

The beam lights torched directly into his eyes which he protected with his raised forearm. A white Juke pulled next to the cab they stood on. The engine stopped. Granick stepped out with a cigarette in his mouth. He wore a red t-shirt, Neythan's worst colour. Black shoes and grey cargo trousers.

"You barely can open your eyes," Granick said. "Are you serious? Do you understand what's about to happen?"

"Straight up," Neythan said. "Am gonna make the son of bitch tell me where my wife and daughter are before I open his chest."

"How are you gonna do that when you can't even stand straight?"

"Don't worry about that," Neythan said. "What's the plan?"

"The exchange is at ten." Granick threw his cigarette on the ground. "At the Cathedral."

"Exchange?" Tracy said.

"I explained to you how this is going to go down," Granick said. "I am only there to get my daughter and leave. Whatever else is up to you."

"Ok. This is bullshit." Tracy said. "Who are we even going to meet? How many are they? You think we are just gonna believe that they got your daughter and go in there off guard. For all we know, you could be working with these people."

"You gonna have to take my word for it," Granick said. "This isn't the time to start this. I am giving Evock the man who has his wife and daughter. That's a fair deal to me."

"Hold on?" Neythan said and stepped back involuntarily. "Where did you say is the exchange?"

"The Cathedral."

"What?" Neythan said.

"The place your Lawyer brought you," Granick said.

"Fuck is with you and churches man?" Neythan said.

"I have my reasons."

"What reasons?" She said.

"Let's just say it's of significance to me and that's the safest place I would want my daughter to see me in," Granick said and lit another cigarette.

"Are you ready for this?" Tracy looked at Neythan.

"I have been ready since the day I left the courtroom."

"I don't think we should go," Tracy said.

"You are right," Neythan said and ran his palm over his face. "I don't think you should go. This ain't your fight, you have nothing to prove." He kept eye contact. "You have done more than I could ask of you. Go home, get in the bath, get some sleep, and wake up tomorrow alive. We don't know what we are walking in to. I am ready but I ain't ready to see you die or get hurt."

"If you are going. I am going with you." She held his hand. "I am in this now and we have come so far. Besides, the police are after me as much as they are after you."

Neythan checked her eyes. They were determined. There was nothing he could do to change her mind but to make sure he dies before she does. He just could not live anymore and watch the ones close to him die. Protect with your last breath.

#

Shy drops hit his head as he stepped out of the car. The thick rainy clouds shadowed on top of him. The breeze felt like the kiss of a perfect woman. He walked forward and passed the gate. The graves extended as far he could see. The gun under his belt on the hip. He walked slowly, reading the surroundings. The days for trust had long since passed with Slakky's death.

The graves were neatly decorated. Nothing caught his attention. He proceeded towards where The Boss had said he would meet him. Only the money was in his mind. As time passed, the drops became denser. Not enough to make him wet but he closed his leather jacket.

Goddy. Godfrey Ritchk. Surrounded by the graves and realising that one day he will have one of his own. Not that night. That night wasn't his time. He was going to stay alive till he held the seven million in his hands.

He heard voices. Turned his head. Nobody in sight. He walked forward. On the corner of his right eye. The Boss stood with smoke coming from his mouth. Goddy approached his Boss.

"You good?" The Boss said with a cigar in his mouth.

"Yeah." Goddy nodded. "What's going on?"

"They are digging."

"Digging what?" Goddy looked at the two men who shovelled mud out of the pit.

"See?" The Boss said. "Someone told that Evock is alive."

The men in the pit climbed out and took their position. Goddy glanced behind him and then at the men. He knew them. He worked with them, but he knew that didn't matter if The Boss wanted him in that pit. "What?" He choked on his words. "That's not possible."

"You had one thing to do." He blew smoke out. "But you chose to disrespect me. You chose to lie." He motioned his hand with force and released his cigar into the pit. "The fuck you think I'm gonna look? Huh?" His voices echoed in the graveyard.

At that moment Goddy realised he had to react first if he was to stay alive. The Boss stared at him with a look that made him almost certain that he was a dead man. The two men started moving apart from each other like they wanted to surround him. Survival mode. Goddy pulled the gun from his waist, "Don't even think about it." He said and took three steps backwards.

"Put that fucking gun down." The Boss said. "You know how this is gonna end."

"I am not dying tonight," Goddy said. "No. Not tonight."

"You are already dead." The Boss gave a nod to the men.

Goddy pulled the trigger after one of the men made a slight movement. Headshot. One man disappeared into the pit. "Go kiss your wife." He said to the other man.

The man's body shook. He looked at The Boss then back at Goddy. He moved back and took off hard as if he raced with the rain.

He pointed the gun at The Boss. "I have nothing more to say except, Slakky didn't deserve to die."

"You know how things work."

"This is how its gonna work," Goddy said. "I am gonna make sure you feel as much pain before you die."

"What?" The Boss said before he fell to the ground. He rolled, screamed, and cursed. Both his kneecaps bled.

Goddy put another two bullets in his stomach. "Now, you will know how it feels."

#

Granick opened the double wooden doors. The benches were empty. The statue of Jesus on the cross looked right straight at the entrance. He walked a few steps forward and bowed with one knee. Neythan just looked but he didn't ask why Granick did that.

Neythan scanned the cathedral. One exit in sight. Not good, he thought. If the guy will use the same door they used, they will be closed in. He pulled the gun from his waist. Walked forward after Granick. His heartbeat steady. His body felt lighter. His vision was perfect, but it didn't feel normal. Tracy was behind him; he couldn't hear the echoes of her footsteps.

"Five minutes," Granick said.

"We need to be near that statue," Neythan said and walked further.

"Why?" Tracy's voice echoed.

"It's a clear view of the entrance from that position and it will provide cover if they come throwing bullets."

"You don't have to worry about that," Granick said. "Nobody is gonna be shooting."

"You must be crazy to believe the shit you just said," Neythan said and approached a table which was covered with a red cloth. There was a vintage metal jug. The silver jug sparkled with the light from the ceiling. Beside it was a silver cup with a lid on top. A huge book was at the corner of the table. He stared at the table before he opened the book. It was the Bible. He couldn't remember the last time he had read the Bible; he knew a few biblical stories. He closed it and opened the jug. There was red liquid in it. He lifted the lid off the silver cup and poured the liquid.

"Evock, don't touch that," Granick shouted. "It's for the Priests."

"What is it?" Tracy said.

"It's the blessed wine," Granick said.

"If this is a church, everybody should be welcome to eat and drink, right?" Neythan swallowed all the wine from the silver cup. "Good wine." He hummed and nodded his head.

"Can you just stop touching things and do what we are here to do," Granick said.

"Until the guy comes. I'm gonna be drinking this." He agreed it was a good exception to the whisky.

"You are not Catholic. You really shouldn't be drinking that." Granick looked at Neythan.

"Who said Catholics are the only ones who should drink wine?"

"Ok. Help yourself." Granick said. "You are drunk already, why drink more? Do you even know why we are here?"

Neythan filled the silver cup and lifted it. The door was opened. "Stay behind the statue." He looked at Tracy.

He had a sip and looked at the entrance. A bald man approached. He had a full black suit. It matched with his skin. The man was calm. Not what Neythan expected. He had another sip.

Granick stepped bellow to the levelled floor with the benches. "Where's my daughter?"

The bald man rubbed his hands together. "Where's the money?"

"That wasn't the deal?" Granick said.

"I am talking to Evock." The bald man said.

Neythan had the last sip and he threw the silver cup onto the floor. "Where's my family?" He burped.

"Fuck this," Granick said and reached his back. "Where the fuck is my daughter, Daniels?" He moved closer to Daniels with his gun raised.

"If you pull that trigger you will never know where your daughter is," Daniels said and rubbed his nose. "If I die, your daughter will be dead in two hours." He continued. "Put the gun down and let's figure out where the money is."

Neythan pointed his gun at Granick. "You knew who Daniels was and you didn't say?" He cocked it. "This is the motherfucker who killed Chelsea and her daughter."

Granick turned. "What difference was it gonna make?" He said. "I still gave you the man you wanted."

"No," Neythan said. "This, this here changes everything. You are dealing with the man. You knew all this shit from the beginning." He walked toward Granick. "Where the fuck is my family? You knew all this man. You knew my family was alive. You knew who had them. Where the fuck is my family? I'm gonna remove your knee cap."

"Ok." Tracy interrupted Neythan. "Stop all this shit."

Neythan turned to face Tracy. She had her gun aimed at him.

"Both of you drop your guns." She said.

"Fuck you talking about?" Neythan said.

"I am not gonna repeat myself." She said as she walked forward.

Daniels laughed. "You thought she was on your side?" He said with laughter. "Do you even know who she is?"

"Shut up," Tracy said to Daniels.

"Tracy. What the fuck is going on?" Neythan said.

"Shit. I am never wrong about this." Granick said. "I knew she was lying. I knew it. I told you Evock."

"Put the guns down." She looked right into Neythan's eyes.

Her eyes were cold. Her face had changed. It had a look Neythan had never seen. The gun was aimed at his face. Neythan slowly bent his back to place his gun on the wooden floor. Had he had too much to drink to not understand what Tracy was doing? He knew she was a smart woman but what she was doing had nothing to do with what they had come for.

"Kick it to me," Tracy said.

Neythan watched his gun slide on the wooden floor towards Tracy.

"Now." Daniels straightened his jacket. "Where's the money?"

"Shut your mouth." Tracy aimed her gun at Daniels.

"You don't wanna kill me, Agent Hoover." Daniels smiled. "I am the only one here who knows where his family is, which is our only leverage."

"I don't care about his family," Tracy said. "I am here to clean up your mess. My mission is to recover the Xenner."

"The General knows I am working on it," Daniels said.

"Your services are no longer needed anymore," Tracy said. "Your time is up. You made the situation worse. Police are involved now, and you kidnapped women and children, really?" She cocked her gun. "That wasn't part of the plan."

"If you kill me. His family is dead."

"What the fuck is going on?" Neythan said. "What's this Tracy? Who do you work for?"

"Where's the money?" She said.

"Where's my family?" Neythan said.

Tracy pointed the gun at Daniels. "I will put a bullet in his head if you don't tell me where the money is."

"As far as I am concerned, he's already dead to me," Neythan said.

"Wait," Granick shouted. "I have nothing to do with what's going on. Can you at least wait until I know where my daughter is?" He continued. "Where's my daughter Daniels. I gave you Evock."

Gunshot.

"No," Granick screamed.

"Don't move." Tracy aimed her gun at Granick.

Daniels's body laid on the floor with a hole at the corner of his forehead. It bled.

Neythan just stood. His gun was behind Tracy. It was too far for him to get to it alive. "Who the fuck are you?" Neythan said and wondered how he had been blinded by her deceit. She surely had mastered the art of deception.

"Where's the money?" She said.

"All this for money?" Neythan turned around. "All this? Just for money?" He said. "Who are you?"

"That's what you think." She said. "This was never about the money." She scratched her hair. "You were all just pawns. But you. You tried to be clever without knowing the kind of people you were dealing with." She moved around. "This is way up. Higher than the government."

Neythan didn't say anything.

"Where did you put the money?"

"Why do you need the money if this was never about the money?" Neythan said.

"Because in the money is where the Xenner is." Tracy said. "This was supposed to be a straightforward mission. A bank robbery. We get the Xenner and the money. Nobody would know about the Xenner but the money. Every pawn had to be eliminated. Two were neutralized at the bank. You were supposed to be caught with the money. Daniels was supposed to get the Xenner before the money went back to the bank. You, the last pawn, you were supposed to get life in prison for two murders and a bank robbery." She continued. "The money went missing and everything changed. Now here we are. No games, no nothing. Where's the money?"

"You missed one thing," Neythan said.

"What?" She said.

"I never had the money?"

"This is not a game Neythan. This is way above you." She cocked her gun. "I'm gonna give one last chance to tell me where the money is."

"Where's my family?"

Gunshot.

Neythan fell on his knees. His mouth let out a cursed scream. The bullet had sunk in on the side of his stomach, just above his hip bone. He held the wound and saw the blood flow over his dark fingers. He couldn't feel the side of his stomach. No pain. Just blood.

"This is not a game." She shouted.

Granick just stood in silence.

"I need to see my family first." Neythan groaned.

"I don't give a fuck about your family." She said. "I am on a mission." She cocked her gun. "Where is the money?"

Neythan felt the hot barrel on his forehead. He looked down. The black jeans he wore stuck to his right thigh. His fingers were wet. He looked up at Tracy. He knew it. The reason he had trouble of believing in God. When things seem to be falling in place, life has a way to tremble them down. Was it his time? He couldn't know. He just knew that his family was alive. That was enough to die knowing. "If you're not gonna tell me where my family is, you might as well pull the trigger." He said. "Another thing you missed." He cleared his dry throat. He breathed heavy. "I ain't afraid to die."

Silence. Just Neythan's heavy breaths. Nobody coughed or said a word. Granick was stood next to a bench. Neythan on his knees with a gun on his forehead.

Gunshot.

CHAPTER 23

The sound of the gunshot kept ringing in his ears. He opened his eyes. Felt weak, and stabs of pain on the side of his stomach. He looked further forward. Tracy laid on the floor in an uncomfortable position. Her right foot was beneath her body. Both of her hands were spread wide like she had been crucified to the floor. Her mouth closed but her unblinking eyes were wide open.

Force pulled him up from under his shoulders. On his feet. He pressed his wound harder, it still bled. "Thanks." He said in his breath. He then turned his head from Granick to face the door. A man approached with his gun aimed at them. The man who had put a bullet in Tracy.

Neythan advanced to Tracy's body. He tried to reach for the gun on the floor beside her body, but the clicked sound of the man's gun stopped him.

"Don't." The man said.

"Who the fuck are you?" Neythan said and observed the man. He couldn't have been older than Neythan. He wore glasses and a navy-blue full suit. Scruffy curled ginger hair covered the man's skull.

"DCI McCunt." He flashed his badge. "What's going on here?"

"Not the fucking police again," Neythan said. "You know where my family is?"

"What?" McCunt said. "Didn't they die?"

"No." He said. "This motherfucker on the floor knew where they are."

"Daniels?" The Detective asked.

"Stop playing dumb with me," Neythan said and realised the Detective lowering his gun slowly. "If you aren't working with Daniels. How the fuck are you here?"

"That doesn't concern you."

"Listen, Cunt." Neythan pressed on his wound. "By now, my family only has an hour and a half of life. If you aren't gonna tell me where they are. Let me go."

"I know a place where we can check," McCunt said. "After this, you and I have a lot to talk about."

"Where?" Neythan said.

"I have been tailing Daniels for the past three days," McCunt said. "There's a farmhouse he has been visiting at least twice every day."

"Where's the farmhouse man," Neythan said. "Time is ticking."

"Somewhere in Easington," McCunt said. "I can take you there."

"Let's go," Neythan said.

#

The tears of the sky felt heavy as they dropped on his skin. The ground was already wet. A BMW X5 flashed lights before he opened the door to the back seat. "We gotta move," Neythan said and pressed on his wound. It felt like the bleeding drained the Jack Daniels out of his system.

"Let me check that," Granick said and removed Neythan's hand from the wound.

Neythan groaned as Granick lifted his t-shirt. He still bled. It wasn't the first time he had been shot. Wasn't even the second time either. But this time it was different. He had everything to live for and everything to lose.

"It could have hit your kidney," Granick said. "You will be fine. Just the meat." He smiled.

McCunt laughed.

"What you mean just the meat?" Neythan said and slid down to rest his head and relieve the pressure from his wound.

"Nothing major was hit," Granick said. "We need to stop the bleeding though."

"You got something Cunt?" Neythan said.

McCunt pressed the breaks on the red light and turned his head to the back seat. "Don't call me that mofo."

"The fuck?" Neythan said. "I will put a bullet in your head."

"Are you threatening me dickhead?"

"No," Neythan said. "I am promising you."

"I should have left that bitch put one in yours," McCunt said. "Fucking ungrateful mofo."

"Ok. Enough of this. Christ." Granick raised his voice. "Detective," He said. "Do you have something we can use to stop the bleeding?"

McCunt remained silent for a moment. The windscreen wipers moved fast like they would quit at any minute. The sound of thunder was louder than the splashing water that ran away from the ever fast spinning wheels of the car. He then stretched his left hand to open the dashboard. "That's all I got." He threw the duct tape to the back without looking.

It hit Neythan's noes. "Thanks, Cunt." He said.

When the tires skid. The force threw Neythan's body forward. His face sunk into the back of McCunt's head seat. He felt the crack of a pulled muscle in his neck. Granick's head connected with his knee.

Neythan and Granick breathed and groaned as they tried to get back to their sitting position.

"Let that be the last time you call me a cunt," McCunt said and then accelerated.

"Jesus Christ," Granick said. "You could have killed me."

Neythan laughed hard and then moaned like he had just remembered that he had a wound. He pressed it and laughed again before he swallowed air. "I like you, man." He said. "You got balls, real balls." He adjusted himself. "But the next time you pull breaks on me like that. You better make sure I am dead."

McCunt didn't respond. He took a left turn into a small road. Dark. No traffic lights. The rain hit the windows like they would crack. The wind and the flowing water on the road posed a challenge on how fast the car went. McCunt didn't mind. He stepped the accelerator like he fought with it.

"Lift your t-shirt."

"Careful holy man." Neythan said.

"I know what I am doing." He bit the role of the duct tape.

"Shit?" Neythan said when Granick pressed on the wound. The duct tape went around his body. It was tight. It was necessary.

Granick kept rolling the tape. Again, and again. Round and round. Then bit with his teeth to cut it. "Right." He said. "You can breathe, can't you?

"I will be alright," Neythan said. "Thanks, man." It felt like someone sat on his stomach. At least that had dealt with the bleeding but not the bullet.

"How far left?" Granick said as he wiped off the blood from his hands.

"Not far." McCunt said.

"That's not an answer." Neythan said.

Nobody responded. Thick darkness. Strong winds blew across them.

"So, Detective." Granick said. "Which branch are you under?"

"South Yorkshire." McCunt said.

"What are doing up north?" Granick said.

"The reason is set next to you?"

"Don't talk like I can't hear you." Neythan said.

"Are you after the money as well?" Granick added.

"No." McCunt slowed the car to make a turn. "I am homicide. It turns out Evock killed an army operative and two civilians. Wait." He said. "What do you mean as well?"

"The civilians had names." Neythan said. "Daniels killed them."

"Daniels wanted the money." Granick said.

"That makes sense." McCunt said.

"What do you mean?" Neythan coughed.

"The Bank Manager told me that the police knew everything that went down about the robbery." He turned the heating off. "Daniels was involved."

"The lady you killed was some type of agent. She knew Daniels." Neythan said. "The SIB Operative knew Daniels." He learned toward the front. "Why would the army be involved in this?"

"The army?" McCunt said with a sharp voice.

"What's a Xenner Detective?" Granick asked.

"Why are you asking?" McCunt said.

"The agent lady said that was the whole reason for the robbery," Granick said. "To get the Xenner. That's why they wanted the money."

"Is the Xenner with the money?" McCunt turned his head.

"Yeah. That's what she said." Granick looked at Neythan.

McCunt pulled the car to the side of the road. Killed the engine. Exhaled. Rubbed his head. Checked the interior mirror. Turned to the backseat with the gun in his hand. "Where's the money?"

#

He stood faced the window. On the eighth floor. The lights of London where like angels in the darkness. An hour had passed. Special Investigative Operative Kate Hoover had not reported mission.

The building was as silent as the darkness outside. It was the Ministry of Defence Headquarters. The General sighed and rubbed his face. He understood the weight of the situation. The longer the Xenner stays in a civilian's position the higher the risk. He loosened his black tie and unbuttoned the collar button.

The General heard the door open. He didn't turn around. He then heard a shuffling sound which must have been a salute. "At ease soldier." He said.

"Permission to speak freely, Sir?"

"Granted."

"We have reason to believe SIB Hoover is K.I.A, Sir." The soldier said.

"Go on."

"Hoover has not reported mission and she's not responding."

"You have worked with Hoover, Lieutenant." The General said. "I take it you know her very well. Do you think there could be a possibility that she could go AWOL? Maybe the mission proved a challenge too hard for her."

"No Sir," Lieutenant said. "If there's anything, she loves challenges. She's a very smart Operative, one of the best undercover Legends we got, Sir."

"Are you absolute with your conclusion Lieutenant?"

"Yes, Sir."

The General looked down on the streets of London. Vehicles still moved. People still walked the streets. It was like the City never sleeps. He checked his watch. Not too long till midnight. It was time to send in the flood. Taking down a country needs very precise moves and a closed execution. Risks are high. The weight is even greater. The nucleus of an unthinkable mission was the Xenner. Take down the military defence. Blind the army. The country will have no resistance.

"Lieutenant." The General said.

"Yes, Sir."

"It's time we open the Special Program."

"The Flood?" Lieutenant said with a dry voice.

"Yes." The General said. "There are twenty-four operatives in the shadows right now." He rubbed the back of his head. "You let them know this is a national security threat. Level three. Apprehend the subject. I want the subject alive. Minimum damage to the subject."

"Who's the subject, Sir?"

"Evock." He said. "Neythan Evock."

"The police are all over him Sir."

"That's why I am sending these Operatives." The General said. "The Flood Program is carried by ghosts. The best this country has ever produced."

"Time frame?"

The General cleared his throat. "Seventy-two hours." He said. "Open the program now."

"One more thing, Sir."

"I know," The General turned to face the Lieutenant. "That's why you are here. To make sure MI5 does not smell this program. Nobody should. We need the Xenner in our hands to make sure we proceed with the mission."

#

"You still wanna play fucking games?" Neythan raised his voice. "Pull the trigger or drive. I am done with this police bullshit. Every fucking shit. I want to get to my family and any of your fucking concerns mean less than the steam off my shit to me."

McCunt just kept his eyes on Neythan and the gun raised. It wasn't the time for interrogation. It was time for death and life. Long as Neythan's lungs expanded, he only had one thing in mind. Alisha and Tanya.

The silence in the car was overshadowed by the music of the raindrops as they hit the windows and the body of the car. Thick darkness. Lightning in the sky like Zeus was turning over in his bed. Echoes of distant thunder added to the melody of cursed weather.

"We have less than forty minutes now lads," Granick said. "We need to keep moving."

"Evock." McCunt said. "I don't think you understand the weight of this situation."

"I do," Neythan said. "That's why you need to start moving because my wife will be dead if I don't make there in time." He leaned forward to connect his hand with the barrel. "If that happens. You gonna wish you had pulled this trigger because I am going to kill everyone you ever knew, and everyone involved in this."

McCunt cocked the gun. "Are you threatening my family?"

"I don't do threats," Neythan said. "I make promises." The gun felt unsteady on his forehead. He swerved his head to the right and motioned forward to connect with McCunt's teeth. The loudness of the gunshot felt like it originated from the inside of his head, like a continuous sharp, loud echo that scratched his earbuds. His vision blurred but the gun had fallen behind him.

The echo kept repeating inside his head like a screaming devil. The grip on his throat was no illusion or was his knuckles as they lifted McCunt's chin with a force which made him sound the horn with the back of his head.

"Drive." Neythan now had the gun in his hand.

Granick just sat on his seat wearing, on his face, the look of a lost child.

McCunt groaned and adjusted in his seat. He spat and turned the key. The car took off like it tried to escape from Neythan's wrath.

Silence. Granick must have thought it was a good idea to sing a hymn. At first, Neythan wanted to punch the singing mouth but the hymn relaxed him. It took him to the day of Tanya's birth. A baby born two months early with less than half the weight of an average baby. She was beautiful and fragile. Three more months she stayed in the hospital. He could not forget the spirit of hope he saw in his wife's eyes every single day as fragile Tanya fought with all her mighty, to see the sun.

A tear escaped his eye. He had to carry that hope with him now. It had to be that night he would see Alisha and hold the fragile Tanya in his hands. Sometimes the sins of the father indeed bring pain and sorrow on his family, just to torture the father. He had realised that. There's no greater pain than which is caused by guilt and blame. It's deeper than grief. It's like an eternal fire burning inside one's heart. It can't be escaped or be removed. You live with it and you die with it. But, fortunately for Neythan. There was redemption. If there was still time.

CHAPTER 24

Rain. Darkness. Granick beside him. McCunt drove, headed to the only place he had to be. The only place worthy of drawing his last breath. He checked his watch. Twenty minutes before midnight. His heartbeat gradually increased each time he checked the watch. "How far left?" Neythan said and checked if he still bled. He wasn't. Granick had done a great job.

"We are getting there." McCunt said.

Neythan closed his mouth before words escaped. He had to be patient, or he would've ended up putting a bullet in the back of McCunt's skull. The DCI didn't know how to answer questions, he thought.

"What's this Xenner everyone is going crazy about?" Granick coughed.

Neythan met eyes with McCunt on the interior mirror.

"It's an advanced military technology." McCunt cleared his throat. "I thought it was just a myth until now." He said. "It's a very dangerous, theory-based, weapon."

"What do you mean theory-based?" Neythan said.

"It has never been tested." The Detective said. "It can override any military software, database and system. It can activate any missile or weapon from anywhere to anywhere in the world." He existed A19. "In the wrong hands, the world would not be safe. Especially in the hands of people who don't know what it is." He looked on the interior mirror.

"If it's military technology." Neythan scratched his hand. "Why did the army steal it?"

"That's what we need to figure out?" McCunt said.

"What do you mean we?" Neythan said.

"What you don't get is, you need me," McCunt said. "You are not going to walk away from this. Especially now, you have put down two Operatives." He stopped on a red light. "An army is gonna come after you. Well, that's what I would do because you have proved to be a challenge."

"But why would l need you?"

"You can't give them the Xenner without knowing who they are and what their motive is," McCunt said. "That means we have to come after them because they will be coming after you. And this time, it won't be a beautiful nurse or a sky employee. It will be soldiers with guns and one intention. To put you down." He cleared his throat. "This is what I do. I find ghosts, but this is far beyond that we can understand."

Neythan sighed.

"Your family will never be entirely safe if we don't take out this threat," McCunt said. "This isn't just about you. It is about this country and everyone in the world. What that technology can do is beyond destruction." He glanced back. "It's called the Judgement, meaning the one who has it will be God, by definition."

The smell of manure travelled his nostrils. The car slowed. He checked his watch. Twelve minutes before midnight.

"The house is within sight now." McCunt said. "End of this fence."

"No lights." Granick said.

"Dim your lights." Neythan said. "Get closer and then switch them off."

Neythan heard pig sounds, horse sounds and some other sounds he couldn't identify. The rain still poured, and the darkness was thicker than the clouds. They got closer. McCunt switched the lights off and moved closer. The sound of the rain and wind could not help them hear if there was any movement or screaming in the house.

"Stop here." Neythan opened his door. "Let's get out."

Heavy drops washed him. He felt the resistance from the wind. "Detective," Neythan said. "You're not going to walk in there with a badge, are you?" He laughed and placed the gun in McCunt's hand. "Let's space up. The last thing we want is to be surrounded."

They slowly walked closer. McCunt to his right and Granick to his left side. The rain stung his eyes. He kept wiping his face and kept his ears open. It was still hard to get a clear view of the house even though they got closer. The darkness covered it.

A faint thunder from the sky produced a blink of light. Neythan stored the flashed image in his head. There were two buildings. The smaller building was further to his left side and the bigger building was straight ahead of him. It was about the same size as his house. He thought they could be about five bedrooms in that house and possibly a basement. McCunt and Granick had been swallowed by the darkness, but he knew they were there. Hopefully.

He had picked up Tracy's gun. He now had a fully loaded pistol in each hand. He refused to dwell on the revelation which backed his belief that trust is a weak man's game. It was a good lesson. Never to compromise your beliefs or values no matter of who or what might seem true. The revelation at the Cathedral had affirmed that.

The pain on his bullet wound had not disappeared but he had managed to suppress it. He was close to the building. About ten metres away. Rays torched his eyes. Brighter than dawn. He closed his eyes to adjust to the light. A mistake, as something hit the metallic post beside him. Glanced ahead before he jumped to the ground. Three men aimed their machine guns at him. The bullets splashed the water from the ground as he rolled for cover.

Behind a tractor. He weighed his options. No option. The bullets hit the tractor with the same rate at the raindrops from the sky. A pole light was in the middle of the yard, just a few feet from the main door of the big house. Neythan moved slowly with his elbows crawling in muddy waters. He had no visual. He crawled further. Moved his head past the big tire which covered him. The men advanced toward him.

He looked up. Aimed and fired. Darkness clouded. He stood and ran to the front of the tractor. The men still fired which made it easier for Neythan to assume their position. The firing stopped.

He wrestled with the wind as he approached the door. His right kick proved too strong for the door. He aimed his guns into the hollow corridor when the old wooden door displaced on the floor. With silence, he stepped on the broken wooden pieces. His hands firm. The trigger slightly pulled. Ready to fire at any movement.

The corridor was clean. It had a polished red floor. Nothing on the walls. Distant music played. He walked with his shoulder against the left wall. A glance back to the door. Nobody. Quick shuffle of feet as he passed the right door. Didn't notice anyone.

#

Turned the door handle. It was locked. A look on the window. No visual but the lights were on. McCunt moved three steps back and fired two rounds beneath the door handle. He had stirred the wrong cup of coffee. Before he made it to the door. The door spat bullets toward him. With the cover of the wall. He fired back.

It took him about six rounds to choke the door from spitting more bullets. He charged toward the door. His shoulder connected with it and gravity pulled him and the door to the floor.

He spun to his right and found himself under a table. He looked ahead. Just an opened door. Stood up. A body laid on the floor. Three holes in its chest and blood flowed to its feet. McCunt stepped on its face toward the opened door.

He removed his wet hair from his face. It had gone from curled to a ponytail. The wind had taken his glasses. His vision was slightly blurred. He just wiped his eyes. And wiped again.

He moved towards the kitchen. He heard shots fired near the front of the house. He wondered how many people were in the house. He had used the back entrance like Evock had suggested he do. He hasted toward the gunshots.

Past the kitchen into another room. Two strides were all he took before the wind blew past his face with a force which knocked the gun from his hand.

#

"Shit." Neythan said. Magazine empty. He slid the pistol under his belt. Peeked his head out for visual but a bullet that hit the door frame, just beside his ear made him push against the wall like he wanted to sink in it.

He had seen at least five people. With the same attire as the Russian Boss's man. Same guns and same language which he couldn't understand a single word. He only knew they wanted to stop him breathing. He knew the position of every man in that room, but he wasn't sure if he had seen them all.

First, he had to take out the one close to the door he stood. Maybe seven bullets were all he had left with. On a different day, it wouldn't have been a problem but at this moment, his strength was also becoming a problem. Maybe it was the blood he had lost or the bullet inside him. He didn't know and didn't care. He just sprang from the wall into the room. He sunk a bullet into the man's ear. Caught the body before it hit the ground. The dead body proved to be a bullet saving shield.

Against the wall. Corpse shield covered him. Almost. Too much heat came towards him which made it impossible for Neythan to get space to aim a target. It wasn't long until that heat exploded the corpse's head and took off an arm.

He fired a shot. Hit the fireplace wall not the target.

The shield was getting torn apart. Few feet ahead of him. An AK 47 cuddled the red floor. He advanced. Slowly. And he fired back. Just for cover.

"Fuck." He breathed. The torn shield fell on his feet after a bullet pierced through his chest muscles. Just above his armpit. Missed the shoulder joint but made Neythan drop his gun and feel the coldness of the red floor with the side of his face.

#

"Drop the gun." Vichk said. The shiny silver of the knife reflected the light from the bulb which hung from the ceiling.

"Ok," Granick said and placed the gun on the cemented floor. A smell of urine made his insides turn. He was sure it wasn't just urine, but he couldn't tell what else it was. "I got Evock." He wiped the water off his face. "Where's my daughter?"

"You make another step; I will slice her throat." Vichk pressed her mouth to make sure she doesn't scream. "Where's he and where's Daniels?"

"You think I care about her?" Granick made a step forward. "I just want my daughter. Where's she? I brought you Evock. That was the deal."

"Daniels?"

"Turns out the mighty Daniels isn't of the rain." Granick said. "I left him in the car."

Vichk kept the long knife on her throat.

Granick scanned the room. Almost empty. Just a toolbox filled with blades like the Russian was about to have the tied woman into a torturing session. He knew the Russian. He was one of the two who came to his house and gave him a beatdown before Vienna disappeared. "What you gonna do with her?" He pointed at the woman in the chair.

"Make her talk."

"About what?"

"Where the money is."

Granick made another three steps forward. "Evock is here now and I think it's in your best interest if he doesn't find his wife tied up with a knife on her throat."

"Where's he?"

"He's looking for her right now. In the house across from us."

"Where's the money?"

"With Daniels." Granick said.

"She's useless to me now then." Vichk said before he slowly slid the knife against her throat.

#

McCunt ducked as the man loaded another attempt on his head. A left hook sunk in the man's stomach. The landing of the hook was strong. It made the man involuntarily bent his waist to protect his stomach which brought his chin within reach. McCunt released a ruthless uppercut with his right hand.

Clean connection. The blow carried the man's body into the air. It had seemed like the window would break his fall but all it did was revenge what the man's skull had done by kissing the man's throat with the remaining piece on the bottom corner of the window frame, it sucked the blood from the side of his neck.

McCunt smiled. Even broken windows fight back.

He picked the gun up and walked from the room. He breathed heavy. The gunshots from the entrance of the house had stopped but he kept going. Slowly this time.

Opened a door. Nothing in.

#

He had landed on the AK47. They had stopped shooting, but they advanced toward him. He waited.

They got closer. He felt their shadows above him. He waited. His eyes closed. He felt a foot which pressed against his back and shook his body. He felt the trigger with his finger under his stomach. He waited. He heard them talk but he couldn't understand what they said. Maybe they confirmed he was dead, or they talked about something else. Or maybe they talked about his wife and daughter, or maybe to finish him off. He then felt fingers below his ear.

He turned and pressed the trigger. Bodies fell on top of him, he kept firing till the gun clicked. He breathed. Threw the gun on the floor. Pushed a body off his face and wiped the blood from his eyes.

There was immediate silence, but the distant music still played. He struggled to move his legs as bloody, dead bodies piled on top of his knees. He pushed another body off his waist and tried to sit up. His left arm was weak.

Neythan groaned and summoned all the strength he was left with to sit up. Then he heard footsteps behind him. The AK47 was empty. The pistol on his waist was empty. The other pistol could have been somewhere but not in his hand.

He closed his eyes and inhaled. Hold. Then exhaled as he opened his eyes. Was it his time?

He tried to turn back. He couldn't. "Come look into my eyes before you pull that trigger." He coughed. "We all gotta die someday." He heard the footsteps approach. No word was said. The footsteps passed him, then he looked up. The gun was aimed at his head.

They both laughed.

"Damn," McCunt said. "You look like you swum in blood."

"Help me up man." Neythan said and wiped his face.

"Fuck." Neythan breathed and supported his arm around McCunt's neck as he stood up.

"You alright?" McCunt said.

"Yeah." He said. "You checked every room?"

"Let's check what's up these stairs there." McCunt helped Neythan on his feet.

"Yeah," He moved forward. "That's where the music is coming from."

McCunt nodded and followed Neythan up the stairs.

They moved without hesitation. Both his arms held the AK47. Ready to fire.

Up the stairs. There was only one door. It was closed. No voices. Just the music. He kicked the door, but it pushed him backwards. Not enough force.

"Move back." McCunt said. He charged towards the door. He fell with it on the floor. Screams erupted.

Neythan ran in. There she was. Coiled on the corner of the bed. Pillow around her arms. Tears on her cheeks. Mouth wide open and a scream which gave warmth to his harm. She kicked her legs. He stopped and just looked at her for a moment. He dropped the gun. "Tanya." He shouted but he smiled.

The screaming stopped. "Daddy?"

He knelt. Rested his elbows on the edge of the bad. "Come." He opened his arms. "You're safe now."

She gave Neythan a strong, unblinking stare and then sprung towards him. She fell into his arms and send him on his back. She cried.

Neythan held her. Relief. Happiness. Joy. All that was not close to a description of how he felt. It was like healing. Like a miracle. Like she had risen from the dead. It was life. Life. She was alive. Damn.

"Where's mama?" Tanya managed to say between sobs.

Neythan stood up with her. He looked into her teary eyes. "When was the last time you seen her?"

"At the accident."

Neythan looked at McCunt who had now stood up. "She's outside sweetie." He coughed. "Let's get out of here."

"Wait." She said. "I met a friend."

"What?" Neythan said.

"Vienna." She shouted.

Neythan heard some movement under the bed. He looked down and saw a bald head. He stepped back.

"This must be Granick's daughter." McCunt said and helped her up.

"Where's he?" Neythan said.

"Let's go." McCunt walked.

#

The wind had calmed, the rain had become shy. Neythan inhaled the night air. His shoulder bled. The duct tape was still tight. He scanned the area. Tried to focus in the thick mist of darkness. No sign of Granick.

Tanya stood beside him. He held her hand with the same arm that bled.

"Where's mama?" She looked up at Neythan's face.

Neythan sighed. Sat on his heels, looked into his daughter's eyes. Her face, hair and clothes were covered with blood. Tears in her eyes. "Sweetie..." An echoed gunshot interrupted him as he turned his head to the direction where the sound originated.

"What was that?" McCunt said and raised his gun.

"Stay here Tanya." He held both her hands. "Don't move. I will be back." He stood up despite her plea for him to not leave.

"Where are you going?" The Detective shouted.

"There's a building across from us." Neythan kept moving towards the building. Gun hoisted. His legs felt heavy. He moved. Kept.

The naked bricked building wasn't as big as he had thought it was. Squared maybe. Leaned his head against the wall. Looked up to the swallowed sky. Just faint drops kissed his bloody face. He listened. Nothing. "Open the door." He whispered to McCunt.

A big stride carried him inside.

A man stood in the middle of the room. The hand which held the gun shook. He didn't turn back to check who had come in.

Neythan moved closer. When he got beside Granick, he saw it. "No, no, no, no, no. No." He whispered. Heat travelled around his body. Saliva filled his mouth. "No." He roared till he felt the pain in his throat. He looked at Granick. He looked up. He looked in front of him. A nightmare. He fell to his knees. Breathed heavy. Tears flowed. He couldn't stop them. He looked at her. Soaked in blood. Her head tilted up. Deep. Visible cut divided her neck.

Neythan rested his forehead on the cemented floor. He knocked the floor with his head a couple of times while he screamed. He didn't know what to do. He felt like he couldn't breathe, think, or talk, or even call her name. His nose blocked. His palms felt warm. Too warm. Everything was hazy. It seemed like all his eyes could see was smoke. He couldn't feel himself. Alisha. Alisha. Alisha.

He stood up. Rage. No thought. His right hand dislocated on the wall. He punched again. And again. He couldn't speak. He felt some-one's hands around him. His elbow must have sunk into the person's head. "No." He roared.

"Evock." McCunt shouted. "Evock. You need to stop."

Neythan turned. Heavy breaths. Tears in his eyes. Coldness in his veins.

"Police will be here soon." McCunt said. "And, you need to be gone before they get here."

Neythan looked at Granick. He walked toward him till they were stood toe to toe.

"I am sorry." He swallowed saliva while he trembled. "I was too late."

Neythan said nothing. Just stared at Granick. He felt his hand slowly bulge into a fist. A distinctive sound snapped his attention.

Neythan turned his head. Behind the chair. Behind the nightmare. A body laid on the floor. In the pockets. A phone rang.

"I will get it." McCunt walked to the body and searched the pockets. "Hello?" He said. He nodded. Looked at Neythan and removed the phone from his ear. Pressed on it.

"Evock." The voice said now on the loudspeaker.

Neythan recognised the voice. The voice from the tunnel.

"Bring me the money before dawn." He said. "Your son seems stable. Peaceful. Rested." He breathed into the phone. "He's going to rest in peace by dawn. Your choice."

"You are dead," Neythan said and sniffed.

"Dawn. The money or your son's dead." He hung up.

"I am going to the hospital." He headed toward the door.

"What?" McCunt said. "Look at you man. You might not even make it to the Hospital." He walked forward. "You hear that? You need to disappear and take care of your wounds."

"I ain't leaving my son." Neythan said. "You hear me. I ain't leaving him. None of my blood is gonna die today." He fell against the wall. Held his shoulder.

"Listen." McCunt helped Neythan up. "Take my car and get somewhere safe. I will take care of this mofo. I am going straight to the hospital after this." They walked out of the room.

The mud made the walking harder for Neythan. The rain had departed as if it had only come to take away Alisha's spirit. His hands grew weak. He grew weak. His mouth got dry.

Tanya ran towards him. He sank his knees in the muddy waters as Tanya wrapped her hands around his neck. He put his left arm around her. Tears began to flow.

Tanya screamed and pushed herself away from Neythan like she had seen a monster behind him.

Neythan turned. "What's wrong Tanya?" He looked at his daughter.

She looked at Granick who had now stood beside Neythan and McCunt. "Daddy?" She breathed heavy. Pointed at Granick. "That's the policeman who gave us to the men who brought us here."

"What?" Neythan used all his reserved strength and got on his feet. Pointed his gun at Granick.

The blue flashing lights were within sight as the sirens got louder.

"Not now Evock." McCunt said. "Look around you. You got to move."

Neythan breathed. His heart raced. He caressed the trigger. He looked at Tanya who stood at a distance and then at Granick's daughter who was stood on Granick's feet with her eyes fixed on the gun.

Neythan breathed. Looked into Granick's eyes. "It's not over." The waters on his feet splashed as the gun landed on the ground. He walked toward Tanya. He picked her up and headed to the car. The darkness swallowed him toward an uncertain future.

EPILOGUE

The wet soil reflected the scorching sun. Chilled breezy stung his already red eyes. He folded his hands behind his waist. He still mourned the uncertain death of Brian, so was the few people who were present. A tear dropped on his black suit. He just sniffed and avoided to wipe his eyes.

Vienna stood beside him and Kiesha was beside his daughter. He stared down at his daughter. The enormous black hat covered her head and her shoulders. He argued with himself if everything was worth it. Well, he now had Vienna by his side. Which is all he wanted. Could anybody in his position done the same? He couldn't answer that.

The few days he had spent with Neythan and what they had been through together. Granick had concluded a picture like any good policeman would do. He had understood what type of man Neythan was. If, by any chance, Neythan blamed him for the events that took place. Neythan would come for him.

It was time to disappear. Granick had already had that in mind. This time he had to. Neythan was not the type of man who would let his transgressors walk on earth with breath in their lungs. Granick knew that, but what would he have done differently. He only sacrificed for his own blood as any man should.

"Dust to dust." The Priest said. "Ashes to ashes." He closed his Bible.

That's all Granick heard from the Priest's speech. Everything else had sounded like rushing waters.

He raised his head and noticed Lisa. The old man who rubbed her back must have been her father. The old lady who covered her mouth like she rubbed her nose must have been Lisa's mother.

He watched as people walked to the mount of soil beside the grave. In a line. They all did the same thing. Pinched a handful of the wet soil, muttered a few words, then released it into the grave.

He walked after Kiesha. Vienna between them. His mind still replayed what had happened two nights before at the farmhouse.

He dug his fingers into the soil. Filled his fist. Looked down to the casket. Glistering brown wooden frame. It seemed like it was coated with honey by how the sun shone against it. He closed his eyes. Prayed in his heart. Said a few words in his heart. Opened his eyes. "Rest in peace mate." He walked off.

He walked toward the tree which Kiesha and Vienna were under. Good block from the sun. The purple flowers floated in the air as the breeze shook them from the tree. A healing scent. The fallen flowers covered the wet soil. It must have been a Jacaranda tree.

He wiped off tears from Kiesha's cheeks. Her shiny, thick lips still looked as seducing as how her black top reviewed the cleavage. He then held her long-nailed fingers after he tested her lipstick.

Granick looked at Kiesha and worshipped her beauty. Blood rushed in his body that his heart vibrated as he dropped his right knee on the ground. Tilted his head to look in Kiesha's eyes.

"What are you doing Ray?" She moved her eyes everywhere like she wondered if anybody saw what she saw.

He cleared his throat. "I have never been so sure in my life." He felt steam around his face. "You brought joy, love, and meaning into my life. You are home to me. Your love, in your heart, that's the only place I wanna be in for the rest of my life." He reached the inside of his pocket. "Kiesha Vadhino." He paused. "Will you bless my life by giving me the honour of marrying you?"

Kiesha muted. Granick could feel her hand shaking. She opened her mouth but not a word came out. She breathed. "I am pregnant." She said with a grin coated with tears.

"What?" His heart calmed. "Really?" He slid her thin finger through her mother's ring.

ACKNOWLEDGEMENT

I would like to thank you for taking your time to read this book. I'm grateful. I only ask you to kindly spare a few moments and leave an honest review about this book. Your review matters and it will hugely impact on the reach of this book to other readers.

I also want to thank my sister, Tinti, my first reader. She helped making the book become what it is now.

This book is sponsored by

Active Life Transformation

Printed in Great Britain
by Amazon